a *Dream* of Light

AMELIA GRACE

Also by Amelia Grace/Julieann Wallace

Amelia Grace (print and ebook)
<u>Adult fiction</u>
The Girl with the Flaxen Hair
The Colour of Broken
All the Colours Above
A Dream of Light
The Book Keeper

Julieann Wallace (print and ebook)
<u>Young Adult</u>
You Before Me

<u>Middle Grade Chapter Book</u> (print and ebook)
Captain Vertigo, and unfortunately... Fart Man
(a superhero with a cochlear implant)

For Children
<u>Picture Books</u> (print books)
Forever and a Day, Love Mama
Henry Bear
Darth
Who Said?
Lily's Lollies
THING
THINGY

Ménière's disease (print and ebook)
(donating profits to medical research)

Vanilla Swirl (children's print book)
Blueberry Swirl (children's print book)
Dear Ménière's - letters & art (#1 on Amazon)
Ménière's Woman
Daily Ménière's Journal
It Will Change Your Life - a cochlear implant journey

Amelia Grace is the pen name of Australian author, Julieann Wallace. Her best-selling adult novel, *The Colour of Broken* was longlisted to be made into a movie, twice and was #1 on Amazon in its category.

Julieann is also an artist and secondary arts teacher, empowering students to be change-makers to create a better world for themselves and for future generations.

When she's not writing, teaching or creating art, Julieann tries not to scare her cat, Claude Monet, or her mini sausage dog, Pablo Picasso, with her terrible cello playing. Her deaf cat, Jameela, was her #1 cello music fan.

Julieann lives in Brisbane with her husband. She is the mother of three amazing grown-up children and has a gorgeous grandson. She has a cochlear implant and is an Ambassador for Ménière's Australia. She is also the subject of the Brisbane Portrait Prize in 2025.

www.julieannwallaceauthor.com

For my husband, with love xx.

A catalogue record for this book is available from the National Library of Australia

PROUDLY

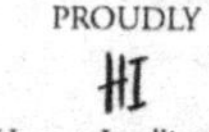

Human Intelligence.

Aim at heaven and you will get earth thrown in.
Aim at earth and you get neither.

C. S. Lewis

The *Change*

2030.

The year my mother's Meniere's disease was cured with nanobot biomedicine-technology. *Personalized* healing, where the disciplines of biomedical science and technology met. The treatment was declared a triumph for the medical field. And the incurable, horrid, debilitating disease that had taken away her quality of life, her dreams, her friends, sentencing her to living in fear of a horrendous vertigo attack, every moment of every day, had ended.

Mother 2.0, I called her. Living the life she was meant to live.

And that same year, *all* incurable diseases were eradicated, and the blind could see, the deaf could hear, the paralysed could walk. Life was beyond what was imagined for people whose bodies had betrayed them. It was deemed a miracle, falsely attributed to humankind, instead of the Ancient of Days who gifted humans with intelligence to be able to make medicines and invent technologies.

2030. The year that some awakened to the truth of the new atomic bomb that is Artificial Intelligence. Soulless. No moral code. "Hallucinating". Lies. Digital deceit. The deception from the lawless one. The stealing of human creativity—the essence of humanity. The deepfakes that spiralled people into a world of paranoia and darkness where multitudes didn't know who they could trust. Where countless people didn't know what was real. Where they didn't even know themselves anymore. Manipulation of one's memories. Panoptic gaslighting. *Deepharms...*

2030.

The year there was a shift where some welcomed a love for the truth, if they had not already embraced it.

2030.

The year I was *changed*. The year I was restrained and injected with cell repair nanobots for disease removal. My mother and father were terrified I would develop hereditary Meniere's disease as I aged. They wanted to prevent it so I would not suffer. So I could live my life to the fullest. It would also extend my mortal lifespan to at least 120 years. Maybe more. It was defying the Hayflick limit of 80-90 years, where in the final phase of cell division, the third stage, *senescence*, cells stopped dividing entirely. Until cellular division ends and undergoes apoptosis. That is, death.

The cell repair nanobots was experimental. I'm an experiment. With guaranteed happiness. *Guaranteed happiness...*

The pharmaceutical giant had developed the "technology cures" with the promise that humanity would never suffer from illness or disease. Ever. They said it was heaven on Earth.

All you had to do was to agree to their conditions, and pay them a monthly mandatory "donation" as "thanks".

Except, illegally mixed in with my concoction of disease prevention was the immortality elixir of self-building nanobots, repairing and enhancing telomeres.

Death would be no more.

Welcome to the new age of the immortal human. Different to transhumanism, where artificial intelligence and human intelligence merged in 2029, to enhance human capabilities, of which I was a loud voice of dissent before the *Change*. AI. It doesn't know when its information is wrong. It doesn't *think*. That's why it was merged with humans.

I'm an immortal human, imprisoned in this Earthly vessel with cell repair nanobots. Against my will. Against my rights. Against the Universal Declaration of Human Rights declared by the United Nations for all of humanity in 1948.

Article 27
Everyone has the right freely to participate in the cultural life of the community, to enjoy the arts and to share in scientific advancement and its benefits.

I did not *freely* agree to participate in their medical scientific advancement, nor freely agree to their conditions, paying them a monthly "donation" as "thanks". My parents had signed the non-disclosure agreement for me, under false pretenses, being led to believe that it was *just* the disease prevention treatment I was being injected with.

Now I'm twenty-eight years old. For the remainder of Earth time. Til the very ugly end. And Earth time will end.

And I hate being frozen at twenty-eight years of age. I hate watching the demise of society. I hate watching human immortals struggle to pay their bills. There is no generational wealth to pass down. I hate watching the profound economic impact. I hate watching the Earth scream for help under the exploding population that believes it cannot die. A delusion. They will die. There is no cheating death, escaping from the realities of time and eternity.

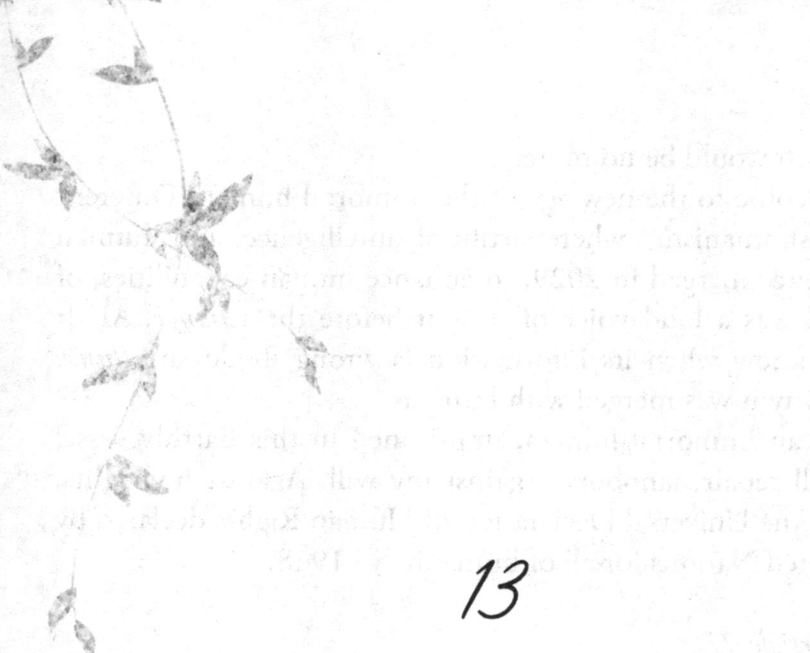

13

Monday.
2151.

I've been twenty-eight for one hundred and twenty-one years. And I want out of this social and physical experiment forced upon me. I've wanted out since I was made aware of the unethical bio-nanobot intrusion. I was told it was simply to cure any disease that was inside me, or would present inside of me, and not for immortality.

They lied. I am immortal. An *Immortal Human*, as we're known. But we can never disclose our immortality.

Humans aren't meant to live as immortals on this Earth. The length of our days is eighty or ninety, on average. Yes, extremely rarely some live until around one hundred and twenty, but they are long ready to step into eternity, where true immortality exists.

A young woman sits on the white leather sofa, presumably

waiting for someone. She fidgets nervously, knotting her fingers together in her lap. She does not wear the glowing *Life Watch*, also known as the *Death Watch*, her days of remaining life counting down. Is she a chosen one for continuing the human race? *A Pure One*. Like when life first started on Earth, free of technology or vaccinations.

She looks this way and that, her red hair falling over her shoulder, and then our eyes lock; her green eyes to my honey-brown, lost together until the elevator doors close…

I am being summoned…

The elevator rises swiftly with the smoothness of glass to the thirteenth floor of the apartment and office building. The high-pitched ding alerts me to the arrival at my destination. The metal doors open.

Mr. Moretti stands waiting for me. His usual black, slick hair is ruffled as though he's been running his fingers through it in exasperation, or frustration maybe.

'Welcome, Mr. Harris. Please hold the elevator and exit. The time has come.' His voice is deep and gravelly. His face without emotion. Not an ounce of happiness, or peace.

I push a button to hold the position of the elevator and lock it in. With a cautionary mindset and a jittery stomach, I follow my stressed boss to his spacious white office. He is the one who injected me in 2030, changing the length of my life.

'Sit. Please, Mr. Harris.' He indicates to the black chair in front of his desk.

I hold my gaze on his round face, trying to read his expression to give me some sort of indication as to what surprise is about to be bestowed upon me. He gives nothing away.

He clears his throat. 'Mr. Harris, our clients have been declining. What is the reason for this?' His dark eyes pierce mine with the intention of making me feel intimidated, without success. When your life has no end date, there is nothing to be afraid of. Except boredom, and that dark depression that litters your days like a punishing wave, relentlessly washing over you with feelings of emptiness, depleting your self-worth... if you let it.

He stands and sways before he catches his balance, placing his hands onto the desk then leaning towards me as a threat. He is drunk. Again. His mind clouded with a film of alcohol bouncing around from cell to cell. He won't remember anything I want to speak to him about. He won't remember the truth I am about to tell him.

I breathe in through my nose and calm my heart rate before I find the words to impart to him. 'Mr. Moretti, from my observations, there's a rumour that says that some people who use Elevator Thirteen do not return to use it again. I fear we are acquiring a bad reputation,' I answer, my voice even. 'If this is the case, then it is not the fault of the elevator, but of the organization. Your product is working well, but the non-disclosure clause is working against it. People distrust you. There is nothing to gain in secrets and NDAs. It just makes people suspicious. It you allow me to diversify, and to deliver people to other levels, that will take away the stigma of Elevator Thirteen.'

Mr. Moretti lowers himself to his chair, clasps his hands together in front of his now passive face and peers at me. He narrows his eyes and clenches his teeth, forcing his jaw bones to expand on either side of his face. 'Then fix it as you see fit, Mr. Harris. The organization will go into receivership if we don't act promptly, and be seized by another company. And you know what that means for you. You have exactly thirteen days to rectify the problem. If there is not a satisfactory outcome, your worst fear will become a reality!' His voice is stern and threatening as his eyes pierce mine like a dagger.

I cringe inwardly. The are levels of fear. I have three. *Level 1*. My immortality and the hatred of it and the rage that it causes in me. I never chose to be like this. *Level 2*. Being alone because of my immortality. I cannot even explain how that feels. *Level 3*. Being the subject of science or technology experiments. That is my worst fear. The immortal seekers walk amongst us. Searching and finding. And people disappear.

'Your review will be in thirteen days' time, at 13:00. Do not be late. You are dismissed, Mr. Harris. And… I, ah… wish you every success in your endeavors.' His dark eyes grow wide with humour and a bead of sweat runs down the side of his face.

I stand, bow to him and turn on my heel and exit his office. I am in deep trouble. If the business closes down, my dream of Light will be destroyed, along with my hope.

Re-entry into my elevator shell is most welcome. The smell of bergamot calms my erratic heart as I close the doors and shut my eyes, blacking out the visual of his burning eyes that haunt my mind. I open my eyes and release the express button and allow all floors to be accessed, then sway as the elevator starts to descend. It stops at the tenth floor.

Mr. Haydn Brown enters with a blonde woman close behind him. Their Life Watches glow with numbers. The countdown. How many years, days, minutes, seconds, they have left. Unless there is a fatal accident. The Life Watch, also known as the Death App, cannot predict that.

'Good day to you both. What is your destination, may I ask?' I look at the blonde first.

She peers at my name badge, and then at Mr. Brown.

'I'm with Hayden, Alex. Wherever he is going, I am,' she replies, sliding her hand along her skin and under the collar of her blouse.

I feign a smile at her before I look at Mr. Brown.

'Sir?' I ask, raising my eyebrows.

He does not look at me, but keeps his eyes on the blonde, watching her hand.

'Thirty-nine, the viewing platform, thank you, Alex,' he says, moving closer to the woman.

I turn and program the elevator to ascend to the thirty-ninth floor. Express. They will be delivered there without interruption. I keep my eyes on the floor numbers as they illuminate. They need privacy and… I disagree with what he is about to do. My body tenses at the repulsion. I have been reprimanded for speaking my mind, at times.

As the elevator door dings, Mr. Brown quickly removes his wedding band and slips it into his pocket. He grabs the woman's hand then, and they quickly exit the elevator to the viewing deck, or more precisely, the restricted area of the viewing deck.

I expect to be summoned to pick them up within the next ten minutes. Yes. Ten minutes, after the lust deed is done, his pleasures of the flesh sated. I shake my head.

The doors close and I descend the bowels of the elevator shaft, returning to the ground floor. The heartbeat of the Great Hall. A world heritage listed building that has stood in the city since 1880, one of the world's oldest remaining exhibition pavilions with a soaring dome. In 2045, it was extended, so that it had thirty-nine levels built on either side of the dome, for residence and business, the new build, using brick, timber, steel and slate to complement the original materials.

It swarms with people in business suits, casually dressed residents going about daily activities, and visitors and tourists wanting to ride the elevator to the thirty-ninth floor to catch a glimpse of the city skyline, and of the famous dome.

All mortals check their Life Watch at some stage. The predicted date and time of their death. A reminder of how much time they have left to accomplish what they want to do.

The *Time Keepers*, aptly named.

It's marketed as a technology tool for happiness. And users sign a non-disclosure agreement, also agreeing to make a compulsory monthly "thank you" donation. Except, as an observer, I know it takes away their peace of mind, enjoyment of moments, and leaves some in a continual state of anxiety, shortening their original intended natural life span.

There are mortals who refuse to wear the technology. The *Hippies*. A term borrowed from another time. People who reject the social norms.

I look down and smile. The absence of *Transhumans* in our district creates an ambience of safety of sorts. There's no technologically enhanced humans connected to the cloud with AI chips implanted into their brains. Humans and machine merged together producing a homo sapien species with vastly increased intelligence, strength and lifespans. They call themselves gods. And the world fractured when they populated the globe, chasing power and control at all costs with their inflated egos and arrogant, misplaced thinking. They see themselves as the superior species, and caused destruction and wars whilst seeking to eradicate the *Pure Ones*, who they see as a threat. The world's safeguard. Protected humans. The *Chosen Ones,* destined to reset humanity if AI self-detonates. And it will.

She still sits on the white leather sofa, alone. I didn't expect to see her in the same chair, waiting. This time her fingers are spread wide across her forehead. She looks at her wrist timepiece, an old mechanical, self-winding analogue watch, powered by the natural movement of her wrist, then checks her fold-up cell phone, as thin and as flexible as paper, and taps her foot on the smooth polished timber floor.

She looks up and her green eyes connect to mine.

'Madam, may I help you?' I ask, projecting my voice like honey to draw her in, as elevator operators have been taught to do.

She considers me for a moment before she shakes her head vehemently, her red hair bouncing this way and that.

'I'm completely aware of the comings and goings of all in this building. Perhaps I have the information that you are after Miss… ?' I wait for her to fill in her name.

She looks away from me and ignores my offer of kindness.

I frown. Is it because of Elevator Thirteen?

At that moment, the elevator doors close and I lose contact with her.

The doors open on the seventh floor. A group of women enter. Their Life Watches all glow a happy green, the colour of well-watered grass, differing with remaining days left. My breath catches at the time on one Life Watch—*7 days, four hours, 3 minutes*. It glows red.

Her hand fumbles as she rushes to pull her long sleeve over her watch, concealing her impending death. I dare not look at her face. But I have to. It's part of my job. She gives me a small smile, her eyes portraying a deep sadness. An unspoken language is there as well. Her soul song. Her written story that she wants to say, but can't, because courage and acceptance is the only emotion that is acceptable by *The Life Watch Society*, lest they collect you and deliver you to their "retreat" to hide the "emotional" people. Her inner being is shattering in hopelessness. Despair. And she isn't allowed to show it, or express it. The non-disclosure agreement. I send a prayer of love and comfort for her.

'Good day, ladies. Where can I drive you to today? A dream holiday? To the secret wives' club? The anti-stress lab? What tickles your fancy?' I ask in my melodic, smooth voice, smiling. 'The immortality lab?' I smile, then add, 'just kidding'. I watch the woman's left eyebrow raise.

They women return my smile and visibly relax. 'I'll take the floor with a personal masseur, thank you, Alex,' one woman says, smiling at me, her eyes twinkling. The women laugh and the atmosphere in the elevator changes. It feels like a spring day gathering of women who are best friends.

I return her smile and look down at the elevator floor before I pull a card from my pocketful of business cards, and hand it to her. 'Madam, take this card. I can highly recommend the magical hands of David. If you return in the next five days, your wish will be granted,' I say and incline my head. I observe her Life Watch add five days to her life expectancy.

'Why, thank you, Alex… so kind of you,' she says, elated.

I nod, then speak to the women as a group. 'Floor ladies?'

'Guess,' another cajoles.

'Hmmm… by the mood in the elevator, and the happiness on your beautiful faces, I choose the ground floor—a most popular request for those leaving the building and adventuring outside to have some fun. Please correct me if I have misinterpreted the atmosphere.'

The women break out into rapturous giggles.

'Ground floor then, it is,' I add, as the elevator begins its descent to the hub of the building.

'Enjoy your adventure,' I encourage, and bow slightly to them as they leave the lift in laughter, and to the sound of thanks from their lips.

I lower my head and smile. Elevator Operator Operation Popularity is underway. The boss will be pleased. Perhaps he has the antidote to human immortality to offer me. Then I could wear the Death App… the Life Watch, and know that true immortality was coming with God, our Creator, overflowing with love and grace.

I take a small step to recede into the elevator when our eyes meet again; green eyes to honey brown. I look at my gold pocket-timepiece, a windable analogue fob watch devoid of modern technology, then back to her. She has been waiting for quite some time now. Forty-five minutes to be exact. Maybe it is a guy and he has stood her up? Silly man if he has done that. It's disrespectful. He should have let her know, at the very least.

She stands, folds her arms and starts to pace the floor.

I set the elevator doors to open, and step onto the timber floor of the building. 'Really… I can help you. I have access to other officers throughout the building.' I incline my head. 'Video surveillance etcetera. I can contact anyone you wish. Who are you waiting for, Miss…?' I am waiting for her to tell me her name.

She looks briefly at me, then turns away, her colourful floral dress swishing around her. She is agitated. Annoyed. She sighs, then turns to me again. 'Miss Finnigan. I'm waiting for Christopher Collins. Do you know of him?' she asks, her voice assertive.

'But of course, Miss Finnigan. He is well-known amongst staff.' For reasons you don't want to know, I want to add, but don't. 'Let me contact security to see if he's in the building,' I offer with sincerity, maintaining eye contact with her.

Reluctantly, I turn away from her and speak into my communicator, but freeze mid-sentence as I see Mr. Collins approach.

He is dressed in his usual black business suit, white shirt, black tie. He runs his hand through his short dark brown hair, then over the one day growth on his face. His Life Watch is glowing green. He does not smile at Miss Finnigan, and acts as if he doesn't know her. I have seen him do this to other women. His self-interest is his priority. He will break her heart.

Miss Finnigan looks at me and smiles with dancing green eyes and my heart lightens. Her mood has lifted and she is now full of energy. I smile crookedly at her and nod my head slightly before I return to my elevator office.

The doors close at once and the elevator ascends to the thirty-ninth floor, no doubt to collect Mr. Brown and his liaison. I look at my pocket timepiece. Twelve minutes.

When the elevator doors open, they stand beside each other, casually, as if they were mere acquaintances catching the same elevator together. Although, she straightens her clothes, giving away the fact that some interlude has caused her clothes to become disheveled. He stands with his hands in his pockets, pretending not to notice what she is doing. Except a lopsided smirk decorates his face. Then he pulls out his wedding ring and slips it back onto his finger and looks at his remaining life days. 20,415 days. His Life Watch flickers red and the numbers change. 19,392.3 days. The impact of betrayal shortens lifespans. Mr. Brown's smirk vanishes and his demeanor stiffens.

He enters the elevator before the blonde woman and stands beside me, keeping his distance from her.

The shine from Mr. Brown's wedding band catches my eye. Immediately, I feel sympathy for his wife, although I have never met her.

'Welcome. It is a beautiful day outside. I am certain the air is fresher at this height. Which floor would you like to arrive on?' I ask in a jovial voice while looking at Mr. Brown, avoiding eye contact with the blonde—she's emitting a negative energy after her liaison with the unfaithful man beside her. She knows she is part of the equation. She knows he is married. Neither of them have the right to dishonour his wife in the most intimate way possible. I close my eyes as I feel the hurt his wife would feel. The betrayal.

I open my eyes again at the sound of his voice. 'Ground floor, and?' He looks at her and raises his eyebrows.

'I have an appointment on the third floor, thank you,' she adds, removed from the situation.

I nod and push the buttons as requested. The blonde exits the elevator without even a sidewards glance at Mr. Brown. As we arrive on the ground floor, Mr. Brown taps the side of his nose twice when he looks at me.

'Certainly, as always,' I enunciate clearly, nodding my head. Patron confidentiality is a given, although it is written in our work contract. It didn't mean I agree with what he did.

An unusual quietness roams the ground floor. It appears as if it's a ghost town, except for Mr. Brown walking away. The elevator operators stand outside their treasured offices waiting for clients to ferry between floors.

But the quietness isn't to last. Within five minutes the ground floor becomes chaotic with bodies busily lining up at elevators to return to their business. I smile. I love the eagerness and the excitement that bounces around people. They are all on a mission of sorts. Hands in pockets, phones at ears and mouths communicating, or the invisible technology embedded into brains for communications, or projected into the area before them. Contact lenses or glasses that record and track everything. Revealing every detail about a person who is recorded in the government data base. Everything. Unless people take evasive measures to stop tracking their lives, their careers, their earnings, their food consumption, their health status, updated every hour. Eyes search the numbers above elevators for the next elevator available.

Then, out of nowhere, a group of men approach elevator thirteen and enter.

Loud. Boisterous. Obnoxious.

Not to worry. The elevator will fix that. And like a magical mist in the air, the moment the doors of the elevator close, they are silent. Totally different men.

'Where am I taking you, gentlemen?' I ask in my business-like manner. No humor. No bling. All my t's crossed and my i's dotted.

I notice Mr. Brown amongst them. 'Tenth floor, Alex, thank you. You know you're lucky to have a job here. We're all very capable of pushing a stupid little button ourselves,' he spits, distaste evident in his words.

His true colours are ugly. I could easily take him down and expose his character with my knowledge about him and his numerous illicit rendezvous. 'That may be so, Mr. Brown, but I have been employed to serve you, and serve you I will do with thankful heart. This job puts food on my table, a roof over my head, and clothes to conceal my nakedness. Besides, I am ambitious, and will be working on the thirteenth floor within a year. Mark my words, Mr. Brown,' I add with a contrite voice. The thirteenth floor. Part of the plan for my dream of Light. I stare into Mr. Brown's eyes and plant the seed of curiosity. He narrows his eyes at me, feeling something, but confused as to what. He will be back. He will beg me to help him.

The ding of the doors herald the exit of the men. A few good ones amongst them.

The day continues slowly. It's because of the thirteen elevators. All in competition with each other. Our use is dependent on timing—which elevator is where at which time. Unfortunately, my elevator seems to have poor timing. Plus the fact that I lost my temper with a badly-mannered-stuck-up-good-for-nothing-who-dickey three months ago didn't help.

The short story of the occurrence had grown and twisted to such an extent that little of the truth was left in the anecdote of the event on that day.

At 4:45PM, a woman approaches me. She's the one from in the elevator with a group of women this morning. She shows me her glowing red Life Watch. 'Is there really an immortality lab?'

I narrow my eyes are her. 'And if there is, are you sure you want to live forever on the Earth?'

She nods.

I gesture to her to step into my elevator. She stands at the back of the elevator car, her face ashen. 'Thank you,' she says, her voice barely audible.

I want to tell her that her friends and family will die. And that she'll be the only one left. But I am forbidden to speak of these things.

The elevator doors open on the thirteenth floor and I take her to Mr. Moretti. And that is the last I see of her.

The close of the business day creeps upon me as I am lost in the social and unsocial graces of people. I head to the staff quarters, change into my own clothes and remove my honey brown contact lenses. My eye balls are free at last. I blink several times before I close my locker and make haste to the freedom of the concrete jungle.

'Alex, bud, come for a beer with the rest of us elevator pilots?' Jack says, his voice high with energy as he slaps me harder on the back than I expect him to.

I run my hand through my hair and watch him in earnest while I make my decision. 'Sure. Thanks, Turner,' I say, smiling at him. He is a good man.

We enter the bar and settle on our first and only round of drinks. We have strict rules about alcohol consumption, even out of work hours. I lift my scotch to my lips and freeze as warmth runs through my blood.

It's not alcohol that affects me.

It's a person.

I turn my head to the right and catch the sight of flowing red hair.

It's Miss Finnigan. And she sits alone. She wears the same floral dress from this morning, except an elegant shawl wraps around her shoulders.

I excuse myself from the table of elevator pilots and nonchalantly sit beside her. She smells exquisite, like honeysuckle mixed with the freshness of innocence.

'Excuse me,' I say in a low voice as I reach across in front of her to some peanuts on the bar. She has an old scratch on her arm. She is a mortal one.

She looks at me for a millisecond then smiles, out of politeness, I assume. Her mood is low. Then she taps the air at me with her finger. 'Aren't you the guy from the elevat—no... you have blue eyes. His were light brown or something... I th-th-think,' she stutters, frowning.

I look into her eyes as green as emeralds and shake my head slightly. It is better that she doesn't know who I am, or what I do. I turn my head away from her and sip my beverage, slowly, then return my face to hers and hold my drink up to her. I look into her eyes once more. 'Here's to a better day tomorrow,' I declare.

She smiles shyly at me before she raises her glass and clinks it against mine.

'Emily,' she says and proffers her hand to me.

'Liam,' I add, as I take her hand in mine.

Her eyes widen and she takes a short, sharp breath when our hands touch. I smile crookedly at her, aware of the powerful force of energy that passes between us.

I think back to a letter my father left for me before he stepped into eternity. Letters of advice and wisdom.

My Dear Liam,

My son, you will meet the one. You will know when you meet her. It will be as if your entire being has been charged with a surge of energy. And it's like you feel you know her already. Do not ignore the sign.

Love always,
Dad

Will Emily understand that connection we both shared?

Or perhaps, she's an unbeliever in the Creator, not aware of the spiritual dimensions that co-habit the Earthly and heavenly spaces.

But, putting all this aside, she and billions of others on the planet have what I want. Mortality. Not this Earth physical life of immortality, frozen at the same age I have been journeying on.

My mother missed the message about God's grace. *For by grace you have been saved through faith. And this is not your own doing; it is the gift of God, not a result of works, so that no one may boast.*

I lower my head as I eat the peanuts and keep my eyes on the bar. She is itching to talk to me. I can feel it.

'So, Liam, where's your girlfriend tonight?' she asks.

'I'm in between gigs at the moment,' I answer, hoping she will get my humour.

'Gigs? You call your girlfriends, gigs?' She has venom in her voice.

I turn to face her and nod with a smirk on my face. 'Only when they're not keepers,' I add to fuel her fire.

'And have you found any… keepers… Liam?' she asks with sarcasm dripping off her words.

I raise my left hand at her and point to my bare fourth finger. 'Does it look that way to you?' I ask, raising my eyebrows, maintaining eye contact.

'With an attitude like that, you're not likely to, believe me,' she spits, raising her left eyebrow at me, with a look of disdain.

'Your temper seems to match your hair, Emily. I'm glad to see the old adage is true!' I fire back at her while brushing my thumb over my chin.

She stares at me and narrows her eyes. She's angry. There is no doubt. She throws the remainder of her drink down her throat, slams the glass down onto the bar, huffs at me, and leaves in a storm.

I swirl my drink in the glass and finish it, then return to my colleagues at the table to the sound of their laughter and pats on my back. I'm now the butt of their jokes. It's been an entertaining evening at least, even if it is me who is the entertainment.

The mist has descended by the time I leave the bar. Street visibility is low and the light from the street posts strains to illuminate barely a meter around them.

I pull the collar of my coat up to cover my neck and tilt my head downward to avoid eye contact with others walking in the mist of the night, their Life Watches glowing green. I will my feet to pick up the pace. I have to be back at my apartment by midnight, lest the unthinkable happens and my protector seeks me out.

I ascend the steps of my apartment in record time. I never choose to ride the elevator at any time except for work. It is claustrophobic and inescapable—like this human body I am trapped in.

Wishing I had a cloak of invisibility, I enter the apartment and close the front door behind me with the faintest of clicks. I still, as I hear the arrowed voice, aimed at me with the precision of a crossbow.

'Where have you been?' The voice is low and dark, with each word pronounced separately, threatening my mind.

I turn, and smile at Dudley to soften his heart. 'At the bar with my work colleagues, Dudley. My curfew is midnight, and I'm well within the parameters of this time, thank you. How was your day?' I ask to distract my protector. He takes his job too seriously, at times.

'Uneventful, thank you, Liam. And that is the way I like it, as you know. I don't like picking up the pieces after you.'

I cover my face with my hands and roll my eyes at his comment. One is entitled to lose one's temper with the condition of being an immortal human after being twenty-eight-years-old for one hundred and twenty-one years.

'I managed to beat the cat in a staring competition today,' Dudley continues. 'Victorious at last. Matisse was most disgusted, shook her leg and walked off. She is sulking in the reading chair as we speak.' There's humor in his voice.

'Nicely done, then. I had a meeting with Mr. Moretti today.'

'And… was it an interesting… discussion. Did you ask him about the antidote to that vile concoction you were forced to take?' Dudley raises an eyebrow at me.

'No. His mind was clouded with alcohol, buzzing around killing off some brain cells. I'll open that discussion when he is not so intoxicated next time.'

'Very good, Liam. Although alcohol is also called the truth serum. Perhaps it may be to your advantage to ask him while he is under the influence.' Dudley stands, his hand on his lower back. 'And now I must retire for the evening. You know I need my beauty sleep, lad,' he says, raising both eyebrows at me and chuckling to himself.

'Aye, that's for sure, old man!' I joke with my protector. My third protector. The previous two had died of old age. The first protector had been assigned to me by my mother to ensure that my good works outdid my bad works. She had tasked my original protector to train the new protector, Dudley, who will also train a new protector to take over when he dies. I hate attending the funerals of people I have grown close to. Their mortal deaths are like rubbing salt into my wound. And I'm jealous. They have what I want. To return to my true home.

'Aye—there'll be no cheekiness from you about that. You know we don't get to choose our body on the Earth. Now make haste and prepare for bed. Something tells me you met a person of interest today. Your mood has changed. You will need to mend that surge of power that is still residing in your veins. Good night, Liam!'

I lower my head and smirk at Dudley's remark. Is it that obvious about my connection to Emily? 'Night, Mr. Castoro—sogni d'oro,' I call after him.

'Sweet dreams to you, too,' he replies, waving his hand in the air as he disappears up the stairs.

I run my hands through my dark brown hair and look towards the ceiling of the apartment, clenching my teeth. I let out a low growl in frustration. How much longer do I have to remain as a human immortal? I have already had enough "life" at one hundred and forty-nine years now.

I close my eyes, allowing the memory of the last moments with my mother to come to the forefront of my vision.

'Liam, why have I given you Earth immortality?'

'Because you believe that I keep making bad choices, Mama…'

'Why is that?'

'Because you think I'm impulsive and keep repeating my mistakes. You think the experiences on Earth will provide everything I need to obtain spiritual eternal life. But I disagree with you. It's God's grace and belief in our Saviour that has my name in His Book of Life.'

'But are you learning courage, temperance, wisdom, justice and patience, Liam?'

'I already have those, Mama. My belief in the Lord

teaches me those things. I do them because I want to, not need to.'

'But what if you truly don't have them?'

'Let us not talk about this anymore, Mama. I'm stuck here on the Earth anyway. I will continue to live in the confines as a physical immortal on the Earth, unable to become a human mortal to die, and unable to enter the spiritual realm as an immortal spirit. I will never see God, unless He intervenes.'

'Forgive me, Liam. I couldn't possibly imagine that you would be imprisoned in the dim light of the Earth. I thought the immortality drug would wear off. But I have tried to compensate you. I have assigned a protector to watch over you. Patience, Liam… you must learn patience, and remember that Love has no boundaries, anything is possible. Until we meet again, remember my love for you, my son. I will be here, waiting for you…'
'I forgive you, Mama, as God does. And yes… with God, anything is possible.'

I squeeze my eyes tight as I recall her last breath. Mama loved me with her whole heart. She always told me that I look like my body had been sculptured by *Alessandro Algardi* himself—my nose perfectly straight, lips well formed, my jawline chiselled. But like Dudley said, we don't get to choose our Earth body.

I shake my head to rid my mind of my memories, turn off the light and make my way to my bedroom, where I enter the mindless routine of showering and preparing for sleep.

Once I climb into bed, I reach for the glowing energy ball of the Earth that sits on my bedside table. It's supposed to be a kind gift from "Here now. Here forever". But to me it's a reminder of love and hate. I love the Earth created by God. I love that I get to be a witness to the work of His hands. God's fingerprints. Over all of creation. Over the heavens and the Earth. Over me. And I hate that I am stuck here. I place the glowing energy ball onto my bedside table, squeeze my eyes shut and clench my jaw. I shake my head at the ugly, sheer ungratefulness that fills me. Every moment spent on the Earth is an opportunity to see God's love in action. And I should be thankful for that.

'Forgive me for being a selfish jerk, Lord,' I whisper. Then I reach for the box of letters my mother has left me, and take one out.

> *To my dearest Liam,*
>
> *Be careful. Don't stay in the physical dimension of the Earthly realm as an immortal human, unable to return to the Light. The Light is your rightful place, your true home. You are a sojourner, blessed to witness God's creation in the form of a human, given the opportunity to spread the light on the Earth. Find the antidote for your immortality. And come home. Forgive me for what happened to you.*
>
> *Love, Mama*

I flick away my tears. I cannot see how I can return to being a mortal human. It's an impossibility. I have grieved the loss of control over my life and accepted it. But still, my throat tightens from the deep emotion in my chest that tries to escape. I have always thought that reaction was hatred and anger. But now I realize it is grief. And loss.

For one hundred and forty-nine years I have been on the

Earth, plagued by physical torment, chained to the laws of gravity and craving to be able to return to the Light. To freedom. To love.

I inhale deeply—that sacred breath humans have been gifted with. I turn my head and stare at the glowing Earth energy mass. I lift my hand to it and watch as the fourth state of matter arcs to my fingertips like bolts of lightning, lighting my entire sleeping room as if it is daylight. My fingertips tingle under the warmth until the plasma retreats back into the glowing ball of energy. I turn it around. The Earth globe was meant to be an icon of allegiance to Earth immortality. But I can only see it as an allegiance to God's Earth.

I sigh. How long will I be subjected to this living nothingness cut off from my spiritual homeland? What is the antidote to immortality?

I close my eyes. "Caro Dio, possa io avere coraggio, temperanza, saggezza, giustizia e pazienza – Dear Lord, may I have courage, temperance, wisdom, justice and patience,' I whisper. Patience and acceptance; those attributes I have learned, but self-control was the essence of temperance, self-control in all things, and I am still working on that one. 'And my dream of Light, being in Your unimaginable, indescribable presence one day, where no eye has seen, no ear has heard, and no mind has imagined what You have prepared for those who love You. And trusting in Your timing and wisdom, in Jesus' name I pray,' I say, feeling comfort from my spiritual connection before I slip into the unconsciousness of sleep...

12

Tuesday.
12 days.

Blinding light enters through the white plantation shutters of my bedroom. The sun, my wake-up call provided by nature. Free of charge.

I roll over and cover my head with the pillow, wishing I had more time to sleep. I chuckle. Here I am. An immortal human, thanks to a repulsive injectable concoction that contained self-building nanorobots that roam my body, curing diseases as they develop, including removal of aging cells. If biomedicine was that good, why doesn't it include the cure for the need of sleep? But I guess, my tiredness reminds me that I am human. My only wish is that I can die like a mortal human.

I rise from bed and saunter to the kitchen with eyes full of sleep. Dudley is there staring at me as if I am the walking dead.

'Welcome to the land of the living, Liam Harris. Your breakfast awaits you. It's about to be devoured by the manipulative cat as we speak.'

I look over at the table, adorned with a bouquet of delicate pink peonies from Flowers for Fleur to honour my mother. Matisse is sitting on the dining chair like a human, eyes focused, ears pointing forward, and a paw about to swipe a piece of my bacon off my plate. I push her off the chair and sit, and then feed her a little bacon to satisfy her predatory skills. Matisse with the bacon blues is not a good sight to suffer, and the assault on one's ears is akin to torture.

Dudley joins me at the table. He looks at me as if I have forgotten something important.

'Put me out of my misery, Dudley. What have I done, or not done?' I question, cocking an eyebrow at him.

'I want to know of the letter from your mother,' he replies, piercing my blue eyes with his.

I look at my cup of tea, pick it up and take a sip. 'She told me to find the antidote to nanobot immortality. And to come home,' I reply almost in a whisper without looking at him.

'Indeed you must. You cannot dilly-dally and meander your way through immortality on the Earth, Liam—it is not meant to be. And I for one would not want to be locked upon the physical realm of the Earth for eternity. It tortures me as it is.'

I look at Dudley in all of his physical ugliness. I can see how difficult it must be for him to be accepted by a human society that is so bent upon shallow vanity. It takes an incredibly special person to look beyond his human shell and into the beauty of his heart and mind. I am no doubt still his only friend, beside the cat that tries to dominate him. 'Yes, I'm aware of the short comings of life here. Not only do we battle the physical heaviness of our body, we battle the daily judgment from others, purely based on our looks. Everyone seeks to fit in somewhere, they seek acceptance, yet the answer to that search sometimes seems out of reach, and some give up. Please accept my apology for having to be my protector. It can't be pleasant for you.'

'Liam… as your protector, it's not my happiness I seek, but yours. But I do accept your apology none the less, thank you,' Dudley says in a calm voice, staying a moment longer connected to my eyes than he should.

I nod and look away from him and tuck into my breakfast, grateful that Dudley has become such a great cook. Goodness knows he's had enough time to perfect his culinary skills. His initial attempts at cooking when he first moved in with me left much to be desired.

I stand and bow to Dudley before I leave the table to prepare for my day's work, as is respectful to give thanks to the one who has served.

While I change into my day wear, the twelve days remaining to achieve Mr. Moretti's goal ruminates in my mind. And the twelve days to achieve my goal. I wonder if Mr. Moretti can see what is coming his way. I want to believe it is impossible to see into the future. But I know better. God allows some people to see what is to come. The prophets. I, on the other hand, am simply an instrument for things to flow and change. An enabler. To me, things just seemed to fall into place perfectly, like missing jigsaw pieces. I don't know if it is a gift, or whether it is just using my emotional intelligence to guide others.

I pull the white T-shirt over my head and onto my shoulders, pausing as I see the floral tattoo on my left pectoral muscle. The nanobots keep repairing it, returning my skin to blemish free. They haven't quite finished the repair of this one yet. The reversal of my tattoos continuously reminds me of my human immortality, and the self-building nanobots, repairing and enhancing telomeres, repairing any damage done to my body. A cut is repaired in four hours. Bruising, two hours.

My memory returns to the day of my nanobot procedure, deceptively upgraded to an immortality procedure. *It will only hurt for a moment*, they had said about the physical pain of the process. I cut my finger two days later, and found it healed in four hours, instead of the natural one to two weeks. I confronted my parents. Then we confronted the doctors.

The physical scars healed, but the psychological scars hurt every day. I am chained to this Earth until the end of Earth time. I narrow my eyes at the ugly reminder of not aging. Stuck here at the forever age of twenty-eight. The Earth is a mess. Fighting between good and evil. Truth and lies. I want to become mortal so I can die, my spirit returning to my Creator. I let out a long sigh.

I'm a marked man. By mortal humanity. Like everyone who was chosen and signed the NDA and secretly become immortal. It seemed to turn some into ugly people who thought they were lawless. Uncountable for their actions. But everyone is accountable for what they say and do. They will discover that in the end. And there will be an end. Eventually. They need to wake up from the delusion of their self-imposed power.

I have no intention of revealing my immortality. It's best that only Dudley and I knew my history.

I shake my head. Human immortality is revered. Little do they know how suffocating it is. If only they knew the depth and breadth of being subject to eternity on the Earth and its ramifications and shortcomings, they would not seek it. And I certainly have no intention of remaining a prisoner of the curse.

I pick up my work satchel and sling it across my chest, then enter the kitchen to wish Dudley a good day.

I walk to the front door, and just as I'm about to open it, Dudley calls over his shoulder, 'Wear your acid wash jeans to work today, Liam. They will serve you well, later!'

I pivot to look at him.

He remains standing at the sink washing dishes. He makes no attempt to turn and make eye contact with me. After a moment

I take a deep breath, then returned to my room and change into the said jeans, shaking my head in wonder about the sudden order to change.

When I turn the door knob to leave the apartment, Dudley calls over his shoulder once again, 'Enjoy!' Then I hear him chuckling to himself. Annoying!

A biting chilly wind sweeps along the busy roadway as I walk to the Great Hall. I pull the collar of my thick coat higher, covering my neck.

'Remember to keep your neck covered while walking in the open, Liam…'

'Why, Mama?'

'Always keep your neck covered when you are outside. Your human immortality has a specific scent, and it makes you a wanted man for scientific experiments.'

'Yes, Mama. I will remember.'

I lower my head and focus on the footpath in front of me. The brisk walk to work will be good for my mind.

I skip up the steps to the Great Hall building and enter the revolving door, then the door immediately on the right that leads to the staff quarters.

The other elevator operators are already busy polishing their black shoes so that the lights reflect off them, shining their brass buttons on their navy double breasted coat with gold piping on the sleeves, and doing the obligatory final check for imperfections and donning their navy coloured attire for work.

'Top of the mornin', Alex. Gold star for being on time!' yells Aidan. An immediate cheering and clapping echoes throughout the locker room.

I look down and smirk at their energetic cajoling this morning before I press my finger to the scanner to unlock my locker, to start my own morning ritual of preparing my uniform for the day.

After checking my uniform in the mirror, I leave for Elevator Thirteen, enter it, and ride the elevator up to the top floor, ensuring it is in fine working order.

Once it comes to hover on ground level again, I put on my white gloves, open the double doors, step out and wait in the elevator foyer in anticipation for the start of the day.

There is a rush of people as business commences for the day. I watch each of the elevators fill with people, wondering if they'd like to share.

A lone man approaches and looks pointedly at me.

I gesture for him to step in to my elevator. He hesitates before he takes a step.

'Good morning, sir. It's a lovely day outside. Which floor would you like to proceed to?' I close the elevator doors.

He closes his eyes and pulls up the sleeve on his business shirt. His Life Watch glows red.

'Do you need to see the funeral directors on the sixth floor?'

He shakes his head.

'Would you like… more *time*?' I ask, raising an eyebrow at him.

His bottom lip quivers and he nods his head.

I push button number thirteen, and the elevator pod rises. 'Are you sure about this?' I ask. I want to tell him not to do it. But I am forbidden to.

'I'm certain.'

The elevator doors open on the thirteenth floor. I follow him out then guide him to the office that he seeks. We enter.

'Mr. Moretti, I would like to introduce this man to you. He

wishes to speak to you about more *time*,' I say, inclining my head, my insides repelling at the spiel that I hate with every fibre of my being.

Mr. Moretti closes his eyes before his head bobs to me in the affirmative. He turns to the new client. 'Welcome. Our experience in extended time, and our ability to resolve matters of time is second to none. I have an appointment available now if you wish to speak to me about it.'

The man nods.

'Mr. Harris, can I offer you tea or coffee while you wait?' he asks.

This is my cue to leave the office. 'Thank you for your offer, Mr. Moretti, but I must get back to work. Perhaps another time I will be able to have coffee with you,' I reply formally, as per my given script, before I stand and shake his hand.

I turn to the man and proffer my hand to him. 'I wish you the entire best, sir. You are in good hands with Mr. Moretti,' I say in a smooth, calm voice, as per my script, and return to my elevator and coast down to the ground floor.

She is there again, the girl with the red hair.

I politely smile at her, tilting my head towards her. 'It is a beautiful day, Miss Finnigan,' I muse, connecting my honey-brown coloured eyes to her green, holding the connection for as long as I can.

'Yes,' she whispers, and smiles at me with the shyness of a child, then stands as she sees Mr. Collins approach.

She walks towards him with a spring in her step, her ivory coloured long skirted dress flowing behind her. He looks at her but does not return the beaming smile she offers him. And when she presents him with a small parcel in a bag with enthusiasm, he holds up his hand and looks away in disapproval.

Miss Finnigan drops her arm by her side and follows him as he walks towards Elevator Thirteen.

'Good morning, Mr. Collins,' I chirp as he steps over the threshold.

He simply nods at me and stands at the back of the elevator.

I smile at Miss Finnigan. 'Which floor, Miss?' I ask, expecting her to wait for Mr. Collins to give the answer.

'Floor eight please, Alex,' she answers, and then looks at Mr. Collins for reassurance of her floor choice. He nods ever so slightly.

'Sir?' I ask, playing along with his game of deception, so as not to upset the client.

'Ah… same,' he replies, looking past me and at himself in the reflective surface of the elevator wall. He stands with his hands in his pockets, pretending he does not know the young woman who stands in the elevator with us. He is deceiving himself. The worst type of lie.

With the sound of the door ding, Mr. Collins takes the parcel from Miss Finnigan's hand and passes it over to me. 'For you, Alex… enjoy,' he says in a low, monotone voice before quickly exiting the elevator.

Miss Finnigan gasps. I look into the bag and see a beautiful silk tie in a shade of ocean blue. She would have spent a good portion of time choosing it for him. Men's choices in tie colours are ridiculously over-indulgent.

I glance at Miss Finnigan with a look of apology on my face. As she returns my gaze, I see her tears well. She quickly blinks them away to conceal the hurt he has just dealt her. She hurries after him with her head held low, like a puppy that has just received a scolding.

When the elevator doors close, I take a deep breath, then exhale slowly. My heart breaks for her. But unfortunately, it's human nature for some to be scum. And that is what Mr. Collins is; utterly and purely.

The elevator comes to a stop. The doors open on the tenth

floor. Mr. Haydn Brown stands, waiting with his hands in the pockets of his gray suit. He brushes his rough chin with his fingers, leans forward a little, and steps into the elevator and inclines his head to me.

I nod back. 'What is your destination, sir?' I ask, articulating my words fluently.

'Aaah… three, please,' he replies, preoccupied.

He rummages through his pocket and pulls out his foldable mobile phone. He looks at the screen before he puts it to his ear. 'Darling, how are you?' he asks in a cheery voice before his face freezes. His mouth drops open. He leans over with his hand on his chest, and squeezes his face as if in pain. Then he drops the phone down by his side before he places it back to his ear.

'Yes. Yes. We must talk. It's not what you are thinking… it's not like that… we can work through this. I love you, Jayne… please let me explain…'

I stop the elevator. It would not be right to allow others into the lift while Mr. Brown is in the middle of a domestic dispute. He has his pride to maintain, and I will not let him be destroyed by others seeing him in his weakness, although it is tempting to let him suffer for his wrong doings. So, his wife has discovered his infidelities. Nothing is ever hidden. The truth always surfaces.

He folds his phone and places it back into his pocket, then runs both hands through his hair in despair.

'Mr. Brown… I can help you. What would you like me to do?' I ask, remaining calm and in control, creating a supportive, kind energy in the elevator. I don't approve of what he has been doing, deceiving his wife, but… love your neighbour, as you would yourself.

Mr. Brown looks up at me, his eyes red. Emotional pain is etched onto his face like an engraving with the words of his guilt. His chin quivers. 'Help me? How can you help me? You are nothing but a worthless, useless, lowlife, elevator operator,' he spits out at me, his words of venom trying to poison me.

He takes one step toward me, his eyes burning his wish of death into me, anger fuelling his look, making him as ugly as hell.

I remain calm, lift my hand, remove my white glove and touch his arm. My hand warms as my prayer for him of repentance travels under his skin to his brain to his amygdala, the centre of his anger emotion. Within an instant he steps back from me and tears fall down his face, all anger gone.

'Help me, Alex,' he says, his voice weak. 'I beg of you. Please, help me…' he pleads.

My heart softens for him, and I nod in compassion. Turning to the shiny brass buttons on the wall, I press number thirteen. This pitiful man's life is about to change.

Is it a good thing or a bad? Whatever it is, it is not my position to judge. I am simply the delivery boy to the Establishment, as I am employed to do.

Old Mr. Moretti greets us in the reception room of Suite 13 on the thirteenth floor. He opens the door and gives me a knowing smile, exposing his perfect false teeth while looking over the frames of his dark rimmed square glasses. 'So good to see you, Mr. Harris, please come in,' he croaks, gesturing the way for us to walk.

My body shudders at physically being in this room, by giving Moretti what he wants. But I have to bide my time.

I look back at Mr. Brown. His eyes are fixed on the floor. He is the perfect example of a broken man. He does need fixing, but not here. I feel like I'm betraying him. A guilt I will have to deal with. An act I can't keep doing. It's chipping away at the pieces of my soul, my spirit.

Arriving in a small soundproof office, Mr. Brown and I sit opposite Mr. Moretti, who has positioned himself behind his black desk. The fluorescent lighting shows every line and wrinkle on Mr. Moretti's face, and the grey regrowth of his hair. He must be about seventy-five years old. For a moment I wonder if he is a human immortal, or just the deliverer of the concoction.

'How can I help you today, Mr. Harris?' he asks, his pen poised in his hand, ready to take notes. He peers over his glasses at the unresponsive man beside me, then looks back to me and winks in approval of my delivery.

'Mr. Moretti, I would like to introduce Mr. Hayden Brown to you. He has found himself in a spot of trouble, domestically, and would like some help to sort it out. I have brought him to you because I know of your success in dealing with matters such as these,' I explain fluidly, nausea rising at the repulsive spiel that it scripted for me.

Mr. Moretti closes his eyes before his head bobs to me in the affirmative. He turns to Mr. Brown. 'Hayden, Mr. Harris has done you a favor by bringing you here. Our experience in family matters, and our ability to resolve... misunderstandings... disagreements and the like, is second to none. Alex will require your wife's phone number... I assume it is your wife by the wedding band on your finger, and she shall join us for remediation... yes?' It is a question and statement in one, worded so he would not refuse treatment.

Mr. Brown pulls his business card from his wallet and hands it to me, pointing to the phone number on the back of the card. I look into his eyes and see his tormented, guilty conscience. But is his torment and guilt for his betrayal of his wife, or for getting caught?

I give him a nod and tuck the card into my suit pocket. Looking at Mr. Moretti, I wait for the next instruction that can only come from him. 'Hayden, Mr. Harris, can I offer you tea or coffee while you wait?' he asks.

That is my cue to leave the office. Mr. Brown looks down and shakes his head.

'Thank you for your offer, Mr. Moretti, but I must get back to work. Perhaps another time I will be able to have coffee with you,' I reply formally, as per my given script, before I stand and shake his hand.

I turn to Mr. Brown and proffer my hand to him. 'I wish you the entire best, sir. You are in good hands with Mr. Moretti. I shall send for your wife and bring her here to sort this out with you,' I add in a smooth, calm voice, as per the script I have to say, adding details of his wife to suit his situation.

Mr. Brown simply presses his lips together. He knows he is in deep trouble with his wife. I want to tell him that you reap what you sow, and that it all catches up with you in the end.

Wisdom. I know I have wisdom. But how many more times must I prove it?

I release the elevator floor lock the moment I re-enter my elevator office. With a jolt, I feel the metal rectangular prism rising at speed.

The doors open on the thirty-eighth floor—the penthouse, owned by the extraordinarily rich, Mrs. Luciati. Elevator Thirteen is hers to enjoy alone. Whenever she summoned it, an over-riding circuit cut out other floors purely to service Mrs. Luciati at her beck and call.

'Mrs. Luciati,' I call to her, in my most endearing voice. I truly like her. She is sixty-seven, and is the closest person to an Earth grandparent I could ever have.

I hold my arms out to her and take her hands in mine, look her up and down and exclaim, 'Graziosa e bella! Your beauty is the light of my day. Where are you going today?'

She links her arm through mine as we walk to the elevator, our eyes interconnected without skipping a beat. 'Grazie, Mr. Harris, my favourite elevator operator. I'm taking Selena to the dog park for some socializing. She has a boyfriend, you know!'

I pat the well-groomed, white Maltese dog, being careful not to upset the pink bow in its fur atop of its head. 'Ooh, Selena, watch out for those boy dogs. They like to do a special dance!'

Mrs. Luciati bursts out laughing and bops me on the arm. I look at her and smile.

The elevator descends the intestines of the building to the ground floor, where Mrs. Luciati walks off briskly in her black fur coat, black long boots and bright pink hat, and Selena walking beside her on a lead. Anyone would think that Mrs. Luciati is meeting her boyfriend at the park. Perhaps she is?

I turn back to the elevator and remember Mr. Brown, sitting out the long wait, pondering his fate of when he will meet his enraged wife, which reminds me to contact her, so I can deliver her to floor thirteen also.

I have taken my sweet time in contacting Mrs. Brown on purpose. The longer Mr. Brown has to reflect on his misdoings the better, only in that it will make him sweat, thinking about how to explain his infidelity to his wife, I hope.

I pull Mr. Brown's business card from my pocket and enter his contact number into my fold-up phone, as thin and as flexible as paper. Some people choose to use their brain microchip to call up the interconnectivity on their life online, or project it onto the back of their hands or in front of them.

'Mrs. Brown. This is Alex Harris. I found your husband crumpled in pain earlier today after your conversation with him. I have taken him to a counsellor, who requests your presence to declare your next move with your husband. The situation is in your favor, Mrs. Brown. Mr. Brown will agree to any of the conditions you choose. But do come quickly before his guilt turns to anger, in which case it will be harder to reason and negotiate with him. Come to Elevator Thirteen. I'll be waiting for you.' I end the connection with her, not giving her a chance to decline the invitation to meet her deceitful husband.

Now I will simply wait for her.

Two customers in one day to the thirteenth floor. Mr. Moretti will be pleased. But not me. I hate being in cahoots with him. I am accountable for my actions and that accountability and its awareness and implications grow stronger each day. It's like I'm being dishonest with myself. I hate my actions enforced by the man.

The next hour goes rather slowly with very few clients joining me for a joy ride in my elevator office. I do, however, get the opportunity to watch people, playing my game of are they mortal, immortal or a Pure One? Timekeepers or hippies? They are fascinating. Their quirky little mannerisms, their insecurities, the masks they wear to deceive others into thinking they are someone they are not.

What do they gain from doing that?

What do they lose from doing that?

How abhorrent can their own self be?

And is it forced, or self-imposed by a need to be accepted by others, or even to protect themselves? I know the answer to that. I also play that game.

I recognize Mrs. Jayne Brown walking on the polished timber floor to Elevator Thirteen before she introduces herself. Her quick step gives her away; a quick step of urgency that means whatever she has to do she wants over and done with quickly. She holds her expression in a robotic fashion, pushing the pain of Mr. Brown's infidelity behind a mask to carefully conceal the bubbling erratic, devastating emotions just under the surface of her skin, I assume.

'Jayne?' I query as she approaches, choosing not to use her surname to hide her identity from those who loiter about the elevator platforms.

She bobs her head and narrows her blue eyes at me.

I indicate with my hand to step into the elevator. She stands directly in the middle of the confined space, her demeanour as cold as ice.

The moment the doors close and the elevator starts to move, I turn to her. 'Mr. Moretti is the gentleman attending to your husband, Mrs. Brown. He is a highly sort after counsellor in situations such as this. I can assure you that you will be very pleased with the outcome he will offer you.'

Mrs. Brown does not look at me. She is a woman scorned and her fury is palpable.

She follows me in silence to Mr. Moretti's office. I open the door for her and look around the office. Mr. Brown is absent. It's probably for the best. This way, Mr. Moretti can speak with Mrs. Brown without the fire that will burn savagely when Mrs. Brown sets eyes upon her unfaithful husband.

'Mr. Moretti, I would like to introduce Mrs. Jayne Brown to you,' I say formally, gesturing appropriately.

'Thank you, Mr. Harris. Can I offer you a cup of tea or coffee?' Mr. Moretti asks right away, whilst raising his left eyebrow giving me the cue to leave.

'Thank you, but no, Mr. Moretti, I must get back to work. Perhaps another time I will be able to have coffee with you. Elevator Thirteen is busy!' I say, as scripted.

Mr. Moretti does not smile. He simply maintains eye contact with his raised eyebrow until I have finished talking, and then adds with the lowering of his eyebrow, 'Very well. Good day then, Mr. Harris.'

I bow slightly to Mrs. Brown. 'You have my sincerest thoughts for the best for you, Mrs. Brown.' I breathe out steadily, about turn, and exit Mr. Moretti's office to retreat to the solace of my elevator, deep in thought about the cruelty of human nature and the consequences of failing in self-control, not only to the self, but to those whom we love and who matter the most.

I start to see the Earth in a dim light. Its people and the choices they make, not the bright light of beauty in the days of

Earth's creation, filled with love from the Creator. I pray that everyone will one day see and feel the true freedom, the uplift, the soaring spirit, the surrounding light energizing their spirits, and the pure acceptance of their being without the judgment one feels every moment in the dominion of the physical Earth.

I crave to become a mortal human. Not the immortal human I am.

If only I could die.

It is impossible to take my own life once I had gained immortality. It comes with self-building nanobots that repair any damage I do to my body, sustaining the Earthly immortal life.

Sometimes I wish to see how my life will unfurl. To see how I will release myself from human immortality. But then again, the futuristic psalmists, nor the seers nor the prognosticators, know anything. They only feed you information from the clues you give them, with your body language. Wisdom prevails. If someone tells you your future, does that then become the self-fulfilling prophesy? And besides, had I been able to see my future spread out before my eyes, there would be no joy, as I would know what is coming.

Yes, I like that I have no idea about what is going to happen to me from one moment to the next. In that moment, I am starkly reminded that my window for transformation to becoming a mortal is closing. Like Mama's letters tell me. Her letters of regret and repentance and advice.

Perhaps I can't become mortal again on my own. Perhaps guidance will come, in whatever form, for I know that all things are possible. I just have to have faith and humble myself, being thankful for this opportunity of learning, trials, and polishing until I am ready to become mortal to enter the spiritual realm, in my designated time.

The ding of the opening doors resonates through me when I arrive back on the ground floor, pulling me from my contemplative thoughts. I'm confronted with the reality of no queue for Elevator Thirteen. But I do have one patron who decides to enter my humble elevator, as all the others are in service. He has no choice if he is in a hurry, and it looks like he is.

He flicks his overgrown brown hair and paces in front of the elevators in his long brown shorts, dark green hoody and red converse shoes. He sees me waiting for him. He sighs and looks away before he drags himself towards my elevator and steps inside.

'Hi!' I say. 'Which floor?'

It will be a residential floor for sure. I've seen him in the elevator lobby many times. In fact, I've watched him grow from a wee lad, but he has never ridden in Elevator Thirteen with me.

His skin pales and sweat starts to bead on his forehead. 'I-I-I need to get out of-out of thirteen, please,' he stutters while shuffling from foot to foot.

I look at him with concern in my eyes. 'Why? Is it the number thirteen that bothers you?'

'N-No. I heard that some enter thirteen and never return... let me out, please!'

'Sure, but know that the rumor is untrue. I hope to be able to help you out next time,' I say with gentleness of soul, piercing his blue eyes with my honey-brown eyes.

I watch as he sets a quick pace out of my elevator and heads to Elevator Seven. Johnno the operator looks at me and shrugs, then disappears into the building transporter. I watch the numbers above the doors illuminate as they whizz by each level. It stops at floor twenty-seven. I put the floor number to memory in good faith that he will ride with me one day.

I cast my gaze out the large glass windows opposite my elevator. The sun has started to set, spraying the sky with shades of red, orange and yellow, with a tinge of purple. I note that Mrs. Luciati has not returned with Selena yet. It's highly unusual for her not to return in the daylight hours with her dog. I look at the timber floor and feel an uneasiness in my gut. There is something wrong.

At once I enter Elevator Thirteen and shut it down from service, locking it with my key. I'm well aware I can lose my job for putting it out of commission during work hours, but Mrs. Luciati is far more important than the two or three other patrons who will use my elevator in the next forty-five minutes.

Without thinking about my elevator operator attire, I exit the building. The cool wind blasts onto my face and caresses my neck.

'Always keep your neck covered when you are outside,
Liam. Your immortality has a specific scent, and it makes
you a wanted man for scientific experiments.'

I clench my fists as I realize the huge risk I'm taking, going outside without covering my neck. The risk of being exposed as to what I am. But I have to be courageous. Mrs. Luciati is in trouble. I can feel it. Her need is greater than my self-serving preservation and my fear of becoming a research subject, where they experiment with different ways to kill me, to see if I am truly an immortal human.

I stampede across the busy roadway and into the park, stopping at the entrance, then head straight to the dog park. That is where Selena would have met her boyfriend.

I follow the signs and am greeted by the sight of people crowding around, all focused, some visibly upset. And I see Mrs. Luciati's black boots amongst the jungle of legs.

She's in the centre, shaking. And Selena is lying on the ground, covered in blood.

'Excuse me, please,' I assert as I push my way through the concerned onlookers. I squat next to Mrs. Luciati and hold her hand in mine as I lay my other hand on Selena.

Selena isn't breathing. Her life has left her, her open eyes allowing the emptiness of her soul to be seen.

I place my hand over Selena's eyes, one at a time, and close her eyelids, wondering why, out of all of these obvious dog lovers, no one has already done that!

'Rest in peace, Selena.' I feel Mrs. Luciati place her weary head upon my shoulder.

I kiss her forehead. 'I'm sorry for your loss, Mrs. Luciati. Let me carry Selena's body back to your apartment and prepare her for burial for you.'

Mrs. Luciati sobs deeply and her pain vibrates through my body. She stands while I gather Selena's damaged, bloodied body in my arms and hold her close. I walk by Mrs. Luciati's side in slowness, back to the apartment building, and then slow more, almost to a stop. On the pathway directly before the revolving doors of the Great Hall, are three men dressed in black, giving off an air of superiority. Dominance. They are dark-haired and tall, and narrow their eyes at me.

My skin prickles. Three immortal seekers. Wearing scent detectors on their uniforms. No Life Apps. My heart accelerates. Mrs. Luciati stops walking, wipes her tears away, straightens her back, lifts her chin, then we proceed once again.

I look away from them, glad to be holding the blood covered Selena. She is my protection from being discovered as an immortal human. The scent of the dog's blood, thick in the air, will be enough to overpower my immortal scent that their artificial intelligence air analyzer can detect. I become quintessentially conscious of my exposed neck. My mother has made it very clear to me to always cover my neck when out in the open. It did not take long for the immortal seekers to track me the very first time my neck is left exposed.

For a moment, I wonder if any of them is an immortal

human, employed to help the trackers find immortals.

Dudley will be furious that I have disregarded my life by helping Mrs. Luciati. He is possibly storming out of our abode right now, following my GPS to come to protect me.

'Mrs. Luciati, let's proceed to the elevator before the night chill catches us,' I encourage, to distance us from the immortal seekers, who have taken a great deal of interest in me.

She nods, and we enter the lobby of the building. I unlock Elevator Thirteen and enter it with my present company. One alive. One dead. As I turn to push the button for the thirty-eighth floor, my unwelcome visitors scrutinize us.

'Friends of yours, Alex?' asks Mrs. Luciati through her waterfall of tears and sobs of heartbreak.

'No, Mrs. Luciati. Not my type at all,' I respond. Although I suspect I had more in common with one of the men than I care to admit.

Upon entering Mrs. Luciati's apartment I am guided to the laundry. I place Selena onto a towel and proceed to clean her bloodied body with a damp cloth, returning it to its previous whiteness, blow drying her fur and covering her in the sweet smelling powder on the shelf that I know Mrs. Luciati uses on Selena for grooming.

I ask Mrs. Luciati to find some linen to wrap Selena's body in, but before that, I encourage her to brush Selena's fur and say her final farewell. I stand back with my head bowed while I watch Mrs. Luciati in her grief. She sings to Selena and speaks of her love to her. Then finally, she kisses Selena's head, stroking her with trembling hands and gives in to the sobs that overtake her fragile body.

When Mrs. Luciati steps away from Selena, I step forward and carefully wrap the body in linen with gentleness and respect— she was a creation of God, after all.

'Rest in peace, dear Selena. Thank you for your duty in being a woman's best friend,' I utter, kiss my hand and place it onto her wrapped body, and close my eyes.

I smile at myself at the joy that enters my body. We have treated her with honour and respect. 'Selena would be happy, Mrs. Luciati. She would be wagging her tail at the loving care in her preparation for burial. Would you like me to make the funeral arrangements for her?' I ask, to try to help ease Mrs. Luciati's pain.

At first, she doesn't answer. 'Thank you, but no, Alex. You've been so helpful and sweet in coming to rescue us, and in taking care of Selena. I don't know how I could ever thank you.'

'I am honoured to be able to help you, Mrs. Luciati. Let me know if there is anything else I can do for you,' I respond, feeling Mrs. Luciati's deep sadness at the loss of her beloved pet.

I make her a cup of tea and make sure she is settled before I leave her apartment.

Once I am back in the elevator, I look down at the blood splattered over my uniform. A mess as it is, it has saved me from being detained. There is no doubt about that.

Elevator Thirteen arrives at the ground floor and heralds the end of my shift. But before I open the doors, I fuss about ensuring it is clean, free from any of Selena's blood, and smells of bergamot once again, as I like.

Content that the smell of death in my elevator is removed, I open the doors—to the sight of the three men sitting on the white sofa.

I look briefly at them, my heart pounding in my chest. I turn to my left to walk to the staff area to rid the blood stained clothes from me. They follow me. I feel their presence and hear their quickening footsteps.

I stop in my tracks and face them. Courage. 'Can I help you, gentlemen?' I ask in an authoritative voice, meeting their eye contact. Their eyes narrow as they look at me, scanning my eyes, my face, my neck, my hands, my body.

'Ah, no... we thought you were—' the tallest one narrows his eyes at me. '—someone else. But we are wrong. Aren't we gentlemen?' He looks at his companions. 'Please forgive us for following you.' His voice is deep. He dips his head at me.

I incline my head but say nothing as I watch them leave the building, their faces burned into my memory for future reference. I wonder how much they knew about me, or even suspect. And for once in this elevator operator career, I am thankful for the honey brown contact lenses that prevented them from penetrating the windows of my soul to possibly discover my human immortality.

I back away before I face the staff door to add my fingerprint for entry. As soon as the electronically secure doors close behind me, I start to unbutton my blood soiled uniform and head for the showers, where I stand and let the warmth of the water wash over me, soothing my panicked state.

I change into my white button-up shirt and acid wash jeans as advised by Dudley this morning, remove my honey-brown contact lenses and gather the plastic bag containing the blood-stained uniform. I don my long black coat before I head out into the cool night air, remembering to pull the collar of the coat up to hide every skerrick of skin on my neck.

I drop my uniform off at the dry cleaner and make my way to the bar. I hope I have not missed my elevator colleagues. They give me some sort of normalcy in this immortal human life.

As I enter the bar, I spot them sitting at the usual table that some occupy five nights a week, for an hour at the least. I join them, their glances and nods acknowledging my presence.

I recount the dog episode to my work friends, some responding in revulsion at the preparation of the dog for burial, some full of compassion, patting me on the back.

I sit back in silence then, and look around as I listen to the banter at our table, until my eyes are drawn to the bar.

She sits there again, this time with the repulsive Christopher Collins.

He sits closely to her, practically drooling over her while he runs his fingers up and down her spine, suggestively.

I walk over to the bar and sit on the stool beside her. I indicate to the bar tender for my usual scotch, then lean over in front of her to help myself to the complimentary peanuts, brushing my arm lightly against hers, giving her a jolt—enough of a shock for her to drag her eyes away from Collins and to look at me, as intended.

'Ooooh… apologies. Would you mind pushing the nuts this way, thanks,' I say in a cool and calm manner.

As soon as her eyes lock mine, she smiles. 'Liam, hi!' she says, a little too enthusiastically for my liking.

What is going on? 'Oh-ah-Emily, is it?' I reply, trying to sound as if I barely remember her name. She bobs her head up and down, her red hair bouncing around her.

'Liam, this is Chris,' she says, but doesn't elaborate on how they are connected.

I proffer my hand to him. 'Nice to meet you, Chris,' I add, looking him in the eyes. He takes my hands and blinks. Excessively. Trouble. He quickly looks away from me. His unease at my presence is palpable.

I lift my scotch to them both. 'Cheers!' I add, then return to the round table of my comrades, ensuring that Emily is within my range of sight.

I slouch back into my seat and watch as Christopher slugs his liquor and slams down the shot glass onto the counter and demands another one, more loudly than necessary.

Emily looks at him, her eyes wide with fear. He runs his hand up her back and under her mid-length hair and strokes her neck before he moves closer. He leans forward and runs his nose along her jawline, and kisses her just below her ear lobe, placing his other hand on her thigh and inching it higher up her leg.

Emily scowls and pushes his hand away from her, then squirms away from his close proximity. He stares into her eyes and laughs in her face, grabbing her jaw and pulling her towards him, planting a covetous kiss on her lips.

A tear rolls down Emily's cheek as she sucks in a gulp of air and moves her head slowly from side to side, her eyes wide with terror. Collins slams another shot of liquor down his throat, then stands with his large hand around Emily's upper arm. He whispers into her ear before he pulls her off the seat and starts walking with her, shooting an intimidating smile at those around him, making them look away.

Cowards. Abruptly, I stand and follow Mr. Christopher Collins out the door, leaving a little distance between us until I feel it is the appropriate time to act.

He drags Emily down a dark alley, knocking a bin over in his drunken state, and laughs like a hyena.

'Let me go, Christopher... let me GO!' Emily yells.

I see her twisting and writhing to release herself from his grip, until he pushes her up against a wall.

He shoves his face into hers and starts to unbuckle his belt. 'I'm gonna give you what you want, Emily!'

Emily's eyes are large with fear. She gasps for breath, her body shaking.

Without a sound, I step directly behind Mr. Collins. I smell liquor emitting from his body while his face is filled with the ferocity of a lion about to pounce on its prey, seeking to devour and destroy.

'Step away, Chris, while you can. Take your hands off the girl!' I threaten in a deep voice.

'No, Liam, leave. He will kill you!' Emily chokes the words out broken with fear.

'I would much prefer to fight and save you, than to run away from a coward and watch you suffer at the hands of this piece of filth!' I say with venom, staring at the face of the low life.

With a deafening yell, Collins turns on me, pushing me back with force, giving him precious time to turn back to Emily.

He pushes her hard into the wall, cracking her head on the bricks.

I lunge at him, reefing him away from her and sling him into the bins. He falls to the ground swinging air punches. I step onto his useless arms and bend over and grip him around the throat, positioning my thumb and forefinger on either side of his windpipe.

'If I were you, I'd leave. NOW!' My voice is grave, my words slow and articulated perfectly, full of rage. I have to expend a great deal of energy to keep my fury contained to stop me from doing some serious damage to Collins, or even killing him. It would be so easy to kill a mortal. His Life Watch glows. Yellow. 16, 790 days. I catch my breath. His time isn't up, but it's a warning. There are laws about taking the life of someone before their time, as they aren't able to prepare for their death. To get their affairs in order. But still, accidents happen, and the Life App is based on biometric data and biological health. It cannot predict a future physical death caused by environmental factors. It cannot see the future.

I turn my head away from him, my eyes water and fill with disgust. I am not his judge. It is not my place to take his life, no matter how much I hate what he was about to do. Besides, his lifespan is far more limited than mine. He has a much shorter opportunity to make peace with himself and to find where he belongs. I turn my head back to him and pierce his eyes with mine, planting the seed of his own self-judgement and shame that will make him reflect on his actions. His Life Watch glows. Green. 15,768 days.

He tries to avoid my eye contact like a dog with its tail

between its legs. He will be back to see me in the elevator. I give him one final shove then release him.

He scuttles off like a marked man with paranoia, constantly looking over his shoulder at me. I watch until he disappears into the cover of the night.

I turn to face Emily. She has come to and is struggling to stand. I race to her side and help her to her feet and steady her while she staggers. She holds a hand to the back of her head and winces.

I support her weight as she tries to walk. The fifty metres back to the bar seems a lot further. I shudder as I feel the icy wind wrap around my exposed neck, reminding me of my unexpected encounter with the immortal seekers earlier. I keep my head down on high alert. I'm not used to feeling so vulnerable.

I shield Emily with my body when we enter the bar. I don't want other patrons looking at her with pity, or to think the worst, labelling her. I grab my long black coat, and hers, then head out the doorway with her to a waiting cab.

'Hospital?' I ask, concerned for her. She could easily have fractured her skull on the wall and be concussed. The sound of the thud of her head as it hit the brick wall was sickening to hear.

'Home. My mother is a nurse. She will know what to do. Thank you,' Emily says with her eyes closed, her hand supporting her head.

'Are you certain?' I ask.

She nods and gives her address to the driver.

The night mist has already set in when I open the door to the apartment I share with Dudley. It is dark inside except for a low light in the kitchen. I breathe out in relief that I will not be having a post-mortem conversation with Dudley about the busy day that had unravelled, and what I could have avoided.

I fill a glass with water at the kitchen tap and lean against the bench top while I drink deeply to satisfy my thirst.

'Interesting day, Liam...'

It is Dudley. I turn. He sits in the wing chair in the corner of the darkened room. His legs are crossed and his hands are joined together at his chin. His eyes are dark and brooding. I'm in for a treat.

'Interesting is not a word that I would choose. I would say more random. Incidental. Totally left field. Odd. But far more than just interesting. Of course, from your point of view, watching with your technology from the safe confines of this apartment, it could be interesting for you. However, I did expect a visit from you when the three men showed their ugly faces,' I add to Dudley's summing up of the events of the day.

'You were in no danger what-so-ever, Liam, the blood from the dog saw to that, and those coloured lenses you are compelled to wear at work saved your sweet little butt!' Dudley rises from the wing chair and takes slow precise steps towards me. His stare is deadly serious. He is certainly unimpressed by my heroics today. 'Your time is running out, Liam,' he says as he pokes me in the chest with his long, bony index finger. 'You left the girl. You should have stayed with her.'

'I left her with her mother, who is a nurse,' I reply to his accusation.

'But is she okay?' he asks, piercing my eyes with his.

'I don't know, you tell me—you are the one who likes to predict the future based on my movements, Protector!' I rebound.

'I can only see things when you are there... you know that, child!' he retorts.

I pace back and forth in front of Dudley, place my hands on top of my head, close my eyes and take a deep breath. *She was with her mother.* 'Why are you so concerned about the girl,

Dudley? I meet many every day!'

He turns away from me then and waves his hand through the air. 'Maybe she didn't come away from the attack as well as you thought. I'm turning in for the night, and I suggest that you do, too.' He walks away. Matisse saunters after him in her catwalk manner, no doubt after a warm place to sleep tonight.

I give a low growl in exasperation. Emily told me she was okay and her mum is a nurse? I shake my head. I'll find out how she is tomorrow.

I head for the shower to cleanse my immortal human body then retire to my bedroom. I slide between the soft, white, cotton sheets of the bed and gaze up above me.

The ceiling is awash with swirling energy. I looked to my left and focused on the glowing Earth energy mass. I close my eyes before reaching for it. It's further away than it usually is, but I manage to pull it to me.

The instant my hands gets close to it I feel the energy connecting with me. The fourth state of matter arcs to my fingertips like bolts of lightning, lighting my entire sleeping chamber as if it is daylight. I see it. Even with my eyes closed. My fingertips tingle under the warmth until the plasma retreats back into the glowing ball of energy. I lift it and turn it around. I wonder how the self-building, repairing nanobots react to the slight power surge.

While mesmerized by the iridescent blue and green colours, I reflect on what I had experienced today, especially after the confrontation with Christopher Collins and the energy it had taken to control myself from hurting him. No matter how much I hate what he was doing, I have no right to deal with him like I am a vigilante. To help Emily, yes. But not to physically attack Collins.

My mind wanders back to Mr. and Mrs. Brown and the man with the red glowing Life Watch. The young boy was right.

They had not returned. They had not been seen and it was bad publicity for Elevator Thirteen. I will deal with it tomorrow.

I place the energy mass back onto my beside table. I need to sleep. Not because my mind needed it, for being human immortal meant that my mind is forever engaged. I sleep only because it is a haven to switch off to the reality of my life. And, I sleep out of respect for the generous chance I had been given to possibly become mortal, so that I can die and enter the heavenly realm.

I close my eyes. 'Caro Dio, possa io avere coraggio, temperanza, saggezza, giustizia e pazienza – Dear Lord, may I have courage, temperance, wisdom, justice and patience,' I whisper. *Patience and acceptance; those attributes I have learned, but self-control was the essence of temperance, self-control in all things, and I am still working on that one.* 'And my dream of Light, being in Your unimaginable, indescribable presence one day, where no eye has seen, no ear has heard, and no mind has imagined what You have prepared for those who love You. Trusting in Your timing and wisdom, in Jesus' name, I pray,' I say. I hold my breath. 'And Lord, help me to find my way back to my mortal self,' I add, then relax, breathing, that sacred gift He has given us. Feeling comfort from my spiritual connection, I slip into the unconsciousness of sleep.

11

Wednesday.
11 days.

The steady drizzle of rain cloaks the city as I arrive at the opulent historic building where Emily lives with her mother. One hundred and twenty-one years of learning has given me a sharp eye for detail, and an uncanny ability to recall facts associated with the city. This building holds secrets unknown to the occupants, all of them mortal humans.

I push the security button. It lets out a low hum.

'Hello, Liam.' It's Mrs. Finnigan.

'Hello. I'm checking up on Emily. May I come up to see her, please?' There is silence on the other side of the intercom and I think I have lucked out, until the click of the security door releasing the lock catches my attention.

With haste I enter the building and run up sixteen flights of stairs to Emily's mother's apartment.

Breathing heavily, I knock on the door. Within a short amount of time, Mrs. Finnigan opens the door and invites me in.

Emily is sitting on the sofa in front of the fire place with a blanket covering her legs and a cup of tea in her hand. Forlornly she stares into the fireplace.

'Hi,' I say gently as I approach her.

'Hi,' she replies, but does not look at me.

'How are you feeling today?' I ask, hoping for an honest answer.

'Oh… you know, sore here and there, still with a massive headache, feeling sorry for myself, and angry at my vulnerability with my choice in men.' She frowns. 'I was so stupid. So, so, stupid!' She rebukes herself and a tear rolls down her cheek. She swipes the tear away with the back of her hand, presses her lips in a hard line and shakes her head.

'It could've ended far more catastrophically for you. You know that, and I don't have to go into details for you. Is there anything I can do for you, besides beating him up, which I did… a little… last night. ' I look down and smile to myself, triumphant in not taking his life.

She shakes her head while still looking into the flickering fire. Then she looks at me. 'I must thank you for helping me,' she says, her voice choking up, the reflection of the orange flames in her green eyes.

'It was my honour. But do yourself a favour, and have some self-defense classes,' I say before I touch her arm. My hand warms on her skin as my prayer of healing for her pain and emotional trauma enters her cells.

She looks up at me and deeply into my eyes then. Mother would have said it was our souls touching.

But we can never be together.

She is mortal.

I am not.

She is forbidden.

'Take care,' I whisper and bow my head slightly to her. Then

I leave after a brief conversation with Mrs. Finnigan.

All seems well with Emily. I don't know what Dudley has been going ballistic about? I wish he had been more specific about his concern.

The Great Hall is a short walk from Emily's apartment building. So I pull up my collar, lower my head and walk at a brisk pace to the Coffee Pot Café to pick up a caffé medici. I wrap my hands around the chocolatey orange coffee and continue on my journey to work.

I hear the immortal seekers before I see them. Two of them walk in time, the other is out of time, like a song with a missing beat.

I focus my eyes downward and stiffen my collar upward. They are on a direct path, coming towards me, and it will not look good for me to turn and retreat from them.

Instead, I reach into my pocket and pull out my sunglasses to cover my exposed blue eyes, and then spill my latte over my hands to cover any immortal human scent I may be emitting.

The immortal seeker in the centre of the trio looks at me with his head cocked sideways, frowning at me as he comes closer. He touches the arms of his companions and they focus on me.

Time seems to slow like a drifting leaf as they approach me. I "accidentally" drop my latte and it splatters on the ground. It's an attempt to conceal my scent. I raise my arms like overacting a drama scene, with a loud sigh, before I put my hands on my hips and pick up the cup and lid.

I turn then, and walk back to the Coffee Pot Cafe where the aroma of coffee beans saturates the air. There is no way they will be able to pick up on my immortal scent here. And they wouldn't dare arrest me whilst I am amongst the patrons, who will then become witnesses to their job, exposing them and alerting people that immortals walk amongst them, filling them with fear. I have never thought in one hundred and twenty-one years, that coffee would ever become my life saver, but it has.

While I stand in the long queue, the immortal seekers wait outside the café, watching me, pacing within their small space. I sit at a table inside the café and read the paper while I sip on a cappuccino at a snail's pace, in the hope they will tire of waiting, and leave. My strategy works. I call a cab and am delivered to the entrance of my place of work. I have no intention of being abducted as an immortal for the purposes of science.

I can't even think about being a research subject without dry retching. It upsets my being with an unbearable ugliness.

High on caffeine, I change into my work uniform and present myself with calmness at Elevator Thirteen. The up and down day of the elevator day has already begun, and I am fifteen minutes late.

Alert, I watch the comings and goings around me, waiting in earnest for a visit from the boss. My prediction is that he will be standing in front of me within the next three minutes.

And I am not disappointed.

'Mr. Harris, step into the elevator and close the doors.'

I stare at him for a moment, then blink, and step inside the elevator with him and close the doors as instructed. He holds his mouth in a straight and serious line.

I am about to be fired from my job. I'm certain of it. I inhale steadily, hoping the elevator will still smell of bergamot from yesterday's cleaning, calming my boss and filling him with mercy towards me.

'Sir,' I say to him, tilting my head in respect to him.

He squares his shoulders towards me in an aggressive-passive gesture.

'Mr. Harris, it has come to my attention that you left your elevator yesterday before the closing of day. Is this correct?' Menace swarms in his words.

'Yes, sir,' I respond, and wait with a straightened back, my hands held firmly by my side, as if standing at attention and waiting for an order from the sergeant.

'And then today, Mr. Harris, you were fifteen minutes late for your shift. Is this correct?'

'Yes, sir,' I respond, keeping my voice even.

Mr. Wilson stares at me, then looks to the wall on his left and presses his lips together in a hard line. He looks back at me. 'Mrs. Luciati phoned me to inform me of your actions with herself and her dog yesterday. She wanted me to give you a raise in your salary for going above and beyond your mere duties of elevator operator, however—' Mr. Wilson's lifts his chin and looks down at me, his intention to unnerve me. I maintain eye contact with him, resisting the urge to remove my white glove and touch his skin to send a calming prayer to the core of his brain. I refrain, deciding I will be using an unfair advantage over him. I must not interfere with the course of consequences for acts. '—We do not reward our employees for feats of heroism, Mr. Harris. I do, though… acknowledge your kindness towards a long term and valued resident of the Great Hall. And for your tardiness to work this morning—do you have a valid reason that will absolve you from discipline?'

My mind races back to the immortal seekers this morning. 'No, sir. It was remiss of me to not adhere to my work responsibilities, and I sincerely apologize,' I reply to his question, inclining my head in respect to my employer.

'Mr. Harris, I must issue you with your second strike against your name. You are aware of our three strikes and you're out policy, are you not?' he questions, raising his eyebrows.

'Yes, sir, I am. Clause 13.13 of the Elevator Operator Contract.'

'Good day then, Mr. Harris,' Mr. Wilson says as he indicates our time together has ended.

'Good day to you, Mr. Wilson,' I return, opening the elevator doors for him to exit, much to my relief. I wait for a count of ten, then close the doors and beeline to the thirteenth floor to make a visit to Mr. Moretti.

He is standing at his red filing cabinet as I enter his office. The glass wall vibrates to the ceiling as I knock three times to alert him of my presence.

'Alex!' he exclaims with joy as he turns at the sound of the knocking.

'Good morning, Mr. Moretti. I have impeded upon you without a new client, and for that I am sorry... I would like to ask how Mr. and Mrs. Brown are doing, and also to ask when I will be able to deliver them to the ground floor of the building. People have noticed they have not returned and are avoiding Elevator Thirteen for that reason.'

'Alex. Do not fret. They are due for release at 1.30 pm today. I shall see you then... yes?'

'Absolutely, without fail, Mr. Moretti. And... thank you,' I add for good measure before I leave to return to my elevator office, sailing it down the elevator shaft to the ground floor.

I open the doors to two men and two women. They look at me with expectant eyes. Expectant eye hoping. Pleading.

'Good morning,' I say and invite them into the elevator, then see the red glow from their Life Watches under their long sleeves. 'Which floor would you like to proceed to?' I ask, knowing very well what their answer will be.

'I don't want to die,' a woman says, a tear trailing down her cheek.

'Would you like... more *time*, then?' I ask, raising an eyebrow.

She nods her head. I look at the other three and they too, nod.

I push button number thirteen, and the elevator pod rises. 'Are you sure about this?' I ask them.

They nod. In unison.

'Be sure to read the non-disclosure agreement,' I say and widen my eyes at them in warning. I'm crossing the boundary of my employment contract. But I don't want them to be what I am. But perhaps they do want to be what I am? But when they have lived for five hundred years, will they still want to be immortal?

The elevator doors open on the thirteenth floor. I follow them out then guide them to the office they seek. We enter.

'Mr. Moretti, I would like to introduce these lovely people to you. They all, wish to speak to you about more *time*,' I say, inclining my head, my insides repelling at what they are about to do.

Mr. Moretti closes his eyes before his head bobs to me in the affirmative. He turns to the new client. 'Welcome. Our experience in extended time, and our ability to resolve matters of time is second to none. I have appointments available now, as individuals or as a group if you wish.'

They look at each other, then one speaks. 'As a group, please.'

'Mr. Harris, can I offer you tea or coffee while you wait?' he asks. My cue to leave the office.

'Thank you for your offer, Mr. Moretti, but I must get back to work. Perhaps another time I will be able to have coffee with you,' I reply formally, as per my given script, before I stand and shake his hand.

I turn to the men and women. 'I wish you all the entire best, sir. You are in good hands with Mr. Moretti,' I say in a smooth, calm voice, as per my script.

I step out of the office and return to my elevator. I lift my hand and turn it over. I have a tremor. It's my body reacting to forcing myself to go against what I believe. I shake my hand out, and it stops. I push the button to return to the ground floor.

She sits on the white leather sofa alone, waiting, twirling her hair around her finger like a school girl. Her long legs are crossed and her knees are showing.

She jigs her leg up and down and looks from left to right and right to left again. She checks her fold up communication device for messages in a quick, abrupt manner.

In the next moment, Mr. Collins appears, worse for wear, probably due to the effects of too much alcohol the evening before. His head snaps quickly to his left when he sees Emily, and his eyes widen in a look of panic. His Life Watch glows green. He looks at it and he makes a calculation after his reaction to her.

Emily stands, and takes quick steps toward him. And as if in a defensive reflex, his hand shoots up at her, his palm facing outwards, warning her off. He looks to his right at my open elevator doors and rushes inside, almost closing the doors before I do.

'Which floor, sir?'

'Eight... wait. Aren't you the guy who was at the bar last night, when I was—' his voice and words are indecisive, either from fear, or alcohol induced memory loss. I frown at him, piercing my honey-brown eyes into his. His face freezes momentarily, then he shakes his head. 'No. He had blue eyes. Mistaken identity. I apologize.'

I press my lips together then smile and nod at him. He thanks me as he leaves the elevator, still unsure of whether I am Alex or Liam.

Returning to the heart of the building I'm greeted by an impatient Emily Finnigan. She is tapping her foot on the wooden floor as she stands directly in front of my elevator. The sound of her tapping barges into the elevator and bounces off the walls before she enters, like a bull at a gate, with her rage in tow.

'Good morning, Miss Finnigan. Floor eight, I presume?' I enquire, absolutely certain that she is headed there on a mission of revenge.

She stands in the centre of the elevator and nods her head at me with determination. I chuckle to myself at her fiery behaviour that matches the colour of her hair. I still, then worry about her. Is she acting out from the trauma of the night before? Is her concussion causing erratic or irrational behaviour?

Out of the corner of my eye, I see her head turn my way with caution. She looks with high interest at my face before she blinks and swallows. 'Alex, pardon me if I am wrong but, you look and sound like Liam, exactly, except for the eye colour.'

I turn my body to face her. 'I am a double agent,' I respond to her.

'You are?' her voice rises with shock.

I'm surprised that she believes me. I push the stop button on the elevator. 'No, Miss Finnigan. I am toying with you, trying to cheer you up. Is there anything I can help you with?'

'No—only if you know how to deal with a freak who attacked me last night and then spent the entire night sending inappropriate text messages to me!' A tear slips from her eye and she wipes it away on the back of her hand. She hands her personal communication device to me.

My heart breaks for her as I speed-read through the messages from Christopher Collins. 'And you are headed there to see him now?' I ask in a quiet voice, not looking at her.

'Yes. It will just be the three of us. Chris, me… and my gun,' she says without emotion as if it is an everyday occurrence.

My heart stops momentarily as adrenalin surges through my body.

Without warning, she bursts out laughing hysterically. 'I'm kidding. I don't even own a gun! I just want to make certain he knows if he ever tries to do anything like that to me again, I'm going to cut his pleasure centre off, cut it up and send it to him in the post!'

Blood drains from my face as she speaks of her intention. I feel faint, then see stars before my eyes. I take a deep breath to restore my physical state. If I had a Life Watch, I'm sure I would have lost a year off my life.

She turns her head and looks at me with eyes full of remorse. 'Again. I'm kidding. I have a personal apprehended violence order I want to deliver to him. His text messages were the perfect evidence I needed to be able to get protection from him.'

'Would you like me to accompany you to his office, Miss Finnigan?' I straighten my shoulders.

'Thank you, but no. It's something I have to do myself. Personally, I want to see the look on his pretty-boy-face as he reads the contents of the envelope,' Emily says in a voice that is barely audible. She burns her eyes into the elevator doors with boldness.

I raise my eyebrows and pilot the elevator to the eighth floor and turn and face Miss Finnigan again. 'Would you like to accompany me to a funeral at 6PM today?' I ask with a cheery voice. I cringe inwardly, disappointed in my delivery of what is supposed to be a sad occasion.

Emily frowns at me.

'It is a dog funeral. Mrs. Luciati invited me and a partner to it. Will you go with me?' I ask as butterflies rampage inside my stomach. I hope the extra information will make more sense to her.

A small smile erupts on her face. The twinkle in her eye reminds me of the flashy diamond rings I have seen so many times on the fingers of women.

'I'll see you at 5.50PM, ground floor, Alex. A dog funeral could be... interesting,' she says as she backs out of the elevator, smiling at me.

I bow my head to her, suppressing the largest smile I have ever wanted to share with somebody else.

For the next few hours my elevator becomes the service elevator with all sorts of trades people coming and going, deliveries being made here and there, jovial conversations between workers and myself. Conversations of a different sort to the usual controlled, carefully worded conversations with clients. It is a welcome intrusion in my day.

Then, at the precise time of 1.30PM, I arrive at the thirteenth floor to collect Mr. and Mrs. Brown. To my surprise, they are sitting, waiting on the red-leather seat next to the elevator doors. I wait for a moment inside the elevator and observe them, overcome with a feeling of awkwardness, panic even, wondering what Mr. Moretti has bestowed upon them to seemingly correct their spiralling lives for them.

I step out of the elevator at the sound of footsteps approaching. Mr. Moretti. He proffers his right hand. 'Mr. Harris. It's wonderful to see you again,' he says, over-smiling at me and shaking my hand in earnest.

I narrow my eyes at him, trying to pick up on any non-verbal cues he is inadvertently trying to send to me. Nothing.

'Mr. Moretti. It is wonderful to see you, too. I have come for Mr. and Mrs. Brown. I believe they are eager to return home today,' I say, still waiting for some sort of sign from Mr. Moretti to guide me.

He looks away from me and towards Mr. and Mrs. Brown. 'Hayden and Jayne, Mr. Harris is here for you. Thank you for coming to see me, and I will be here at any time you need to visit me again. Have a nice day.'

They both look up at him at the same time, nod and smile at him as if it is orchestrated. They look at each other before they stand and hold hands like they are newlyweds.

'You have the tickets, don't you, Mr. Harris?' Mr. Moretti whispers into my ear. I nod, and gesture for Mr. and Mrs. Brown to enter the elevator before I enter after them.

'Mr. Brown, Mrs. Brown, you both look wonderful today. Which floor would you like to go to, may I ask?' I know very well they will choose the ground floor. But it is protocol for me to ask clients who enter the elevator.

Mr. Brown looks at me and smiles. '*We...* would like to go to the ground floor, Alex. I hear that it's a beautiful day outside and I wish to take my stunning wife out for the most pleasant afternoon tea she has had in a while,' he answers, looking at Mrs. Brown with adoration.

'Excellent. It is a most beautiful day outside. Oh, and a courier came by and asked me to give these to you. He said you must read it without delay, or you would miss your flight to your honeymoon destination.' I hand him the bright yellow envelope.

Mrs. Brown gives a little jump in excitement as Mr. Brown takes the envelope from me, and then kisses his wife as if they are the only two people in the elevator.

I turn away from them, and pretend to polish some of the brass decor in the elevator. Even the ding of the opening doors does not distract them from finishing the kiss.

I smile at the waiting clients as the doors open, then clear my throat when they still do not stop their smoldering embrace. 'Presenting the ground floor, Mr. and Mrs. Brown,' I add as a further hint that we have arrived. It is only the applause of the waiting clients that arouse them from the kiss and bring them back to reality.

Mr. Brown holds the flushed Mrs. Brown's hand as they leave, creating a path between the waiting, smiling clients.

That afternoon, I have never been so busy with business men and women, residents and people of all sorts wanting to ride Elevator Thirteen. Mr. Moretti will be exceptionally pleased with my progress.

By 5.45PM, I have changed out of my work uniform and into civilian clothes ready for Mrs. Luciati's dog funeral. I look myself over in the mirror, double checking the honey-brown eye lenses I have left in, for the sake of Mrs. Luciati and Emily Finnigan.

To them I am Alex. Mr. Harris—dark wavy hair slicked down, honey-brown eyes, tall, formal and very efficient at my job as an elevator operator.

The white sofa opposite Elevator Thirteen is vacant as I walk to meet Emily at 5.50PM. She's nowhere to be seen. Anxiety bubbles inside me. Perhaps she will not turn up? I look up to the tall ornate white ceiling, put my hands in my jeans pockets and breathe in deeply before I sit on the white sofa. Is this what disappointment feels like?

I turn my focus back to the sofa. I have always wondered how it feels to sit on it. People occupy it constantly while they wait for others to meet them at the elevators.

I lean forwards and place my arms on my knees, clasp my hands together and wait, hoping that she is running just a little late. I also hope she knows it's very special of me to invite her to the dog funeral. She is the very first woman I have asked out in my one in my one hundred and forty-nine years on the Earth. But then I guess, how many guys ask girls out to a funeral for a first meeting? In hindsight, perhaps it is not such a romantic thing to do.

I close my eyes and berate myself at such a ludicrous scene. She is probably still laughing at my absurdity, wherever she is. At least it's memorable as a pick-up line, if you can call it that.

The gentle tap-tap-tap of shoes echoes throughout the near-empty foyer. They belong to a woman. Men's shoes soundly entirely different to the dress shoes of women, and the timing of the steps also. Men take longer strides.

I open my eyes and see a pair of black shoes near mine on the polished timber floor, then follow the map of her body up to her eyes. Her beautiful green eyes. They connect with my honey-brown lenses.

I smile shyly at her and stand, smoothly. 'I thought you had abandoned me, Miss Finnigan. I was about to go and say my last goodbyes to Selena the dog by myself,' I say to her in a soft, deep voice, maintaining our intriguing eye contact.

She blinks and smiles at me. 'How could I miss the funeral of a dog—man's best friend, or woman's, in this case—a dog who loves unconditionally with all of its heart. And besides, it's a first for me... to attend a dog funeral. It's too extraordinary to miss this opportunity, even with the elevator operator!'

I smile weakly at her and look at the floor. I had hoped she would come to the dog funeral because of me. I return my eyes to hers. 'Shall we then?' I offer her a smile, and indicate to her to step into the elevator.

Within forty-five seconds we arrive on the thirty-eighth floor at the apartment of Mrs. Luciati. The doors open to the opulent entrance of her home. I hear Emily gasp when she sees the interior design and décor.

I place my hand on the small of her back as we step out of the elevator.

'Alex, my darling!' Mrs. Luciati calls in a loud voice as she rushes to greet us, kissing both my cheeks. 'And this beautiful creature is?' she asks, smiling.

'This beautiful *woman*... is Emily Finnigan, Mrs. Luciati,' I say, looking into Emily's eyes as I introduce them.

'Welcome, Emily. It's so nice of you to be here to say goodbye to Selena. Please come this way, the ceremony is about to start.'

We follow Mrs. Luciati through her luxurious apartment to a splendid outdoor area overlooking the spectacular night lights of the city. A cool breeze strokes my skin with the lightness of a feather.

A short man dressed in a black suit with a black and white polka dot shirt stands with his hands together. His eyes are fixed upon the small white coffin in front of him. There are seven people in total gathered together for this special occasion.

'Dear friends, we are gathered here tonight to fare thee well

Selena Luciati. The forever loyal and dedicated companion of Lucy Luciati. It is with great sadness that we say goodbye, but with great joy that we remember the happy times of her life here in God's Great Garden. Selena, we thank you for your service and the abundant times of happiness that you brought Lucy, and we release you to rest in peace. Fare thee well, beautiful Selena.'

'Fare thee well,' I repeat after the dog funeral director, then lower my head in quiet reflection.

I feel Emily move close to me and link her arm through mine. I am filled with an indescribable peace; an Earthly one I have never felt before.

I open my eyes to the sobs of Mrs. Luciati. She has her hand on the small white coffin and wipes away her tears with a white handkerchief. I go and stand beside her and place my hand on her shoulder. 'She is at peace, Mrs. Luciati, and with all of the other dogs you have owned. Life is good.' I kiss her head then step away from her, grab two wine glasses and handed one to her and raise my glass. 'To Selena, the four-legged, bouncy companion that made life easier to live,' I say in a quiet voice, then touch my glass to hers.

'Thank you, my dear Alex,' she whispers, energy drained from her voice.

I walk away as another of Mrs. Luciati's friends approach her, and go and stand at the hand rail overlooking the city. I take a small mouthful of red wine.

I feel Emily's presence next to me. 'That was a lovely ceremony. How did Selena die?'

'Her boyfriend murdered her.'

'What, Mrs. Luciati's boyfriend?'

'No, Selena's boyfriend. Apparently, he had a savage streak that nobody knew about. He overpowered her with his size and strength. He clenched his strong jaws around her neck, flung her from side to side and it was all over in the blink of an eye. Poor

Mrs. Luciati was so distraught as she knelt next to Selena's lifeless bloodied body. It broke my heart. I hope she buys herself a new puppy. She so loves her dogs.' I look into my wine, the redness reminding me of the dog's blood I had smeared over my uniform and hands: the blood that saved me from the immortal seekers.

I look up into Emily's eyes and see a tear falling. I wipe it away with my thumb and she looks away from me. She's beautiful; her creamy white skin and the heart shape of her face.

'I am sorry. I did not mean to make you sad,' I whisper with perfect enunciation, remembering to keep in character of Alex Harris the elevator operator.

'No, it's okay, really.' Emily looks up into my eyes again and lingers there, sending warmth throughout me, and another feeling, like an adrenalin rush. I want to hold her close to me. But I don't.

'Alex, let me steal your girlfriend from you for a moment. I will return her, I promise,' says an enthused Mrs. Luciati as she touches me on the arm.

I smile at her, 'She is not my gir—' Emily's finger is on my lips, stopping me from saying more. She smiles at me. As they walk away from me, arm in arm, I lift my finger and touch the tingling sensation that lingers where Emily has touched me.

It's a whole hour before Mrs. Luciati returns Emily to me. I know where she is the whole time that we are apart, though. My eyes find hers every few minutes, devouring her energy, her presence.

My eyes are closed when she sits next to me on the garden seat, thirty-eight floors above ground level. She smells exquisite, like honeysuckle mixed with the freshness of innocence.

'What do you see, Alex?' she asks in a soft, mellow voice.

I release a long breath and keep my eyes closed. 'I see the wings of angels wrapped around dying people as they breathe their last breath. I see a candy store selling healthy candies. One statement is true, the other is not,' I say with all honesty, open my eyes and smile crookedly at her.

She stares at me in disbelief then bops me on the arm. 'Liar, liar, pants on fire!' she whispers as a slight smile plays on her lips.

I lean in, my lips close to her ear. 'The night is escaping. It is time to go. You know what happened to Cinderella,' I whisper.

Mrs. Luciati walks us to the elevator. 'Thank you, my dears, especially you, Alex. If I had a grandson, I would want him to be exactly like you.' She holds her hand over her heart and looks directly into my being. I wonder what she can see there. Can she tell that I am different to the mere mortals who dwell in her world? I blink and smile with the shyness of a five-year-old. No one can ever tell I am immortal, unless they, too, are immortal humans. And then it is as plain as day. Our skin is blemish free. No freckles, moles, scars, wrinkles or discolourations.

I hug Mrs. Luciati's hand with mine and turn and enter the elevator with Emily.

Despite the dog funeral, it's been a pleasant evening, but one that must come to an end like every other day on this planet. Time is indeed precious for mortals, counted by the human interpretation of passing moments, of breaths you breathe, of eyes blinked, of steps your take, of years upon the Earth, which were numbered. Except mine. There is no end.

My happiness takes a dive and I frown. Moods are funny things, and emotions. They swing to opposite sides of the spectrum so quickly, sometimes so unpredictably, catching you unaware. But you are in control of your emotions, right? Or do your emotions react to people and circumstances around you? It's such a complex mix of feelings that we have to deal with.

I press the button to ferry the elevator down to the ground floor and place my head back on the wall of the elevator, and close my eyes.

Emily is standing opposite me in the rectangular prism of the pod. I detect her proximity. The moment she steps closer I will know it. Right now she is a still as death. Is she nervous about being with me in the elevator, alone? I hope she isn't. I would never hurt her in any way, or make a move on her for that matter.

'Alex is not your real name, is it?' she says, finally.

I keep my eyes closed. 'Why do you say that?' I ask and open one eye to look at her.

'Your acid wash jeans, shoes, shirt, your sandalwood aftershave. The same as Liam's. Your eye colour is not what I see now, is it? It's what you present to the people in this building, daily, isn't it?'

I take a deep breath and shake my head. *The acid wash jeans that Dudley told me to wear...* 'All of the elevator operators wear the same honey-brown contact lenses. It is part of our uniform. They are most irritating to wear. I detest them!'

'So, you are Liam?' she says slowly.

I nod, and my heart races.

She stares straight ahead then leans against the wall, as pale as a ghost, sliding down until she is sitting on the floor of the elevator.

I push the stop button of the elevator and fold my arms. 'Ask away. I'm up for twenty questions,' I say in a quiet voice losing my formal elevator voice, and sit on the floor, too.

She remains silent, and I wait patiently.

'Do all of the elevator operators have an aka name?'

'No, just me.'

'Why do you have the name Alex, here?'

'When I first started, I was given the wrong name badge, and it just stuck. It's sort of a running joke, I guess.'

'Why do you all have to wear honey-brown eye lenses?'

'I can't answer that question due to my contract.'

'I have met you twice as Liam.'

'That's not a question. It's a statement.'

She looks down at her fingers that are knotted together. 'Why didn't you tell me you were Alex from the elevator the first time I questioned you about it at the bar?'

'You were the one who decided I was a different person, not me.'

'But you had blue eyes and you told me your name was Liam.'

'I was telling you the truth.'

'Do you have a photographic memory?'

'Yes.'

'Do all of the elevator operators have a photographic memory?'

'Yes'

'Why?'

'For security reasons.'

'But aren't there security cameras everywhere?'

'Yes.'

'Then why must you have photographic memories?'

'Because photographic evidence can be altered.'

'But memories can be persuaded into something different as well, can they not?'

'If you can be hypnotized…'

'What do you know about Christopher and me?'

'I have a great deal of knowledge about Mr. Collins that I am not able to tell you for confidentiality reasons, and I only know what I have observed of you with your mannerisms, choices, body language, plus a little bit more because of the time we shared at the dog funeral tonight.' I inhale deeply. It's unnerving exposing myself to another person. I never do it.

She smiles then puts her hands over her face. 'What can you tell me about me?'

'Are you sure that you want to hear?'

She takes her hands away from her face and nods. 'Yes—go ahead.'

'That's not a question.'

'Liam, aka Alex, what do you know about Emily Finnigan?'

'Emily Finnigan has red hair, green eyes, and a beautiful smile. She is tall and slender. Men notice her. She can be nervous at times shown by the way that she knots her fingers together, like you're doing now. She's pleasant to all her talk to her, but you can see her summing people up, like you are doing to me now. And that is the end of the Emily Finnigan reading for today.'

'How old are you?'

'Twenty-eight.' Plus one hundred and twenty-one years, so I'm one hundred and forty-nine years old, I want to add, but don't.

'Do you wish to work as an elevator operator for the course of your natural working life?'

'No.' My natural working life has no end date I want to say. Do I wish to work as an elevator operator till the end of Earth time? No.

'Elaborate.'

'That's not a question.'

She rolls her eyes at me. 'If you could choose to do a different job, what would it be?'

'I would like to be a seeker. A healer.'

'Which one, a seeker or a healer?'

'Both.'

'How can a person do that?'

'By study, observation.'

I leave out the word, prayer. People often back away from you if you have faith—a belief in the Ancient of Days who created the heavens and the Earth.

'Are you studying?'

'Bing! Your twenty questions are up. Shall we continue our journey to the ground floor so you emerge enlightened about me?' I say as I stand.

'Only if you remove your contact lenses so I can see your

blue eyes, Liam,' she says to me as she stands, moving closer, placing her hand on my arm.

I breathe deeply as she touches me. 'I can't do that, Emily. Not here. Not now.' I push the ground floor button and the elevator descends. The doors open and I wait for Emily to step out of the elevator first. 'If you wait five minutes, I can go and remove my eye lenses and meet you at the revolving doors, if you like.'

She turns to face me, and nods. 'If I like? I would like. I will wait. Do I call you Alex, or Liam?'

'For you, I will answer, to either. But if I answer to neither, know that it's for a reason.'

She narrows her eyes then frowns at me. I brush my hand over hers as I leave to remove the lenses from my eyes.

She stands to the left of the revolving doors reading her personal communication device and twirling her hair around her finger. I want to do that. Her fitted black dress emphasizes the deep, red-orange colouring of her hair. As I walk towards her, she glances up at me—then does a double take, and smiles.

'Let's get you home, Miss Emily, before the predators are let out to play,' I say, pulling my black, three-quarter length coat on.

She folds my collar over and looks deeply into my blue eyes and then at my lips. I smile crookedly at her.

'Ah—there are the eyes I love, Liam,' she says, almost like a melody. I bow my head and look to the floor and close my eyes feeling self-conscious.

We cannot be together, ever.

She slips on her coat and we leave the building. I pull the collar of my coat up to cover my neck, to cover my scent, and tuck my hands into my pockets. It's safer for her that way.

Emily links her arm through mine and we fall into the same walking rhythm to the cab rank. If I was mortal, I'm sure my heart would have beat as one with hers.

'How's your head?' I ask as we sit in the back of the cab together, a chemical attraction bouncing between us.

She touches the back of her head where she hit it against the brick wall the previous night. 'Funny, I haven't even thought about it since I met you tonight!' Emily says, then looks at me with a huge grin and touches my hand with hers.

For a moment in time her eyes freeze in mine, although it feels like an eternity. Has she unknowingly pulled some healing energy from me?

The cab stops at exactly the precise moment necessary to break the connection between us. With a silent sigh of relief, I slide out of the cab and go and open Emily's door, like a gentleman should.

She steps out and stands directly in front of me with her eyes settling on my lips. Her unspoken question of kissing paints a perfect picture in my mind. No is the answer. I wish it could be a yes, but cards dealt to me say no.

I close the cab door and walk beside her into the building, making sure my hands are tucked into my pockets so she can't entwine her fingers through mine. I need to have some discussions with Dudley about keeping my energy to myself.

We enter the elevator and I lean on the hand rail as Emily stands near the buttons.

She looks at me and her lips curl up. 'Which floor would you like to go to tonight, sir?' Her face is serious and her voice lowered as an attempt to sound like a man.

'Number sixteen please, Miss,' I say and beam at her.

She inclines her head at me, then pushes the button to light up number sixteen, and stands back, as pleased as punch.

Without warning, I lean forward and push every number on

the elevator buttons.

'What are you doing?' she says in horror, her eyes piercing mine.

'I'm teaching you something that may save your life.'

'And what could that possibly be, Liam? Who are you? My bodyguard or something?' Her voice is full of bitterness.

I run my hand through my hair as I feel compelled to tell her my knowledge. 'You have to know that if you ever get into an elevator with someone who you feel uncomfortable with, or you feel threatened by, they are less likely to attack you if you have every floor pressed. There is less time for them to hurt you and you have a possible escape on every floor. I... I... just want you to be safe.'

She looks at her knotted hands and then back at me. The elevator rises and stops at each level for four levels, before she speaks to me again. Her face is full of anguish and pain as she looks up into my eyes. 'Hold me please, Liam. Just hold me.'

I remain where I am, leaning against the hand rail of the elevator with my hands behind my back. I have avoided direct human contact like this for the last one hundred and twenty-one years for a reason. I have only allowed myself to make physical contact through my hands, and briefly at that, to help others. If I hold her in my arms, she will be enveloped by the warmth of my healing gift that wanders over the surface of my skin. It's highly addictive to others. She will be transported to a level of something akin to a drug-induced high. She will either be repelled by me, or unwilling to part with me. This can only end badly, unless... I focus inwards and try to pull the healing energy to the core of my being, leaving as little of the force around me as I can. My healing gift from above is why I want to be a seeker, a healer. And she is seeking me.

I touch each of my fingers, conflicted as to what to do.

I inhale a calming breath and take a small step towards her

and hold out my hand to hers to pull her towards me. She looks into my eyes and I see her deep sadness and pain. How can I not help her?

I wrap my arms around her as she leans into me. I close my eyes and intensify my focus to visualising my healing energy field, pulling it inward away from her as much as I can. She is enveloped by my coat covered body, with no skin to skin contact.

I feel her relax, then tighten her arms around me. I place my hand onto her head then lower my lips and kiss her temple. My mind wanders to visions of our lips touching in a sensuous, lingering way. I have never kissed a woman before, and I have never desired it. But I crave it now.

She is the forbidden fruit.

I feel like I can't win, stuck on the Earth as a forced immortal human, feeling the desires of the flesh, but knowing it is forbidden. My DNA has been altered by AI technology.

The elevator door dings. 'I'll walk you to your door,' I whisper, and release my arms from her.

'Mmmm,' she hums.

I frown. It's my healing energy. She can obviously feel some of it. This is exactly what I was trying to avoid.

She links her arm through mine as we fall into step and walk to her apartment door, like she and I are a "we". She doesn't knock on the door or take out her key. Instead, she turns to me and drinks in my eyes, connecting us again.

I should look away, or knock on the door for her, but I don't want to. I want to stay here in this place of pure elation.

She moves her hand up to the side of my face and touches me lightly. 'Thank you,' she whispers, moving so close to me I am sure that she is in my healing energy zone. But I don't care. I have never felt this awareness before. It's like a drug giving me a high.

She tilts her head and closes her eyes, our lips almost touching.

I blink hard to break my heightened sense of attraction to

her. What am I doing? She is mortal. I clear my throat. 'Good night, Emily. Thank you for coming to Selena's funeral with me… sleep well,' I whisper against her lips as I run my fingers down the length of her hair and step back from her.

She takes a slow breath, gazing at me in a dreamy state. Then she smiles before she opens the door and disappears into her mother's apartment.

I turn and head to the elevator in a brisk walk. The night mist will be coming soon, along with the human immortal seekers of the night. There are more of them lurking in the darkness. I have to get to the safety of my apartment.

Within ten minutes I arrive at my building by cab. The door of the apartment opens without me touching it. Bad news. A reprimand is coming my way. Negative vibes flow from the room beyond the door like a deep resonating double bass infiltrating the air with sound waves of doom. I enter and take off my coat, open the closet door and reach for the coat hanger.

'Sit,' Dudley commands.

I still, mid-action of hanging my coat in the closet, steeling myself for words, accusations and rebukes coming my way. I place my coat on the clothes hanger, close the closet door and sit in the wing chair by the glowing fire, and wait for my protector to talk.

Dear Liam,

Your protectors have been chosen and trained by your previous protectors for you. They are there to shield and guide you. You must listen to what they have to say. This is for your benefit.

Love always,
Mama & Papa

'You have two problems, Liam. One is a menace, and the other will be fatal for me or Emily.'

I inhale sharply. No. That cannot happen.

'I must warn you of the path you are on, and tell you to think about the consequences of your actions, not only yourself, but others involved.' Dudley closes his eyes shakes his head, sadness dripping from him. Dudley has never spoken to me like this before. Our history of communication has always been to mix seriousness with jokes, teasing each other affectionately about our misgivings on the Earth. I did expect him to do a post mortem on today's events, which were numerous, and scold me about the girl. But he did none of those things.

I feel a sense of danger and foreboding coming from the man I have come to love. Something I was doing had to change. I remain in front of the fire place with Matisse curled up beside me, purring each time I touch her. As I look into the mesmerizing flames of the fire, I go deeper into my conscious thought. Is my job the problem, the immortal seekers, or Emily?

My mother and father warned me about the physical realm we journey on before they breathed their last breaths. I must find the letters they left me.

'Thank you. I have a lot of thinking to do, it seems.' I stand up and run my fingers through my hair. The word frustration comes to mind, but that is an understatement. Best if I head off to bed. 'Night, Mr. Castoro—sogni d'oro,' I say to Dudley.

'Sweet dreams to you, too,' he replies, waving his hand in the air as he disappears up the stairs.

After showering, I close my eyes, allowing the memories of my parent's advice to come to the forefront of my vision. I reach for the wooden box of letters sitting atop the desk, and pull out the one I need to read now. The paper of the letter is now stained yellow, not crisp white like one hundred and twenty-one years ago.

To our dearest Liam,

Be careful, don't get caught in the perceived power of being a human immortal. There is no true human immortality. It is a lie. You must find a way to return to the Light, your rightful place, to our Creator.

There are two types of love, Liam. One is true and deep, the other is purely physical. They're also known as love and lust. You cannot have any lustful physical relationships with a mortal. You will fall in true love with one mortal, but you cannot know her in an intimate way. It is forbidden for human immortal bodies to sow their seed with mortal bodies. A mortal and an immortal must never connect reproductive DNA. Do you understand this clearly, Liam? This is the law of the universe, and the research during the production of the human immortal concoction proved the sacredness of mortals.

However, Liam, when you find the antidote to your immortality and become a mortal, and you must find it before it is too late, the physical side of love will come naturally with true love. But only when you become a mortal being... you must be sure. You must look for a sign of mortality.

Love,
Mama and Papa

So the problem is Emily? She is mortal. I am not. She is forbidden. But I know that, so what is the problem? The immortal seekers? Are they good or bad—I have no idea until I have a decent conversation with them, but then that is a risk in itself.

Is it my job? I am good at it. And I work by the rules.

I lay in bed and turn off the light. At once my room is illuminated by the glowing Earth globe. But it now has a companion; a glowing spherical mass of soft red. Dudley has placed it there as a reminder of necessary caution.

I reach for the Earth globe of light and rest it in the firm hold of my hand. Earth is not my eternal home. It's a sacred place I have been privileged to live on, and to witness the grandeur of God's creation.

I've been here for the last one hundred and forty-nine years. Humans have desecrated the beauty and sanctity of the Earth, mining it and polluting it and abusing it for the sake of greed. I don't want to witness it anymore. I clench my jaw as my body tenses at the thought of destruction to the Earth. I want to become a mortal human. Now. And I want the right to be able to return to the spiritual realm, my rightful eternal home.

I place the Earth globe to its stand on my beside table. I am obliged to touch it each night. It's in the contract of "Here now. Here forever".

I rest my hands on my chest and keep my eyes on the ceiling. I focus on my beating heart, and the law of God written on my heart and mind. And I'm so thankful. I want to fuse with that awareness, to stay there in peace, but I know that within moments it will be gone when I drift off to sleep. It's a glimpse, a reminder of my dream of Light.

As the brightness fades along with my joy, I become heavy with the burden of my immortal life, my spirit trapped in this heavy, cumbersome shell of flesh, blood and bones. Instead of dampening my spirit, the thought lifts me to find the antidote of the immortal elixir, and to release all who have been subject to this travesty against their will.

I close my eyes. "Caro Dio, possa io avere coraggio, temperanza, saggezza, giustizia e pazienza – Dear Lord, may

I have courage, temperance, wisdom, justice and patience,' I whisper. *Patience and acceptance; those attributes I have learned, but self-control was the essence of temperance, self-control in all things.* I am learning that with Emily. 'I pray, Lord, that you help me to find the answer to return to a mortal, and to help others as well. And my dream of Light is with me always, being in Your unimaginable, indescribable presence one day, trusting in Your timing and wisdom, in Jesus' name I pray,' I say, feeling comfort from my spiritual connection before I slip into the unconsciousness of sleep...

10

Thursday.
10 days.

'Buongiorno, Liam.'

'Good morning, Dudley,' I reply.

'Hai guardato nella sfera rossa di cautela?' he asks.

'No. I did not look into the red ball of caution you left beside me bed,' I reply, scrutinising his face. He is withholding information from me. 'Do you have one?'

'I gave myself one as well,' he says, not making eye contact with me.

'Ah… twinnies,' I scoff. 'You gave yourself one?' I try to hide my smile at the absurdity. 'And you glimpsed into it?' I ask.

He looks at me, then raises his left eyebrow and shakes his head, his double chin flapping in the process. 'It's not time yet. When it pulsates, it will be time and the message will be released,' he says matter-of-factly.

'Like a ticking time bomb,' I over articulate. I'm not impressed with the red globe. So childish.

'It's a remin—'

'Der. I don't need a reminder, Dudley! Every second of my mind is consumed by this—' I wave my hand over my body now older than Jacob from the Old Testament. Except he died. A. Mortal. Death. '—age of mine and the impossible task of trying to release myself from this… this… torment.' I release my breath in disappointment. I run my hands over my face. 'Si prega di accettare le mie scuse, Dudley. I have brought you to this,' I say, unable to eat my cooked breakfast this morning.

'I accept your apology. You have been in continual danger since innocuously taking the immortal brew one hundred and twenty-one years ago. And hunted by the immortal seekers. We must be more diligent with each step that we take. Hopefully we will be able to diffuse the dangerous situation, and pray to the Mortal-maker to undo what has been done to you.'

'Dudley—how do I pull my healing energy force further into my being so that it cannot be detected by mortals?'

'Infine mi chiedete per la schermatura della forza di energia blu!' he says.

'Yes, finally I have asked you! Just tell me what to do instead of gloating, my dear friend,' I reply with a smirk on my face.

'You must form a small circle with your lips, as if you are whistling, then suck in air to fill your lungs and hold that air inside of you for as long as you can. Your healing energy will then be 99.9% undetectable.'

'Grazie signore,' I say, totally grateful for his information. I pull my lips together to form the circle, and suck in air like a vacuum cleaner.

Dudley's laughter bounces off the walls.

I release my breath and narrow my eyes at him.

He shakes his head. 'Got you!' He grins ear to ear. 'Actually, all you have to do is to inhale deeply through your nose.' He raises an eyebrow at me. 'But you *did* look funny. Imagine doing that in public!'

I load my immortal human body with the food it needs for energy for the day, scowling at Dudley. I have experimented by withholding food for my body to see if it would return me to being mortal. But all it did was turn me to skin and bones with no energy, feeling nauseous.

'Vediamo stasera!' Dudley calls as I open the door to leave.

'Yes, see you tonight!' I call back before I disappear into the outside world.

Two men stand before the doors to Elevator Thirteen. My first clients for the day. They are dressed in jeans and white T-shirts. One a familiar face from the day before.

I incline my head with a smile, then indicate for them to enter the elevator. 'Good morning. Which floor would you like to proceed to?' I say.

'My friend would like to see Mr. Moretti please,' one of the men from yesterday says.

'You, also?' I ask him.

'No. Just helping my friend,' he says.

'And you were happy with Mr. Moretti's service yesterday?' I say.

'He saved my life,' he says then frowns at me. 'You remember me from yesterday?'

In my periphery vision, I notice that he no longer wears the Life Watch, and his friend has his hand wrapped around his wrist, covering his Life Watch. But the red glow seeps through. 'I remember every person who joins me in the elevator. It's my job.' I smile at him, then push button number thirteen.

The elevator rises to the symphony of silence.

'Be sure to read the non-disclosure agreement,' I say like a clash of cymbals. 'Have you thought about the consequences of more *time*?' I say, not looking at them. I'm crossing the boundary of my employment contract. But I don't want them to be what I am.

The elevator doors open on the thirteenth floor. I follow them out then guide them to the office they seek. We enter.

'Mr. Moretti, I would like to introduce these men to you. One was a client of yours yesterday. The other wishes to speak to you about more *time*,' I say. My right eye closes involuntarily then pops open again. Do I have a glitch?

Mr. Moretti closes his eyes before his head bobs to me in the affirmative. He turns to the new client. 'Welcome. Our experience in extended time is second to none. I have an appointment now, if you would like to take it.'

The man in need of more time nods.

'Mr. Harris, can I offer you tea or coffee while you wait?' he asks. My cue to leave the office.

'Thank you for your offer, Mr. Moretti, but I must get back to work. Perhaps another time I will be able to have coffee with you,' I reply formally, as per my given script, before I stand and shake his hand.

I turn to the man. 'I wish you all the entire best, sir. You are in good hands with Mr. Moretti,' I say in a smooth, calm voice, as per my script.

I step out of the office and return to my elevator, remove my elevator operator cap, then run my hand through my hair. It's getting harder to take people to the office of Mr. Moretti. I sigh, then push the button to return to the ground floor.

She stands facing the expansive glass wall looking out into the cloudless day as I step out of Elevator Thirteen.

She doesn't see me, but I soak her in to my memory while she converses on her personal communication device, tapping her foot as she speaks and holding an artist's canvas in her other hand.

She turns and catches sight of me as the elevator doors close, much to my relief. I have to keep my distance from her. She has already had a taste of my healing energy force.

She's sitting on the white leather sofa seat when my elevator returns to the ground floor again. Her chin is propped up by her hand, her elbow on her knee.

She stands and walks towards me, enters the elevator, leans against the side wall and waits for the doors to close.

'Miss Finnigan, which floor would you like to venture to today?' I ask in my proficient elevator voice.

She doesn't reply.

I breathe out, resisting the need to roll my eyes, wondering what game she is playing. She leans over and pushes every floor button on the elevator.

The elevator travels one floor. Stops, and the door opens. The doors close.

'You are either making a point, or you feel uncomfortable with me and may need to escape at some time. Which is it, Miss Finnigan?' I ask, disappointed that she has reacted to me this way.

The elevator travels one floor. Stops, and the doors open. The doors close.

'Perhaps it is both, Mr. Harris,' she answers, piercing my eyes with hers.

The elevator travels one floor. Stops, and the doors open. The doors close.

'You are mad at me because I have offended you in some way, yes?' I ask. She is difficult to read.

The elevator travels one floor. Stops, and the doors open. The doors close.

'Quite the opposite, Mr. Harris! I could not sleep last night.

I had a buzzing sensation that felt like energy bouncing around inside of me. Much like a bad case of anxiety. I also kept getting a vision every time I closed my eyes. So I painted it for you, just to get it out of my head!'

The elevator travels one floor. Stops, and the doors open. The doors close.

Emily turns the canvas around. I try to stop my eyes from widening in shock, but fail. Before me, is the most extraordinary painting I have ever set my eyes on in my one hundred and forty-nine years.

Before me, is the most fascinating captured view of something she could never have seen. In the centre is a large, detailed tree, bearing beautiful fruit, a river and light, everywhere, with arcs of colour haphazardly being thrown off from the centre and flicks of paint strewn across it – gold, blue, scarlet and purple. And Light. The presence of God.

It's my dream of Light.

Is this how absorbing some of my healing energy affected her? It's like she can see beyond her physical surroundings and into my world. My mind.

The elevator travels one floor. Stops, and the doors open. The doors close.

'Miss Finnigan, your painting is impressive, almost mesmerizing, if I may say. The colour palette you used is dramatic, yet delicate. Where have you seen this before?' I ask to quell my curiosity. I raise my chin slightly and look into her eyes, watching her pupils dilate as she looks at me.

The elevator travels one floor. Stops, and the doors open. The doors close.

She starts to shake her head then frowns. 'Nowhere. I have never seen anything like this. My mind became obsessed with the image. And.' She looks away from me. 'And, I felt I was painting it for you. So here it is.' She holds the canvas toward me to take from her.

The elevator travels one floor. Stops, and the doors open. The doors close.

'You know you could sell it and get thousands of dollars for it. You have captured something powerful and breathtaking and… celestial.'

The elevator travels one floor. Stops, and the doors open. The doors close.

'No. I want you to have it. Think of it as a thank you gift for saving me from Christopher Collins. When I look at you, I see my... hero.'

The elevator travels one floor. Stops and the doors open. The doors close.

My chest tightens. I can't let her get attached to me. 'Ah… that would be the "halo effect". It occurs when someone helps you out of a traumatic situation and is a perfectly normal reaction. Thank you for the painting. Can I ask you to leave it with the information desk on the ground floor so I can collect it when my shift finishes?'

The elevator travels one floor. Stops, and the doors open. The doors close.

'Oh, yes, of course,' she answers, biting her bottom lip.

Something else is bothering her.

The elevator travels one floor. Stops, and the doors open. The doors close.

'Miss Finnigan, is there anything else I can help you with?' I enquire in the voice of Alex Harris.

The elevator travels one floor. Stops, and the doors open. The doors close.

She hesitates before she answers. 'No. It's all good. I think I shall have to speak to Liam later. Ground floor please, Mr. Harris,' she requests after sounding cryptic.

The elevator travels one floor. Stops, and the doors open. The doors close.

'Certainly, Miss Finnigan,' I answer, overriding the other ten floors we have not stopped at yet during our conversation, and redirecting the elevator to the ground floor where she exits with a spring in her step.

The doors close and I am summoned to the eighth floor. It is Mr. Collins who waits for Elevator Thirteen. His hands are in his pockets and he is whistling. He steps into my elevator and stands dead in the centre of the platform.

'Good morning, Mr. Collins. Where are you headed to?' I ask in an upbeat voice.

'The viewing platform please, Alex.'

I smile at him and push button number thirty-nine. There is a palpable silence as I stand waiting for the inevitable question to come my way.

'Alex.' He takes his hands out of his pockets. Is that your real name, Mr. Harris?'

'Yes, why do you ask, Mr. Collins?'

'It's just that you're a dead ringer for someone I met a couple of nights ago.'

'Under pleasant circumstances I would hope, Mr. Collins, but your body language tells me otherwise,' I say in a non-threatening tone.

'He left what I would call a… bitter taste in my mouth. I think I'd like to meet him under different circumstances to see if he is still… arrogant,' Mr. Collins adds, clearing his throat afterwards.

'Hmmm. That sounds somewhat ominous, Mr. Collins. I'm sure whatever happened will be forgiven and forgotten.'

He looks into my eyes and I remain calm. He will return to me today before the end of business hours. Of that I am absolutely certain.

Soon after the elevator stops at the viewing deck, Christopher

Collins steps out and into the company of his cockamamie crew; there are five of them. I liked to call them the bad-boys-of-the-office. They invest their time in wild, ridiculous, pointless feats of self-indulgent, self-serving gratifications, either as individuals, or as a group, often hurting innocents in the process. Then they meet up here on a regular basis and gloat about their deeds, offering each other encouragement in feats that err at high risk.

The elevator doors close as their howls of laughter ring out, probably at the expense of an innocent. The elevator coasts down to ground level, the epicentre of the building. It's a busy day. I scour the ground floor noting faces of people, familiar and not.

The elevator operators pass glances of encouragement, with shoulders back and heads held high, a wide stance with feet pointing outwards, their faces bathed in a warm smile.

And then my eyes land upon a person sitting on the white sofa.

He wears a black trilby hat on his head. The newspaper is open and held up to conceal his face. He is old and wears a sterling silver signet ring on the fourth finger of his left hand. A brass-handled walking stick rests against the sofa.

I lower my head, narrow my eyes and connect them to him. 'Superiore del mattino per voi, Dudley,' I mouth to him. It is our regular "top of the morning to you" whenever we meet in public.

He nods ever so slightly acknowledging my communication. He taps his foot three times. His presence is a bad sign. He knows something I do not. He is my Protector. He has come to protect me from something, or someone. Adrenalin in my body surges, awakening my mind so that it is on high alert.

The elevator doors close at the press of the button on the thirty-ninth floor. I am returning to the viewing platform already.

Mr. Collins steps inside and positions himself directly in the middle of the elevator pod again. He looks at the numbers above the doors.

'Welcome again, Mr. Collins. The eighth floor?' I ask, looking directly into his blood-shot blue eyes. Did he drink or smoke something?

He blinks and nods, radiating a low mood.

'You don't enjoy riding in elevators, do you?' I note.

His head turns toward me, his eyes questioning.

'Whenever you enter my elevator car you stand directly in the centre of the floor. The safest place to be,' I add.

He remains silent, unresponsive.

'Where is Miss Finnigan, lately, Mr. Collins? I hope that she is well and has not come down with something. She is always so eager to see you and to be in your company. Her eyes would light up whenever she saw you. I'm quite sure that she is smitten with you, actually.'

Mr. Collins rubs the back of his neck then cups his hands over his face. I have hit a raw nerve; planted perfectly to enter into his subconscious to bring his wrong doings to the surface.

'Alex, I think I have done something terribly wrong. Yesterday morning, Emily delivered a restraining order to me. But I don't know what I've done to upset her!' His voice is taut. He reaches into his pocket and hands the Restraining Order to me, his hand shaking.

I scan my eyes over the words. 'Did you go out with her before she gave you this?' I ask, as I hand the paper back to him and stop the elevator car from descending to the eighth floor.

'Yes. She was with me at a bar. I was drunk, Alex. I can't remember much about the night at all. But what I do remember is sketchy to say the least, except I am sure you were there—but your eyes were a different… colour. And, you… acted differently.'

'Mr. Collins, you are well aware that alcohol will impede recollection of memory, and may even change the details of what you thought that you saw—your brain making up things to connect the missing pieces. Where do you think you saw me?' I ask, curious as to how much he remembered that night.

'In an alleyway, threatening me,' he responds.

'What were you doing in an alleyway?'

'That's the thing. I have no idea!' He places his hands over his reddened face and clears his throat. 'I can't remember parts of the night. It goes blank when I try to piece it together. I worry that… I might have hurt Emily—but I just can't remember! But I must have done something for her to give me this.' He holds up the restraining order with a hand tremor. 'And now it's on my record. I need to know what I did before I lose my mind over it.'

He shoves the Restraining Order back into his pocket and kicks the elevator wall, making the car wobble on its tracks.

'I know a man who can help you with something called Recovered Memory Therapy. He's—'

'I want to be intimate with her, Alex. But I just can't get her to do it with me—' he freezes, then falls to his knees and pinches the bridge of his nose with his fingers. 'Help me, Alex… help me… I know I can't force her into sex with me. But did I do that the other night? Is that why she gave me the paperwork?' His body is shaking.

I remove my glove and place my hand on his shoulder. My finger rests against the skin of his neck. 'Christopher. It is not okay to force intimacy. It sounds like you are obsessed with her, and what you are talking about is… lust, not love. I can help you. I can help you right now, if you wish,' I say, driving a healing prayer through his skin to enter his bio-electrical system, calming him and opening his mind to my guidance.

He nods. I remove my hand from his shoulder, step back and push the elevator button, number thirteen.

Mr. Moretti is sitting behind his desk when I knock on his partially opened office door. I see that he is looking at sealed containers and attaching microchips to them.

He quickly opens a wall safe, places the containers inside,

closes it, and positions a picture over the area, concealing the location of the safe.

'Come in,' he calls in a modulated voice. As soon as he catches sight of me his face lights up with affection. 'Mr. Harris, for what do I owe this pleasure?' he asks, knowing very well I have a special delivery for him.

'Mr. Moretti, I would like to introduce Mr. Christopher Collins to you. He is going through a difficult time at the moment, and I suggested to him that you may be able to help him,' I inform, looking at Christopher Collins as I speak, watching his body language to gauge his reception to Mr. Moretti.

At once, Mr. Moretti reaches forward and takes Mr. Collin's hands in his own, his warm-heartedness spreading to Mr. Collins to put him at ease. 'You are very welcome here, Mr. Collins. My ears, eyes and heart are open to help you on your quest. Please take a seat. And Mr. Harris... can I get you a cup of tea or coffee?'

'Thank you, but no, Mr. Moretti. I must get back to work,' I reply, nodding my head, indicating I understand the cue to leave Mr. Collins with him.

I proffer my hand to Mr. Collins. 'I wish you all the best, Mr. Collins. I'll be back to pick you up once you have finished with Mr. Moretti. You are in very good hands.'

I continue on my way to my elevator, where I head to the ground floor again. I shake my head, disappointed with myself for continuing to work for Mr. Moretti.

When the door opens, Dudley still sits there with his fine black hat, polished black shoes, black and white newspaper, his legs crossed. I smile. He has the patience of a saint. He obviously does not know the precise time that something is going to happen, because then he would have turned up just prior to the event in question.

He taps his foot three times on the polished wooden floor again.

'Godere guardandolo lavorare, Dudley?' I want to say to him, asking if he was enjoying watching me work.

He lowers his paper and looks at me straight in the eye—deadpan, on cue. He is bored. I have seen that look many times before.

I lower my head and chuckle, then step back into the elevator and am transported to the seventh floor.

Mr. Wilson enters Elevator Thirteen as soon as the doors open. He closes my doors and holds its position outside of the seventh floor.

'Good day, Mr. Wilson,' I say, inclining my head in polite respect to my boss.

'Mr. Harris, it has come to the Elevator Operation Department's attention that you have stopped Elevator Thirteen mid-travels on quite a few occasions as of late. Is there a problem we need to be aware of?' he asks, raising both eyebrows at me.

It is a question that contains a double meaning. Underneath the kind words of concern he is in fact conveying to me that the department is watching my movements.

'No, sir, there is no problem. My number one priority is to keep residents and clients happy. I like to stop the elevator if they need deeper conversation, where I can help them, if at all possible. Our people are our business,' I explain in a persuasive manner, attempting to sound genuine.

Mr. Wilson narrows his eyes at me and studies my face, pausing uncomfortably before he replies. 'Very well, Mr. Harris. You are correct. Our people are our business. Thank you.'

He releases the elevator doors, steps out and vanishes into his office.

Satisfied that I have held my own, I close the doors and descend to the ground floor again.

I do not expect to see Dudley standing by the vast glass window when the doors open. He taps his foot three times then stops. Three times, then stops. Three times, then turns to face me.

His walk is slow but determined as he makes his way towards Elevator Thirteen. He stands to the side and looks at his watch before his eyes avert to the right to the three men who have entered the foyer.

The immortal seekers.

Tap, tap, tap goes Dudley's foot.

Tap, tap, tap, I respond on the brass on the wall around the elevator doors. I clench my fists and stiffen my back, waiting for the inevitable to occur. So this is the reason that Dudley has come to my place of work today.

The immortal seekers pin their eyes to mine as they approach, their walk slow and deliberate. They nod once at me as they enter my elevator.

Dudley follows them in. He keeps his eyes hooded after looking me in the eye as he brushes past me. The immortal seekers lean against the handrail opposite me. Dudley is to my right, like a referee of a game.

Except, this is no game.

'Good morning, sirs. Which floor can I take you to?' I ask in a civil voice, pulling my immortal and healing energy inside of me. Dudley holds a subtle smile. He knows what I am doing, and it amuses him. I want to tell him this is not the time to see humour. His head moves side-to-side. I release my energy. The immortal seekers are here to confirm whether or not I am a human immortal. I become acutely aware that my neck is exposed.

Dudley slips me a handkerchief. It has a strong lemon scent. I take it from him and wipe it over my neck, and place the handkerchief in my pocket.

'We hear the viewing platform is quite spectacular… Alex,' speaks the middle man, his eyes focusing on my name badge.

'Yes, quite,' I answer, looking at each of them through my honey-brown contact lenses that would offer me protection in the short term. I press number thirty-nine, and the doors close to allow our ascent to the floor with the panoramic view of the city.

'And you, kind sir,' I turn to Dudley. 'Which floor is it that you would like to pursue?'

'Thirty-nine, also. It appears that it's a popular destination today!' he responds.

The man on Dudley's right turns to him, lowers his head and looks into Dudley's eyes. He tap the hand of the middle man who also turns, and so it spreads to the third one.

Essentially, their attention has been taken away from me and is now directed at Dudley. My protector. My guide. My friend. My confidante. I love him like my own father.

I shift awkwardly on my feet as the silence in the elevator becomes foreboding. Danger is lurking, and the negative energies collide in an aggressive manner in the concealed space.

I look from Dudley to the three men and back again, waiting for an attack of some sort.

'Did your mothers never tell you not to stare, boys? It is just simply and plainly rude!' Dudley suddenly blasts an assault at them, making them retract their attention from him. 'And, if you are going to enjoy the view, I suggest you change your attitude, open your mind and appreciate what you will see. You act as if life is a bother! Do you not realize how many people would love to be able to walk, talk and breathe easily as you do!'

The men remain silent, staring at the ugly old man who rides the elevator car with them.

Dudley closes his eyes closed with a disgusted look upon his face, feigning that his feelings have been deeply hurt.

I chuckle to myself. I'm watching the master at work. He is good. Very good.

The doors open on the viewing platform. Dudley indicates

to the three men to exit before him. But they don't, and Dudley grows impatient. 'Obviously, your mothers did not teach you to obey directions of those older than you. Now get out of here and enjoy the view that you came to see!' he asserts with an agitated voice.

Two of the men smirk as they look down and leave the elevator. Perhaps it is their age. I wonder how old they are. Then the other man and Dudley exit.

They doors close. I am summoned to the second floor, removed from the highly volatile situation that is unfolding between Dudley and the immortal seekers.

He is outnumbered and I feel helpless. I override the elevator computer and return to the thirty-ninth floor, where I hold the elevator there with the doors wide open. I will not leave my protector when I know trouble is imminent.

Dudley wanders about the viewing platform as any tourist would. But I know he isn't there to admire the 360 degree view of the city. He is there to monitor the movements of the three men. He will go where they go, until they are off the radar and we, or should I say, I, am safe. Ultimately, that is why Dudley is here with me: to ensure I'm not captured and used as a science experiment.

I need to find the solution to cure my immortality, and hence, my safe passage back to the spiritual realm, however long it takes. And if Dudley dies, there is another protector to replace him. I cringe inwardly. My mother and father have gone to great lengths to ensure my protection. My safety.

Within a short amount of time the unwelcome passengers are back in the elevator car with me, plus Dudley as well.

'Sirs, I hope you enjoyed the view. Are you headed back to the ground floor, or do you have business elsewhere in the building?' I ask in my professional elevator operator voice.

They look at each other. 'To the ground floor, Alex,' replies the man standing between the two others.

As the car descends smoothly, he looks down at his immortal detector. It's flashing. His fists clench then unclench before he opens his eyes, and narrow them at me. 'I thought I could smell you the other day, Alex.' His voice is thick and threatening.

I freeze momentarily. My first reaction is to look at Dudley, but I don't. I come to the realization that I need to protect him. I am the cause of this confrontation. I should be the one who takes the consequences, not Dudley.

The immortal seeker takes a step closer to me, closing the gap. I suck my healing energy deeper into my body, sure it is one hundred percent undetectable. I will not attack the hunter first. I have been taught to attack only in self-defense. But then technically, if one knew an attack is forthcoming, wouldn't a surprise planned offensive be in defense?

In complete contrast to the man's expectations, I stand straight-backed and place my hands behind me, squaring my shoulders in a gesture that tells them I am not afraid of them.

Dudley leans between us and pushes the stop button on the elevator panel with his walking stick.

We are now frozen mid-floor. There is no escape. The outcome will either be a traumatic and gruesome battle, plastering blood in the elevator pod, giving Elevator Thirteen a terribly bad name. Or, it could end amicably.

Personally, I prefer the second option.

Dudley returns to his position in the elevator and throws his trilby hat in the centre of the floor before he clears his throat.

The dominant man retreats back to his side of the elevator, but does not lean against the rail as the other two do.

'Delivered or created?' Dudley asks.

They look at each other as if Dudley is speaking a different language.

'There is a difference—delivered or created?' he asks again, annoyance and impatience in his voice. 'Were you... born of a human... or grown in a pod?' he rephrases and articulates in slow speech.

'Yes and no,' he responds, pointing to his companions.

'Ah... now we're getting somewhere. Why do you seek Alex?'

'We're collecting immortal humans for a private corporation.' The middle man smirks and cocks his head to the side.

Dudley raises his eyebrows at him. 'And you seek him in an aggressive manner? I suggest you go back to your private corporation and discuss how to attract human immortals to join you. They will more likely be cooperative with the company if they choose to join you by their own decision.'

I look at the men opposite me. They aren't buying Dudley's words. The left man opens and closes his right hand.

Dudley taps his walking stick on the floor of the elevator, and mechanisms of a gun protrude. He points it at them. At once the three men's heads snap to look at him, and their eyes grow wide with fear. 'Grow wisdom in your being, and help others when you can so you can be prepared for whatever is in your future. Make allies. It will be better for you.' Dudley sighs then picks up his hat. 'Boys, when you are outside, day or night, look up. That is where you will find all of your answers.'

Dudley nods at me and I engage the elevator to continue its descent to the ground floor.

The three subdued men abandon the elevator car like young boys reprimanded by a School Head Master.

'Ho molto da imparare Dudley. Ringraziamento per essere stato il mio maestro e il mio protettore. Non vedo l'ora di vedervi a casa stasera,' I say as Dudley retracts the mechanisms on his walking stick, and steps out of my work pod. I adjust the trusty black trilby hat on his head.

He turns to me with his hand on the elevator door to stop it from closing. 'I am your protector, and yes, you have a lot to learn. I will see you later tonight,' he whispers with an ounce of humour in his voice.

I smirk at him, remove my glove and place my hand on his, connecting our kindred spirits before he leaves. This man is my soul-saver, my spiritual deliverer. My mother and father have chosen wisely in their requirements for my protectors.

The thirteenth floor is my next port of call. Mr. Moretti smiles at me when the doors open. Mr. Collins sits on the red leather sofa to the right of the elevator.

When I step out of the elevator, Mr. Moretti proffers his right hand. 'Mr. Harris, it is wonderful to see you again,' he says, over-smiling at me and shaking my hand in earnest.

I narrow my eyes at him trying to pick up on any non-verbal cues he is inadvertently trying to send to me. Nothing. 'Mr. Moretti. It is wonderful to see you, too. I have come for Mr. Collins. I believe he has finished his session with you today,' I say, still waiting for some sign from Mr. Moretti to guide me.

He looks away from me and then at Mr. Collins. 'Christopher, Alex is here for you. Thank you for coming to see me. I will be here at any time you choose to see me again. Have a nice day.'

Christopher Collins looks up at Mr. Moretti with a face devoid of emotion. He nods and smiles at him as if it is orchestrated. He stands and turns to face me. I gesture for him to enter the elevator. Mr. Moretti holds his hand out for me to shake, but I pretend to have not seen it and close the elevator doors to begin our coast to the ground floor.

'Mr. Collins, you are looking better,' I say as he stands leaning against the hand rail of the elevator. It is not the truth, but positive words can change the state of mind of a person.

'Thank you, Alex, I'm feeling pretty good. Mr. Moretti gave me some tickets to the football tonight. I'm feeling pumped!'

Excellent, I haven't been to the football in a while now.' I shift my weight from my left foot to my right foot. 'Just a tip,

Mr. Collins, Emily Finnigan likes to use this elevator. It may be a good idea if you choose a different elevator from now on,' I suggest to him, eyeing his reaction to the mention of Emily's name.

He frowns and shakes his head. 'Who's Emily Finnigan? Should I know her?' he asks.

'Oh, forgive me. I thought I had seen you talking to her at one stage. It must have been someone else. Enjoy the football tonight!' I say to end the conversation.

He steps out of the elevator, smiling. 'Thank you for helping me, Alex. I am most grateful.'

He strolls off at a casual pace, as if he has not a care in the world. I start to question Mr. Moretti's therapy. Besides immortality, what is it that he does with his clients? They seem like different people once they have returned from a "session" with him.

The remainder of the day takes drags on after the mentally exhausting morning of keeping the peace, and preventing a multi-casualty physical fight in the elevator. The cool evening air on my face is a welcome sensation as I walk home, my neck covered.

Dudley's mood is unreadable when I enter the apartment, and it worries me. He works in the kitchen, putting the finishing touches on our dinner. He has become quite the master chef.

'Buonasera,' I say as I lean Emily's painting up against the wall.

'Yes, good evening. You didn't stop by at the bar with your work colleagues tonight, I see,' he says.

'No, I wasn't in the mood. I'm concerned about you,' I say, looking into his eyes to gauge his true feelings.

'I'm not of your concern, Liam. I'm your protector, not the other way around. I made your mother and father a promise, one that I will keep. Now sit yourself at the dining table. I have prepared an exquisite meal for us tonight,' he commands.

I grab the bottle of red wine and two glasses and head to the table. It's already been opened, to let it breathe, I presume, unless Dudley has been sampling it whilst he cooked.

I pull out a chair for Matisse. She always joins us at the table while we eat. I wonder what she knew, and how much she could understand.

'When were you aware that they'd be visiting me today?' I ask, knowing very well that he did not always give in to my request for information.

'Two days ago. A contact had given me the heads-up. Except they hadn't decided on a time until this morning. That's why I had to hang around. Your day was most unremarkable until then.'

'What did you think of Emily's painting? Should I be concerned by it?'

Dudley looks over at it. 'She has talent, for sure. No need to be concerned, though. It could all be a coincidence.'

'What were the three men after, besides the obvious? Do you think there's more to it? What did you think of them?'

'Well.' Dudley sighs. 'One was scared witless, the other did not want to be present, and the dominant one was running the show. He felt threatened by you. They haven't finished with you yet, I feel. We are mulling around in their minds. They have more questions than answers. They will come at you again to persuade you to join them at the private corporation!'

'Emily... may see me as two different people, Dudley,' I throw into our conversation.

'Is that so? Perhaps she is smarter than you think. Perhaps she knows that conversation is quite closed with Alex because of time and place, and that conversation with Liam is open and can be on a more personal level. Don't underestimate her. She's just playing the game that you started!' he says with humour in his voice.

'I'm so tired of this life, Dudley. I'm so tired of watching the Earth fall under the weight of bad environmental decisions by people in supposedly high places. I'm so tired of watching humans treat others badly—'

'What is with you tonight?' he cuts in. 'Your conversation is all over the place. Just say what you really want to say and be done with it!'

I can't look at him after that. It's best not to tell him what is on my mind.

'What is worse? The muddle-headed talking, or the silence?' Dudley asks in frustration.

I remain quiet. I don't know how to express what I want to say about protecting his life over mine. 'Ti sei eccelso con la cena di stasera, Dudley,' I say finally, but it has nothing to do with what I want to talk about.

He looks at me and cocks his right eyebrow at the compliment I had given him on his excellence in cooking.

'And the wine is the perfect accompaniment for the red meat,' I add, trying to break the awkwardness between us.

He starts to chuckle. Then comes the deep belly laugh so contagious I laugh with him. He is right. I am being ridiculous.

I pick up my wine glass and touch it to his. 'To my wonderful friend, my protector, my guide. Life on the Earth as an immortal human would be unbearable if you were not here!'

'Touché. Except, if you would just hurry up and find the antidote to human immortality, you could return to the spiritual realm, and not have to watch people suffer as they do upon this Earth filled with lies, artificiality, confusion and anger.'

I still, and dug deep for courage. I swirl the wine around in my glass. 'I...' I clear my throat. 'I would throw my body in front of you to protect you. It's my choice.' My voice is quiet. There. I've spoken my mind, unsure of how he will react. Our roles upon the Earth are very different, and very particular.

Dudley stands and slams his hand down on the table. I jump, along with the plates and cutlery that bounce, returning to the table with a loud clatter.

I stop swirling the wine and look up at him.

'I. AM. YOUR. PROTECTOR! I have made a promise. I have taken an oath. I am the one who will protect you. No matter what. Even if I die. You must accept your place in this caper, Liam. My time is running out and I want to see you find the solution to your immortality. I want you to find it under my watch! And then we can save other people trapped in this mess. Each day, the self-building and disease-healing nanobots multiply, turning your physical body into a partial cyborg. It must be stopped. You have already been warned!' And with that, Dudley straightens his posture and leaves the table with an abruptness that pierces my being.

And for the first time on my long walk on the Earth, I have to clean up after dinner.

'Caro Dio, possa io avere coraggio, temperanza, saggezza, giustizia e pazienza – Dear God, My I have courage, temperance, wisdom, justice, patience...' I whisper. I press my lips together. I know this is not enough to pray anymore. I believe in prayer. Prayer is powerful. I know that. I have witnessed changes that are not humanly possible in people. I have to pray specifically, naming what I hope for. 'And Lord, I pray the bots would cease to exist inside me, returning mortality back to me, or that I discover how to disarm them, or that you send someone to me who can help me, so I can return to You. In Jesus' name.'

In submission to my reality, I close my eyes and feel the burden of the heaviness of bone, muscle, blood and organs anchored to the Earth by gravity. I also feel the joy of hope in my prayer.

I grab the Earth globe and turn it around in my hand, thinking how accurate Emily's reproduction of my dream of light is in her painting. Is she immortal too and I haven't noticed? She doesn't wear the Life Watch.

I sigh. Maybe the bots are waiting for a biological chemical change in my body that will cause them to detonate. If that is correct, I wondered what the chemicals needed are.

I must be missing something...

I am quietly confident I have learned courage, temperance, wisdom, justice and patience in my one hundred and forty-nine years. I have built emotional walls to keep people at a distance, never allowing myself to become... attached to anyone, other than my protectors.

What else could there be?

I close my eyes and set my mind to search for answers while I am in my unconscious state. The brain is absolutely spectacular at doing that. And answered prayers. They are real.

All things are possible...

9

It's my 54,685th Earth day, including extra days for leap years. I'm one hundred and forty-nine years old, eight months, and twenty days. And Dudley is nowhere to be seen with dawning of the new day. For fifty-nine years he has been up and preparing breakfast before I even see the light of the new day. I'm worried.

I retrace my steps and hesitate near his room. He is murmuring in a faint voice, but I can't decipher what he is saying. It's a dialect I'm not familiar with. His door is ajar, just the tiniest of a fraction. I gaze through the slot and see Dudley kneeling with his hands joined in front of him, in prayer. His head is lowered, as if his prayer is heavy.

I move away and go to prepare breakfast for him. It's the first time in my one hundred and forty-nine years. How hard can it be?

As I place our plates onto the breakfast table, Dudley appears—his face anguished. 'Please forgive me for my lack of attention to your needs, and also to my duty.' He is on the verge of tears.

'It's not as though I am your king, or superior, Dudley. Let me serve you with a thankful heart. Sit down and enjoy my peace offering to you,' I say, feeling sympathy for this remarkable man before me.

He stares at me for a moment, then blinks before he finally takes his seat. Before he pushes his fork into my version of an English Breakfast, he hesitates. 'Did you cook the sausages, bacon and eggs on medium-high?'

'Yes.'

'Did you sauté the mushrooms in garlic butter?'

'Yes.'

'Did you grow the tomatoes?'

'No, I materialized them out of thin air! Of course I didn't grow tomatoes, did you?'

'Yes... did you turn the tea pot three times anticlockwise and three times clockwise?'

'What if I didn't?'

'Did you even stir the tea in the pot?'

'No. I infused the tea leaves with the slightly cooled boiled water so I didn't burn the delicate tea leaves before I turned the pot three times anticlockwise and then three times clockwise... what is up with you this morning?'

He stops chewing and looks at me, then lowers his shoulders. 'My heart is heavy that you would choose to take a heavy beating and broken bones to protect me. Do you not see that I would not be able to live with myself if you did that? My promise to your protectors before me, who made a promise to your mother and father would be broken, and I will be destroyed, Liam, because I did not look after you. You must allow me to keep my promise.' Dudley's brown eyes pierce mine, cutting to the core of my being.

'Dudley... I am, regrettably, a forced immortal human. My body will repair itself after the damage, and although it will be terribly painful, I do not wish you to get hurt because of me!'

He lets out a boisterous laugh. I frown at him, confused by his reaction. 'You are deceived if you think you're stronger than I am. This old ravaged, bony disengaged body is a decoy. It gives me the psychological edge in battle. My strength will outperform yours a multitude of times. This is what I was created for—to be a protector. This is what I do! You have to trust me,' Dudley declares before he places his elbow on the table, and holds up his right hand as an invitation to engage in an arm wrestle.

I roll my eyes before I place my hand in his, and in moments, he has defeated me. I ask for a rematch, and again he wins. He is not the spindly little figure of an old man who looks somewhat like a cripple that he presents to the world. He is a strong seventy-nine year old, in body and mind, prepared to repel and reduce his enemies to mere shadows of their former selves with either brute force, or through his psychological warfare. He is a true protector—totally dedicated to being my minder. He is an immensely beautiful, dedicated person, of soul and spirit.

He withdraws his hand, smirking at me. 'Keeping my body in shape is what I do during the day while you're at work, as well as training the new protector to take my place. We have a personal trainer, and like to outdo each other. Now, would you like a game of chess, so you can lose twice before going to work today?' He smirks.

I shrink at my foolishness and hope he will forgive me. 'Ti prego perdonami?' I say with sincerity, connecting my eyes to his.

'You are forgiven, my friend,' he says in a serious tone. 'You will not be without punishment though. You will be subjected to my cooking until death do we part... well until I depart!' Dudley looks up at me with the slight hint of humour playing on his lips.

'Death by Dudley cooking it is then,' I reply, smiling at him. I hold up my teacup as a toast.

'Put your tea cup down at once! That is so uncouth! Have

you not learnt anything here in your one hundred and forty-eight years, boy?' Dudley chides.

I sip my tea loudly. 'Not. Otherwise we wouldn't still be here! Please excuse me while I change for work.'

Dudley is in the kitchen when I approach the front door to leave. 'Are you expecting to see anyone today, Liam? Matisse says you smell nice.'

'I don't know, Dudley. Just the usual elevator clientele. Follow it on your tracker. It will totally make your day!' I widen my eyes at him. Each day is the same as the day before. It is not something to look forward to. Just something to endure. What choice do I have when I am locked into a contract with Mr. Moretti since the day of my Earth immortality—the day of *The Change*.

'Only if it is consequential, you do realize. Enjoy your day and stay out of trouble,' he adds before I close the door and enter the streetscape, pulling my collar up around my neck.

I enter the foyer of the Great Hall and still. Something feels amiss. It's far too quiet on the ground floor and only Elevator One remains in operation with the night watchman.

I enter the staff door to go to my locker, place my leather over-shoulder satchel in there and suit up for the day. Not a soul is in sight. I look at my pocket timepiece. I'm on time today. Usually it's busy behind the scenes with all sorts of workers getting ready for the day, welcoming each other and bantering. But not today. I slow my pace as a feeling of dread overcomes me.

I feel a tap on my shoulder and turn. 'Alex, report to the conference room immediately.' It's the concierge.

I quicken my step and weave my way to the conference room.

The door squeaks when I open it with caution, and a sea of faces turn to look at me. There are three seats left, and I will inhabit one. At least I'm not the last to arrive.

I sit down and look around at my fellow elevator colleagues. They aren't the usual smiling faces and upbeat people I know. They are a group of people who bounce their feet, cross and uncross their arms, rub their hands on their legs, stroke their beards, flit their gaze around the room, take deep breaths and clasp their hands together. I frown, absorbing their negative emotions, and remain as silent as they are while we wait for the remaining two seats to fill.

The final two people file into the conference room, but when time is relative, it seems to take forever. I look around at the questioning minds. For people who are used to talking for most of the day, their refined skill of striking up interesting and uplifting conversations with others next to none, the silence in the room is uncomfortable. I reach for the glass of water in front of me and sip it slowly, letting the coolness of the water flow over my tongue and trickle down my throat to my anxiety filled stomach.

'Good morning, ladies and gentlemen. It is with a heavy heart that I call you to this early morning meeting today. Unfortunately, I have drawn the short straw and I am the bearer of unwelcome news to some of you.' Mr. Wilson looks down at his notes and places his hands in his pockets before he swallows hard. I watch his Adam's apple rise and fall.

'The Great Hall Body Corporate has decided it is time we update some of our elevators to… self-service.'

Murmurs of disappointment echo through the room.

Mr. Wilson holds up his hand to ask for quite. 'Bear with me. That is, when a person enters the elevator, they push the button themselves. However, to keep residential occupants happy, we will retain four elevator operators for those who prefer the services of a personal elevator operator.'

Gasps echo around the room. Some people shift

uncomfortably in their seats. Nine elevator operators are about to lose their jobs. Their livelihoods. I hope that one will be me. Not because I don't like my job, but because some have families to feed, to clothe, and to put a roof over their heads.

'Ladies and gentlemen, today I will visit you as you work. You will receive an envelope. Inside the envelope is an appointed time for you to see me. During this meeting you will learn the fate of your employment. I am deeply sorry that I have to deliver this news to you, and I wish each and every one of you the best for your future. Thank you. You may continue to prepare for the start of the work day.'

There is a delayed reaction from my colleagues as shock sets in. And then starts the scramble to the door to return to the locker rooms to get changed for the day.

I look up to my right and see the red flashing light on the security camera. We are being watched.

As the second last elevator operator leaves the room before me, I dawdle out the door. This will now be my lot, to act blatantly inefficiently and carelessly in my handling of the elevator, forcing the boss to choose to terminate my employment here, instead of another person, who desperately needs the job for their family.

Besides, I only have one strike to go against my name.

The foyer holds a suppressed ambience for the entire day. Mr. Wilson is true to his word and liaises with everyone, handing them their appointment time.

I do not open my envelope. I place it in the nearest bin.

I observe my comrades carefully as they return from their meetings with Mr. Wilson, trying to surmise the outcome of their future employment with The Great Hall Limited. But I cannot ascertain who has remained employed and who has not. They each continue their day with professionalism as they are trained to do.

Besides the unpredictable news this morning, and of the

growing numbers of people wearing glowing red Life Watches being ferried to floor thirteen in elevator thirteen, the day is quite unremarkable.

Until she sits on the white leather sofa alone, presumably waiting for someone. Her long legs are crossed and her right arm is slung over her leg. Beside her, she balances two parcels wrapped in plain brown paper with string around them, and she focussed on her foldable paper thin personal communication device .

Every time someone enters the building, her head turns towards them, and then turns away and back to her technology.

She sits in the same position for twenty-six minutes until her personal communication device illuminates. She stands to answer it, looking out of the glass window overlooking the park. Then, as if given an instruction, she turns, picks up the parcels and heads my way.

'Good day, Miss Finnigan, which floor tickles your fancy today?' I ask, dipping my head toward her with a gentle smile.

'Thirty-eight please, Mr. Harris,' she replies, narrowing her eyes at me.

'Mrs. Luciati's apartment?' I ask, frowning at her, trying to stifle my surprise.

'Indeed I am, Mr. Harris. She asked me to paint two portraits of Selena for her, and I'm delivering them to her today,' she answers, bobbing her head up and down while looking at me.

'Lovely, Miss Finnigan,' I respond, looking into her green eyes.

Her face flushes and she looks away from me. 'Why weren't you at the bar last night?'

I clasp my white gloved hands together in front of me.

'You go two or three nights after work, don't you? Except last night, you weren't there. Where were you?' she says, before I can answer her first question.

'My uncle needed me last night, so I chose to help him out

instead of indulging in my liking for alcohol,' I reply, lowering my head and looking into her eyes, deeply, curious as to why she is tracking my movements.

'Do you go to the bar every night?' I ask.

'No. I was just hoping that I would see Liam there, that's all,' she answers as the doors ding.

'Be gentle with Mrs. Luciati, Miss Finnigan. She is old and grieving and needs some tenderness at the moment,' I say.

Emily cocks her head to one side and raises an eyebrow at me as she puts her hand on her hip. She is about to rebuke me, but I place my finger on her lips to stop her. 'You are a redhead after all, Miss Finnigan!' I whisper against her ear, sending my energy around her before I step back into the elevator, close the doors and disappear from her view.

Within fifteen minutes, my elevator arrives at the thirty-eighth floor again. I steal myself for the ear bashing from Miss Finnigan. However, she enters the elevator arm in arm with Mrs. Luciati. They look very smug and I wonder what they're up to.

'Good afternoon, girlz. To the beauty parlour, shopping floor, cafe or ground floor, ladiez?' I ask, looking at Mrs. Luciati, avoiding eye contact with Miss Finnigan. I wince inwardly. They are such stereotypical, generalized destinations. But I know that is where Mrs. Luciati liked to venture to in her retirement.

'We, Mr. Harris, are headed to the pet store. Mrs. Luciati has decided to add another family member to her household. And I am privileged to be attending with her to meet the little adorable pup that awaits her.' Miss Finnigan's voice is matter-of-fact.

I smile. She is certainly offended by my earlier remark. The tone in her voice is curt. 'Well, enjoy yourselves, my lovelies. A bouncing fluffy bundle-of-dog will melt your hearts and charm your senses until you find yourself head over heels in love with the little innocent-eyed hairy beast! Shall I expect to meet it soon, Mrs. Luciati?'

'I certainly hope so,' she replies.

'It's not too soon after the passing of Selena, do you think?' I ask, concerned about her state of mind.

'Oh my giddy aunt, Alex! It is never too soon to welcome a beautiful puppy into one's family,' she says, looking at me, and then to Miss Finnigan who smiles from ear to ear. I grin at her and bow my head.

We arrive at the ground floor and they leave the building to head to the pet store down the street. I can hear the tapping of their shoes along the polished wooden floor of the foyer right until they exit the building, arm in arm.

Five minutes later, my elevator door closes. I am summoned to the seventh floor. I inhale deeply. But it doesn't seem to quiet my nerves.

Mr. Wilson waits for me outside his office, pacing from left to right, and back again. He holds his hand up, talking at the interactive communication panel highlighted on his skin. He frowns and nods, often.

I slow as I come near to him, feeling negative energy bouncing off him. I stop and wait for him to finish his connection. He indicates for me to enter his office, whilst he still conversing on his device, and follows me in.

I sit in the black chair of doom. I wonder how many times the occupant of the black chair has heard the words of doom today—the words informing them of the cessation of their employment. Will I be one of them? I hope so. I rest my elbows on the arms of the chair and steeple my fingers in front of me, just below my mouth.

'So, Mr. Harris, it appears that you did not present yourself for your appointment time today.' Mr. Wilson speaks in a low tone just audible to the ear. His Life Watch glows green. 16,425 days flips to 16, 424 days.

'Indeed, it appears that I did not, Mr. Wilson,' I say, looking directly into his eyes. 'I choose to be one of the nine to be made redundant from my position of employment with the Great Hall. I do not have a family or residence which require a steady income, as many of the other elevator operators have, so choose me to walk out that door today and to never return.'

Mr. Wilson hooks his fingers together in front of his face and looks at the list that rests on the desk before him. 'It would seem that you are staying with us, Mr. Harris, although you are the only employee with two yellow cards of warning, and although you are the only employee who did not arrive at their scheduled appointment time.' He clears his throat. 'There are a certain number of long-term residents who have demanded that you stay with us… so we have honoured their request. And besides, you have not finished your mission with Mr. Moretti. He informs me you still have eight days left to fulfil your requirements. And then we shall see about your job security.' Mr. Wilson leans back in his chair. 'Thank you, Mr. Harris. Our meeting is finished,' he says, avoiding all eye contact with me.

I stand at once. 'Mr. Wilson,' I say, bowing my head towards him before I head out of his office to the safety of Elevator Thirteen.

When the doors close, I place both of my hands against the wall and lean into it, putting my forehead against the polished wood. My heart aches for those who have lost their jobs.

I roll my body so that the top of my shoulders now rest against the wooden panel. I look up to the ceiling of the elevator, frustrated by my inability to help those who need it the most, although I have tried. Perhaps I can give my wage to them by sharing it into their accounts as an anonymous person.

The elevator stops at the ground floor. I step out, and to the left of the doors, as we have been trained to do, then look over at my elevator operator colleagues. They give nothing away as to their emotional state. They hold their backs straight and their shoulders square. The closed mouthed smiles on their faces are nothing but professional. It's getting late, and time will soon tell which nine are to leave and which three are to stay, besides me. Guilt starts to chaotically bounce around inside my mind.

A familiar echo sounds throughout the ground floor and enters the building's foyer. It is two pairs of shoes tapping on the polished wood floor, simultaneously. I smile before I turn my head toward the two smiling faces of two women in love. It's Emily Finnigan and Mrs. Luciati, and the new puppy.

They stop in front of me with a contagious smile. I look at my pocket timepiece. 'I do apologize, ladiez, but you have missed your opportunity to ride the elevator. Only residents with furry puppies may enter. Would you happen to have one?' I ask, keeping a straight face while I look at them.

Emily looks at Mrs. Luciati and bursts out laughing. 'Why, Mr. Harris, it just so happens that we do have a furry pup. Montgomery is his name, and he holds the key to our hearts,' Emily Finnigan says, speaking with a plum in her mouth, over-dramatising her words.

I cast my eyes upon the little bundle of chocolate fur in Mrs. Luciati's handbag. I smile and bow to them with my hands out, welcoming them into the elevator. They enter, gushing over Montgomery the Maltipoo, as if he's a baby human.

'Montgomery, meet Uncle Alex,' Mrs. Luciati announces, as the elevator rises thirty-eight levels. I place my hand into the bag and give Montgomery a gentle pet. They are right. The dog holds a key to hearts.

I smile at Mrs. Luciati, approving of her new addition to the family and then look over to Miss Finnigan who looks at me with a "told you so" stare. The elevator doors ding then open, saving me from the stare of death.

Emily Finnigan and Mrs. Luciati leave the elevator, chatting in excitement as they introduce the puppy to his new home.

I blink, absorbing the cherished sight of happiness that flows around them.

Under my breath I pray a phrase of blessings to the predicted long-lasting friendship between the two women. They need each other. And no doubt it has been planned long before they ever met.

The doors close and I return to the ground floor. My shift has ended.

I head to the staff lockers to change out of my uniform and into my regular clothes, my heart heavy. I inhale deeply to steady my emotions as I see my comrades changing out of their work uniforms; some for the last time. Who will not return on Monday?

The silence surrounding us is deafening.

There seems to be an elevator operator code of "not-a-word-said". Eye contact between comrades is fleeting.

Then it occurs to me—Mr. Wilson has included a non-disclosure agreement, preventing them from speaking of their conversations held in their appointment times today.

I'm the last to leave the locker rooms, and the last to arrive at the bar for final drinks as one of the thirteen elevator operators. The women are here as well.

I struggle to hold my emotions together. On Monday night there will be just four of us here, wanting to drown our sorrows, but prohibited from doing just that because of our work contract.

'Hazaar!' they yell as I enter the bar and start to walk towards them at our usual round table. But there is something unusual in the centre of the table. There are ten beer jugs. We only have one glass of beer each, or other alcoholic beverage. Some are either celebrating their freedom, or drowning their sorrows. Or perhaps both.

I join them at the table and raise my glass of beer to them, 'Cheers!'

'Hazaar!' they yell again before they break into boisterous laughter.

I chuckle under my breath and lean back in my chair to study each of the faces of my comrades as they talk and joke around. I'm looking for a quick glance away from others as they laugh. The heaviness of the news of their unemployment will not be totally hidden. It will show in the slightest gestures. But I find none. Perhaps it's alcohol masking the emotional turmoil? I wonder what the deal is that Mr. Wilson made when he delivered the outcome of their employment.

Out of the corner of my eye I detect the flowing red hair of Emily Finnigan as she enters the bar. She sits alone and I decide to leave her that way, although I know she wants to talk to Liam about something. But when she lowers her head and rubs her hands over her face, I sense she needs salvaging.

I slide into the seat beside her without detection when she is looking the other way. I reach in front of her to grab some peanuts. 'Excuse me for passing my arm in front of you. But you do have a bad habit of keeping the peanuts to yourself,' I mumble towards her.

'It's because they are decoration. Nobody *eats the peanuts* at the bar, Mr. Harris! You'll probably get a minuscule piece of peanut stuck in your throat and start coughing your elevator germs all over the place. Or choke to death! I do recommend that you leave the space of one chair between us,' she retorts. She has a bee in her bonnet about something.

'Good evening to you too, Emily,' I throw her way. 'Good to see that Irish blood of yours, mixed with your red hair, is keeping your temper at bay!' I sip on my water and wait for her reply, hoping it would be highlighted with sparks. I like a challenge with entertainment thrown in for free.

She does not respond. So I move down a stool as she had requested. We sit in silence for three minutes, like total strangers.

Then she moves to the stool beside me. It's like playing a game of chess.

'Careful, I might choke on my peanut and cough elevator germs all over you. You are in danger sitting next to me, you know. Or, unknowingly, you might pass on some germs to that cute little puppy of Mrs. Luciati's.'

'Liam, sarcasm is not your strength. Don't engage it in our conversation,' she says in a flat voice.

'Oh, we're having a conversation now, are we?' I ask, looking at her.

'Perhaps, depending on you, of course,' she says, ordering a glass of white wine. I look away from her and sip my water again. Now I am stuck for words. All of a sudden, I don't know what to talk to her about. It's awkward and highly unusual for me to be without verbal communication at any time.

I run my hand through my hair. 'Do you come here every night, Emily?'

'I used to... but since the attack, not so frequently. And you?'

'Perhaps two or three nights a week, on work days, to socialize with my co-workers. We are only allowed one alcoholic beverage a day you know—it's written into our contract,' I say.

'I know… you have mentioned that before… but really? By the looks of them tonight, they have had far more than one drink!' Emily says with wonder in her voice.

I turn around and look at them. They're making a raucous, spilling drinks and up to mischief.

'Aye, we had forced changes at work today. It's their way of dealing with the hand we were dealt,' I say, still looking at them before I look back to Emily's green eyes.

'What sort of changes?'

'You'll see when you come to the building next time... you'll see.' I turn away from Emily towards the bar and order water.

Emily shifts slightly closer to me. 'Liam... I need to spend some time with you... I... I... just need to spend some time with you,' she says to me. Her voice is soft and lacking in confidence.

I frown and turn my head to her. 'You're attracted to me because of the "halo effect". Give it time. It will pass,' I say, trying to fob off her feelings for me, even though I am well-aware it could be that our paths have crossed for a reason.

'No, it's not. When we touch...'

Trouble is brewing. At once I inhale deeply through my nose to pull my healing energy force under the surface of my skin.

'When we touch, I feel... I feel like I am alive for the first time,' she tries to explain as she places her hand on my arm.

I breathe in impossibly more and tighten all of the muscles in my body to hold the healing energy force inside of me. 'Then perhaps we should spend some time together. You'll see then that it's the "halo effect", and will be cured of its magic that binds you to me,' I say quietly against her ear. I too, feel alive for the first time when I'm with her. But we can never be together.

'Son, you will fall in true love with a mortal, but you cannot know her in an intimate way. It is forbidden...'

'Yes, Papa...'

I close my eyes and bring my glass of water to my lips, concentrating on the suppression of my healing energy under my skin.

'Well then, since you are so obliging and have played into my hands so perfectly, how about tomorrow? Saturday, Mr. Harris?'

I choke on my water and cough. I didn't expect her to take me up on the offer so quickly.

'Sure, that sounds like a plan,' I say, smirking at her.

She slips her business card to me. 'Contact me, Mr. Harris. I'll look forward to hearing from you,' she says, stands, and leaves.

Shocked by her audacity, I sit alone at the bar for a while longer before I say farewell to my fellow elevator operators, some for the last time. I know which ones have lost their jobs now. Their drained energy is obvious.

I touch their arms with my fingertips, sending a healing prayer through to their amygdala: the emotional centre of the brain. My eye contact and words in kind are sent there too, strengthening and speeding up the healing.

I pull my collar up, covering my neck as I exit the bar and walk through the cool night air as the mist descends.

Dudley is sitting in his reading chair knitting, when I enter our apartment.

'Buona sera, Dudley,' I say and grin as I place my coat and work satchel in the cloak room.

'Good evening to you also, Liam. Sì sono io lavoro a maglia, fare quel sorrisetto dalla faccia!' Dudley says without an ounce of humour.

'Who said I was smirking at you knitting? Perhaps you're jumping to conclusions,' I say, chuckling under my breath.

'I know you better than you know yourself, Liam. Are you mocking me for taking up the sport of knitting?' Dudley asks, as he puts his knitting down and walks to the dining table with me.

'Certainly not. I was thinking that you could knit yourself a head cover to stop the girls screaming and running away from you!' I say, trying to judge his demeanour this evening.

He pokes his tongue out at me.

'Well, that's certainly mature for a seventy-nine-year-old!' I smile.

'Interesting day at the office, Liam. I see your rebellious antics didn't work in your favour.'

'No, they didn't,' I say, shaking my head. Must he watch my day on his GPS like a television?

'Don't despair. Everything happens for a reason. You'll see.'

'Have you assessed the situation already, may I ask?'

'No, you may not ask,' he answers, raising an eyebrow at me.

'Spoil sport,' I say with fondness to my protector.

'Spoilt brat!' he adds to the flying insults.

'Knitting nerd!' I retaliate.

'Lover boy!' he sneaks in.

I walk to the kitchen, grab the utensils then go to the table and place our knives and forks there, clasp my hands together and wait for Dudley to join me with the dinner plates.

'Tell me what you know,' I say in a low voice after he sits, after he has said grace.

'If I tell you, I'll have to kill you,' Dudley jokes.

'*That*… I would like to see.' I start to eat. 'I miei complimenti allo chef.'

'Thank you, and flattery will get you nowhere,' says Dudley.

'I know that you are a stubborn old mule. My compliment of your cooking is from the heart,' I explain.

He narrows his eyes at me and continues to eat.

'What do you know of love?' I ask, genuinely wanting his opinion for guidance in this very unfamiliar territory I am about to enter, or perhaps, have already entered.

'Ha! You're asking an ugly brute like me?' he bellows. His laughter resonates throughout the walls and his belly bounces up and down.

Then he stills, his joviality quieting. 'Love… or lust?' His voice is deep.

'Both,' I respond.

He sits back in his chair, folds his hands over his protruding stomach and drags in a deep breath.

'Love is kind, love is patient. It does not envy, it does not boast, it is not proud. It does not dishonour others, it is not self-seeking, it is not easily angered, it keeps no record of wrongs. It always protects, always trusts, always hopes, and always perseveres. This definition, Liam, can be found in the Ancient Texts, *1 Corinthians 13:4*—it sums up love perfectly.' He clears his throat. 'Lust… on the other hand…'

He looks up to the ceiling and tilts his head to the left, and then to the right, cracking a couple of neck vertebrae. 'Lust is… how shall I put it? Lust is an intense sexual craving. It's about possession and greed. Lust has, as its focus is, on pleasing oneself, and it's about fulfilling one's desires with no regard to the consequences. Lust is a devastating fire that will devour you and destroy relationships. It's lethal to your soul.'

I raise my eyebrows on hearing Dudley's last words. 'How will I know whether I'm feeling love or lust?'

'Lust is all about you, Liam. You won't care about the other person or their feelings. It will be all about their looks and their body and nothing else. Love, on the other hand… you will want to talk to her, spend time with her, you will be concerned about her feelings, you will be interested in things she does. You will want to be a better person for her. That is how you will know. Why do you ask, boy?'

'I'm just… expanding my knowledge of worldly things, Dudley.'

'Ah, don't ever think that love is worldly. Lust is worldly, but love was defined before there was even a human being on the Earth. Things will come to pass, but love endures forever.'

I ponder his words for a moment. 'I'm wondering if it is the red thread of fate pulling Emily and I together…'

'Hmmm… the red thread… a Japanese legend about an old man who lives on the moon, and when he visits Earth, he shows people their future and whom they're destined to meet, with an unbreakable read thread.' Dudley sighs. 'Hmmm. There is no man who lives on the moon!' Dudley presses his lips together then says, 'Love endures, but a crush will not. Enjoy the journey and see where it takes you. That's my advice. You have taken your immortality far too seriously. Live a little on the mortal side.'

'In that case, I must go and contact someone. Thanks for the advice. You are a rare gemstone in the pile of sludgy rocks, Dudley!'

He snorts, then stands to clear the dinner plates while I go to the study room.

'IDcom,' I say, butterflies rampaging in my stomach. A ping sounds on the augmented reality, and I am projected in a 3D hologram. I scan Emily's business card. 'Write a note to Emily about meeting her on Saturday, 4th of May, at the flowering Jacaranda tree outside Flowers for Fleur Café please. I would like to meet her there at 6.30AM. Thanks, Liam.

Request completed...

Incoming... Emily Finnigan

Dear Mr. Harris,

No civil person gets up that early on a Saturday morning. I will see you under the flowering Jacaranda tree at 7AM.

Emily

#Iamknittingyouascarfforyourneck!

I grin. 'IDcom,' I say, 'write a note to Emily telling her that I look forward to meeting her then, and that scarves look nice around Jacaranda trees! Thanks, Liam.

Request completed...

After rereading our ID communications several times, I

disengage the technology and head off to prepare for bed. Dudley sits in his wing chair knitting under the muted light as I walk past to go to my room.

'Take an extra-long warm shower tonight, Liam. I can hear your heart thumping away from here. Sogni d'oro intossicato uno!'

'Sweet dreams to you, too, and I am not intoxicated!' I reply.

'You have been exposed to the love potion, Liam. Watch out before you see rainbows and unicorns everywhere!'

'Oh - grow up, old one! I'll give you a sip of my love potion. It might fix up your ugly face!' I banter.

'Be careful, Liam. What is said, cannot be unsaid!' he states, chuckling to himself.

'They do say that love is blind, don't they? Buona notte amico mio, tu lo sai che ti amo,' I call over my shoulder as I head to my room.

'Yes, good night, Liam, and... I too, love you,' Dudley says, brushing off the comment with a waving of his hand in the air like swiping at a fly.

The warmth of the water calms my racing heart before I make myself comfortable on my bed. Waves of pleasure stream through me as thoughts of meeting Emily invade my head space.

I inhale deeply. That sacred breath humans have been gifted with. And I relax. I turn my head and stare at the glowing Earth energy mass. I lift my hand to it and watch as the fourth state of matter arcs to my fingertips like bolts of lightning, lighting my entire sleeping chamber as if it is daylight. My fingertips tingle under the warmth until the plasma retreats back into the glowing ball of energy.

I place the Earth globe back onto its holder on my bedside table, roll onto my side and watch it, realising how similar the feeling of love is to the uplifting energy of it.

Energy. A powerful force. The source of energy is love, God's very essence and the core of His nature. His person. My stomach flutters.

I look beyond the Earth energy globe then, and to the lesser red ball of caution. It still glows. The danger has not finished.

Am I heading into trouble by meeting Emily tomorrow, or is danger lying elsewhere?

Dudley did say the immortal seekers have not finished with me yet.

Before I close my eyes, I gaze out the window to see if I can see a sky full of stars. Not tonight. It's obscured by millions of surveillance satellites.

In disappointment I close my eyes. There's nothing better to see the heavens declare the glory of God. The wonder. The vastness. The fact that His fingerprints are all over creation. I release a calming breath. 'Caro Dio, possa io avere coraggio, temperanza, saggezza, giustizia e pazienza – Dear Lord, may I have courage, temperance, wisdom, justice and patience,' I whisper. Patience and acceptance; those attributes I have learned. Self-control, the essence of temperance, I am strengthening, but my patience is waning as I reach for my mortal self. 'I pray, Lord, that you help me to find the answer to return to a mortal, and to help others as well. And my dream of Light is with me always, of being in Your unimaginable, indescribable presence one day, trusting in Your timing and wisdom. And Lord if it is in Your will, please let Emily and I be together, in Jesus' name I pray. Amen.' I say, feeling comfort from my spiritual connection before I slip into the unconsciousness of sleep...

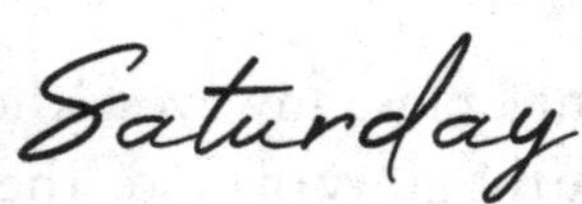

'Matisse approves of your woody oriental aftershave today,' Dudley comments as I walk by him at the breakfast table.

'Tell Matisse she needs to get out more and smell the catnip!'

'She is the Observer. You know she likes to pass judgement on us as we live in her castle. You should bring home a new box for her to sit in and ponder on our human antics. That will keep her happy,' Dudley quips.

'The aftershave masks my immortal scent, that's why I wear it,' I say, as I look for the time on the grandfather clock.

'Of course it does!' Dudley says, winking at me. 'Would you like to carry the antidote to the love potion?' he continues.

I walk out the door, waving to him and shaking my head at him in disgust. I pull my collar up to cover my neck while I walk to the jacaranda tree, even though I'm wearing aftershave. Old habits die hard. And besides, the aftershave has not passed the test of fire in its deceit with the immortal seekers yet. At this point in time, it's still a theory that it may work in masking my scent.

I arrive at the Jacaranda tree before Emily and lean against its trunk. I look skywards at the canvas above me, and into the abundant bloom of trumpet shaped flowers that provide a canopy of a sea of purple, broken by dabs of sky blue.

I watch a flower sail to the ground, but my vision is interrupted mid-flight when my eyes settle on Emily's face as she stands before me. Her grin is wide.

'Good morning, Emily,' I say with a coy smile.

She looks at me, her eyes dancing. 'Good morning to you, Liam,' she says, tilting her head to one side.

I place my finger under her chin, and relish our skin to skin connection. 'Look up. There is beauty to behold,' I say, lifting her chin upwards, but watching her face for her reaction to the canvas painted by nature.

Her eyes widen, and a smile lights up her face, and mine.

'It's magical,' she whispers. Her eyes meet mine and lock, drawn by an invisible divine guidance.

I inhale deeply and close my eyes to break our connection. 'Let's eat, I'm hungry,' I say.

'Huh, men! Always thinking of their stomachs! Let's go inside before you starve to death.' Her sarcastic words are laced with warmth.

I grin and follow her inside Flowers for Fleur Café. The doorbell dingles, and I take the lead to procure our table.

Sunbeams cast a cozy patterned shadow across our tabletop. I sit opposite Emily for the first time in our story together. I look into her eyes before I make a huge effort to avert my gaze and examine the daisy flower centre piece of the table instead. I'm unfamiliar with the emotion of shyness that occupies my mind and feelings right now. It unsettles me. I've been here for one hundred and forty-nine years on the planet, but she has awakened many different emotions in me since we first met. How can it be?

I barely know her, and yet, my reactions to her are akin to the dictionary definition of a high when taking drugs. I'm puzzled, but feeling extremely happy—deliriously.

'Your eyes are more blue today, are you wearing coloured contact lenses?' Emily says while she peruses the breakfast menu, not looking at me.

'No. This is me, in the flesh. Naked, except for my clothing,' I reply, shaking my head and pulling a face at the stupid words I have just muttered. Thankfully, she is still looking at the menu.

'It's very delicious,' she says, and looks up at me and catches me staring at her. 'The food on the menu,' she adds, looks at the menu and back to me. Is she trying to redirect my attention? Does she feel uncomfortable with me?

I raise my chin slightly before nodding in agreement. Butterflies ram into the sides of my stomach. I look back to the menu. 'Have you been here before?' I ask, trying not to muddle my words.

'No, this is the first time. You?'

'Same. Actually, I've never eaten out for breakfast before,' I reveal to her.

She stares at me and freezes. 'Like... never?' Her eyes are wide, her eyebrows raised and her mouth open.

I frown and shake my head. 'No, my uncle cooks every morning. I've never had a need to eat breakfast elsewhere,' I say.

'Not even with friends?' she asks me.

'No.' I don't know what else to say. I just simply have never been out for breakfast before.

'What do you normally have for breakfast?'

'Bacon, eggs, cooked tomato, toast, cup of tea, fruit sometimes as well. And you?'

'Toast and tea in the morning before I hit the art studio. I am *so* ordering breakfast for you,' she says.

I raise my eyebrows, surprised at her assertiveness. 'If you insist, Miss Finnigan,' I reply, playing along with her game.

She smiles at me, then motions for the waiter to come to take our order. As the waitress stands beside her, she points to the items on the menu while making careful eye contact with her, before they both smile at each other.

What plan is she hatching? I have absolutely no idea what she has ordered for me.

Within a minute, two tea cups and a pot of tea arrive. Emily pours the tea for us both, after turning the tea pot three times anticlockwise, and three times clock wise.

'Weird, isn't it?' I say.

'Mmmm?' she says looking up at me, wanting more information.

'The turning of the tea pot. Some people become obsessed with it, are you?'

She stops stirring the sugar into her tea and looks at me. 'Do I look weird to you? No, you'd better not answer that! I like the tradition. It's a little bit fancy!' she says.

I nod with a crooked smile. 'Do you intend to spend your life as an artist? Or do you have other dreams and plans for your life?' I ask with my hands cupped under my chin, looking into her eyes. I'm shocked by a thought that enters my mind, uninvited - maybe you could become immortal like me and spend your life with me. I scrunch my eyebrows together. I hate that I'm immortal. If I'm honest, I don't even consider myself human anymore. I'm inhuman. A monster. I didn't realise until this moment that I have a self-loathing. A self-hate. I try to stop the tremble of fear in my body.

She looks away from me and tilts her head to the side in thought. 'Hmmmm, for now I'm happy painting, dreaming, creating, exploring the beauty in the world. I don't have any long term plans. I like to think of life as an adventure and see where it takes me,' she said, now playing with the spoon on the table.

'What about you? Are you going to be an elevator operator for the term of your natural life?' she asks, oblivious to the fact that the term of my natural life had no end at this point in time.

I look at my tea cup trying to return to the present, then chuckle to myself. 'You'd be amazed by the people I've met, by the connections I've made, and by the satisfaction I get from driving the elevator. It's about the journey through life, like a metaphor for the ups and downs of life too, I guess. It's also about caring for people, being kind to people, even when they're not, and helping them when they feel their situation is hopeless,' I say.

She places one hand on top of the other, flat under her chin and narrows her eyes. 'So, you are saying that you are implicated in using psychological practices on others, is that correct?' she says, and taps her bottom lip twice.

'How does that make you feel?' I ask in the tone of a psychologist, my face deadpan. As I answer her question with a question and it sinks in, she lets out a glorious giggle, and places her hand over mine. I feel the zap of electricity as our life forces meld together, and then the warmth of her soft hand on my skin. Our eyes meet once again and lock in a moment of connection between our souls, and time slows down.

I'm high on the love potion, as Dudley calls it.

The arrival of our breakfast plates break our moment of eye-love. I smile coyly at Emily before I look at the food presented on my plate. It's French toast with a miniature jug of maple syrup with fruit salad on the side. This is a first for me. I have never had French toast before. Emily has ordered the same.

'Pain grillé français Mmmm, je vous remercie - French toast, thank you,' I say.

She widens her eyes at me. 'You speak French, Mr. Harris?' she asks, frowning at me. Her voice is full of surprise.

'A little … nothing to jump over the moon about though!'

I want to tell her that one of the techniques I use to dispel the boredom of being a human immortal is to learn new things. And languages is one of them. But she must never know about the length of my Earth days. For a moment, I wonder if I put on a Life Watch, what it would show on the face.

I devour half of the French toast relishing in the eggy, sweet flavour that dances with my taste buds. Stopping to take a mouthful of tea, I watch as Emily cuts her French toast into mouth size bites, and then places them into her mouth piece by piece, closing her eyes as she eats, each time.

'What do you believe in, Emily?' I ask.

'Oh? How about... what is your favourite colour, or, what was your first pet?' She looks at me with a wry grin. Then she gazes out the window in thought as she realizes that I am serious about my question. She breathes out heavily. 'I believe in happily ever after, family, love. I believe in having convictions. I believe our walk upon the Earth is ridiculously short as compared to eternity. I believe in black jelly beans. What about you?' she asks with her hands resting under her chin, once again.

'I believe my favourite colour is cerulean and that your question is far too deep for 8.15AM. Voulez-vous du thé?' I ask while gesturing towards the teapot between us.

'Wee?' she says, uncertain whether that is the correct French word for yes.

I nod, smiling gently at her, and pour tea into her teacup.

'Where did you go to school?' she asks.

I suck in a sharp breath as adrenaline spikes in my body. I have never been asked where I went to school before. It no longer exists, demolished thirty-five years ago. 'Nowhere, I was home-schooled,' I reply, hoping that home-schooling would be an adequate answer to cover all possibilities and to stop her from questioning my education.

'By your parents?'

'No, by my uncle!' I respond, raising my eyebrows. 'And you?'

'I studied Fine Arts at the College of Art, and paid my way by working at the museum.'

'Ah, history—I have a particular bent towards all things historical. I haven't visited the museum for eons,' I mention.

'Then we must go after breakfast.' She frowns at me. 'If you have time?' she says, her eyes lighting up. Then a flash of emotion fills her eyes.

It's hope. How can I say no? Besides, I'm going out with her today to cure the "halo effect". 'Sure, why not. I'm up for a history lesson,' I say.

After breakfast, I stand from the table, walk around it to her, and hold out my hand for her to take. As our fingertips touch, I bring her hand to my lips and kiss it with the softness of a feather. 'Thank you for my charming breakfast, Emily,' I say, looking directly into the depths of her eyes. 'Let's head to the museum. I want to know what you know.'

She stands, and curtsies with a gentle smile. Her eyes are sparkling. We walk to the cashier, and I take out my digital wallet to pay for breakfast, but Emily pushes my hand away. 'I asked you out. I will pay,' she says, looking at me from under her long eye lashes.

I raise my eyebrows at her. 'I'll pay. I believe in old-fashioned manners,' I say to her, pushing her hand away and holding my digital wallet over the scanner. Her life earnings are limited by her mortality, mine isn't.

'Thank you then, old-fashioned one,' she answers, hooking her arm through mine.

We leave the café and step onto the pavement under the Jacaranda tree once again. I adjust my collar to cover my neck at once. Old habits are hard to break.

Emily stands in front of me. She pulls a blue knitted scarf

from her handbag and arranges it around my neck. Warmth flows through me and my breath hitches. 'There... Mr. Harris.' She's so close I can feel her warm breath on my chin. I want to reach out to her and run my finger along the side of her face and touch her lips with mine.

But I don't.

'Thank you for my scarf, Miss Finnigan. I'll cherish it for always,' I say in a low voice, remembering the hurt she showed on her face when Christopher Collins gave away the tie she'd chosen for him.

'You're very welcome, Liam. The colour matches your eyes,' she says as the windows of our souls lock together.

She steps back from me and starts to walk in the direction of the museum. I watch her as she puts some distance between us, soaking in the sight of her. She makes my heart happy.

She turns around, smiling, walking backwards. 'Are you coming?' she calls with her head tilted to the side.

I look down and smile before I catch up with her. I hesitate before I put one arm around her shoulder. I've never done that before. I've never allowed myself to do that before.

The granite steps leading up to the museum are impressive. As we pass through the Greek columns we step back in time. Emily hurries ahead of me and spins around and looks at me. 'So, where would you like to go, Mr. Harris?' she asks, looking at me through her eyelashes again.

'What floats your boat today, Miss Finnigan?'

'Some sort of art, I believe,' she replies.

'I was thinking the same thing. I'm feeling a little European today. Guide me there, please,' I instruct.

'I'd be delighted to, Mr. Harris.'

She leads me to the west side of the expansive museum where the European paintings are housed, and talks in great detail about each painting.

'Who is your favourite artist?' I ask.

'Without a doubt, it would have to be *Sir Frank Dicksee*. He was such a romantic painter. His work of Romeo and Juliet is my favourite.'

'Ah... the tragic love story. Is it here in the museum?'

'Unfortunately, no. Who's your favourite artist?' Emily is facing me, walking backwards again.

My hands are behind my back and my eyes lock in hers. 'Hard to choose... there are so many. I particularly like Renaissance, and some Impressionism. My favourite piece though is "The Creation of Adam by Michelangelo".'

'Have you been to the Sistine Chapel?'

'Yes, when I was younger—you?' My eyes widen at my error. I did go to the Sistine Chapel when it was still standing, in the 2030s. It's not now. 'I mean... I visited it with virtual reality glasses.'

'Same,' she replies, her voice low.

'It's a pity the Sistine Chapel was destroyed in World War III. It seemed so divinely inspiring.' I swallow the lump in my throat, hoping I haven't given my immortal status away. 'Hmmm... does the museum have Van Gogh's piece called "Starry Night?"' I ask, changing the subject from my knowledge of the Sistine Chapel.

'I believe so, Mr. Harris... this way,' she answers in her guide voice again.

When we arrive at the painting, Emily stands with her back towards it. She spreads out her arms with her palms facing upwards. 'Mr. Harris, I present to you, "Starry Night", by none other than, Vincent van Gogh. What do you know about this artwork,' she says.

I bow slightly to her, smiling towards my feet. 'Well, it's my second favourite artwork, introduced to me by my mother.'

'By your mother?' she asks. 'Impressive. Why did she show it to you?'

I place my hands on her shoulders, turn her around and stand behind her, closely. 'Can you see the vertigo in his painting,' I say quietly into her ear, inhaling her perfume and bathing in the high that her proximity gives me. I want to envelope her in my gifted higher energy to form a bubble, our very own bubble. I want to keep her safe, and keep her happy. I want her to be forever surrounded by my love. I think I need the love potion antidote now, Dudley…

'Vertigo?' she asks.

'Yes. Spinning.'

'I see a stationary swirl, but not spinning.'

'Look deeper, and allow it to spin in your mind.' My voice is soft.

I feel Emily's shoulders lift then lower with her breath. She shakes her head. 'Nope. Can't do it. Can you?'

'Yes. I have hyperphantasia… an exceptionally vivid mental imagery. I can turn it off and on at will. It was mother's favourite artwork because she had Meniere's disease, and wanted to show me the swirls in the night sky. They reminded her of the vertigo she used to get, before her symptoms were cured with bionanotechnology.'

'Wow.'

'She always said that van Gogh was wrongly labelled as insane, or with epilepsy, and that in his letters to his brother, Theo, and his friends, van Gogh described his symptoms that matched Meniere's disease. The vertigo. The tinnitus. The hearing loss. The International Meniere's Research Institute reviewed his seven hundred and ninety-six letters he wrote during his lifetime, and said he suffered from severe repeated attacks of disabling vertigo, not a seizure disorder. Prosper Meniere's description of his syndrome was not well know when van Gogh died, and it was often misdiagnosed as epilepsy well into the 20th century.'

'The spiral stars. It makes sense now.'

'I'll never forget my mother's vertigo attacks. She would have to stare at the wall for around four hours until the spinning stopped. Not moving or she would vomit. She would continuously say the same words over and over. It's easy to understand how van Gogh could be misunderstood as insane.'

'Sorry about your mum. I'm so glad we don't have diseases and illnesses anymore.'

'Same. But I still love this piece of artwork because it brings beauty into something that was utterly unbearable for van Gogh when he was in the midst of his symptoms. Mother would call it, art therapy.'

'Where would we be without the arts? They're all so healing. Even the word heart has the word "art" in it.'

I pull her into a hug. 'What am I going to do with you, Miss Finnigan…' I ran my hand through her hair in a slow movement. It's soft and smells of apple blossom.

'You're the one who creates movement on paintings. What am I going to do with you?' She stands back from me slightly, lifts her hands and places them on either side of my face. She caresses me with her eyes, lingering first on my eyes and then on my lips.

Nervous energy bounces inside me. I take a deep breath to calm myself. 'I'm starving... let's eat,' I say to extract myself from our close proximity and the feeling that I'm spinning out of control.

She sighs then whispers my name. I look into her eyes. She's in a dreamy state. Is it my higher energy force, or the halo effect? I grab her hand and take her to the cafeteria. Coffee would fix her for sure.

We sit at a table by the garden overflowing with spring flowers, creating their own painted canvas. Emily looks over the colourful display and then wipes a tear away from her eye.

'Emily?' I ask, concerned for her.

'It's not working, Liam,' she says in a soft voice.

'What's not working?'

'Spending time with you to make the halo effect vanish,' she replies.

'It will disappear as our day wears on. You will see,' I say, not wanting the halo effect to vanish. I want her to love me. No one on the Earth has ever loved me. Or, more succinctly, I have never allowed a mortal or an immortal to love me.

I reach over and place my hand atop of hers. I'm tempted to send my healing energy under her skin to help her feel better. But I decide against it. I shouldn't interfere with what is meant to be. Or not.

I order our lunch and return to the table.

'Penny for your thoughts,' I say, reaching over and tucking a strand of hair behind her ear.

She smiles at me. 'I just had a vision of a painting that I want to create. Just give me a second to commit it to memory and I'll return to you,' she says, touching my hand.

I smile coyly at her. She closes her eyes and takes deep, slow and even breaths. Her face becomes the picture of serenity, of beauty that shines brighter than the sun. I want to reach out to her and hold her against me again. But I don't.

When she opens her eyes, I take her hand in mine and bring it to my lips, leaving a light kiss like a breath. 'Tu sei bella signorina,' I say in a quiet voice.

'Thank you for whatever you said. It sounded nice... it wasn't French, was it?'

I shake my head and smile, and look over at the flowers. I need to stop charming her so she can get over me. I have to stop playing this game with her. She is forbidden.

'What's your favourite colour?' I ask as our lunch arrives.

'Blue,' she answers.

'What type of movies do you like to watch?'

'Oh, anything with immortals in them,' she says, 'especially the experiments on our Earth immortals on reality programs.' She giggles. 'The immortals act so superior. It's nauseating.'

I sit back in my chair. I can feel the blood draining from my face. What is the knowledge she has? What does she know about Earth immortals? We're all forced to sign a non-disclosure agreement? And more startling. Why do I not know about the reality programs? My throat tightens.

'I'm kidding, Liam. I like romance and some comedy,' she says.

I lean forward in my chair. 'Oh. That's more comforting, maybe!' I manage to say.

Her giggling voice sings to my soul.

What would she think if she knew I am immortal? Would she be repulsed? 'What's your favourite food?' I ask to erase the questions in my mind.

'Fruit, today,' she answers. 'But it changes day to day.'

I nod my head.

'Drink?'

'Tea,' she says, 'the religion of the art of life.'

'Of course,' I say.

Emily smiles at me. She stands and walks around the table towards me, then bends and kisses my forehead, and the side of my face.

I freeze when my heart begins to beat faster. I inhale deeply to calm my heart rate and centre myself. 'That will not help your plight,' I say to her when she sits back down.

'You never know. It depends on what my plight is,' she says, looking into my eyes for far too long.

After we finish eating, I indicate to the waiter to bring the bill. Again, Emily holds out her digital wallet to pay. I look at her and raise my right eyebrow. 'Old-fashioned, remember,' I say in a low voice.

She is just about to protest when I place my finger over her lips.

She grabs my hand. 'Thanks, Mr. Harris, but times have changed. I'm paying!' she says between her gritted teeth.

'I believe we should duel it out with scissors, paper, rock,' I comment.

She raises an eyebrow. 'Challenge on.'

Without further ado we break into scissors, paper, rock. I time my delivery ever-so-slightly later than hers to ensure that she wins, so she can pay the bill, just to make her feel better about our "date". Emily produces her digital wallet. She doesn't have a microchip in her hand.

'I thought you would've had the microchip technology in your hand for payment of services,' I say.

She takes a deep breath. 'I am forbidden to have one.' She looks down and presses her lips together.

She's a *Pure One*. A designed one. Free of technology or of vaccinations. For a moment I wonder when her schedule to procreate is, and with whom.

I blink and clear my throat. I need to change the subject. It's none of my business. She and I can never be a "we". 'Well, Emily, we have done something I wanted to do today. What do you want to do this afternoon?' I ask once the transaction has taken place.

She looks over the flowers in thought, the colours of the petals reflecting on her irises creating a stunning display of colour.

'Let's go and climb some rock walls!' she says, totally throwing me.

I raise an eyebrow at her before I run my fingers over the table in thought. 'Okay…' I say. I stand and push my chair in, and wait for her to join me to leave the cafeteria.

The streets are getting crowded and we seem to be walking against the flow of people. Emily becomes jammed between others and I have to stop and look for her more than a few times. When I finally find her again, I take her hand in mine. She looks down as we start to walk.

'What?' I ask, frowning.

'Holding hands is intimate. I love the feel of your hand around mine,' she says.

'Or... it's a way of stopping you from falling behind as we walk, Miss Finnigan,' I suggest, cocking an eyebrow at her.

'Point taken,' she replies.

We go our own way as we enter The Rock Club and change into suitable climbing gear. I wait for Emily near the booking desk, then she appears before my eyes, wearing a black Lycra tank shirt, black Lycra shorts, and black climbing shoes.

She stops in front of me and smiles. 'You can stop looking at me now. You're making me feel self-conscious,' she says as she rests her hand on my shoulder.

'You just... you surprise me. I never took you for a sporty person. Which room are we entering?' I ask.

'Well, I've done the wall, the boulder cave, the roof climb. But I have never done the team event. What about you?'

'None. I have never rock climbed.'

'And yet you agreed to come here with me?'

'Yes, why not. You only live once.' I say in jest. Her life span is very short. Like the blink of an eye. Mine has no end at this point in time.

'Okay, let's hit the wall since you are a novice.'

'Yes, ma'am,' I say as we enter the Hang Dog Stadium.

An instructor applies my harness. 'Which gym do you go to?'

'I don't.' I want to say that it's my immortal human technology. But don't.

Emily looks hard at me and blinks several times as the instructor finishes with the harness and then breaks into the spiel of instructions.

'Let's climb,' I say and walk off towards the wall.

'Liam, I suggest you start to the left.'

I cast my eye to the left and see a heap of kids. 'No. I'm good. Ladies first,' I say, and watch as Emily mounts the wall, her arms reaching here and there, her legs positioned for balance, and then moving one limb at a time as she scales the wall with ease.

I follow her example and am ready for the next challenge, and the next. The last wall we climb is exhilarating. It is also the last wall we climbed because Emily clashes with another climber. She spirals to the floor, caught up in the ropes and lands awkwardly, sitting on the floor holding her ankle. Her eyes squeeze shut in pain.

I descend the wall at speed and kneel beside her. I run my hand down from her knee to just above her ankle. It's swollen already. 'Let's get an ice pack on that,' I say, picking her up in my arms and carrying her to a chair nearby.

I raise her leg on a free standing cushioned seat as the ice arrives. Emily has both of her hands over her face as I place the ice pack around her ankle with care.

'Please, take me home.' Her eyes fill with tears.

I kiss her forehead, pick her up and carry her to a cab outside.

I slide in beside her after gathering our belongings, and hold her hand in mine. She lays her head on my shoulder and I feel the coolness of her tears soak through my shirt.

'I guess this means no dancing tonight,' I comment to cheer her up.

I feel her smile against my chest. 'I will have to take a rain check on that, Mr. Harris.' She winces in pain.

'You know I took dancing lessons when I was a kid,' I add.

'You did?' she says, her voice a little brighter.

'No.'

Emily hits me on the arm and I feign pain.

I carry her from the cab into her building and the elevator.

'Just as well you know how to operate an elevator, Alex,' she comments.

'Aye. Maybe I could get a job as an elevator operator, Miss Finnigan?' I say.

She smiles and brushes her lips over my neck, creating a silence between us. I want to turn my head towards her and let our lips touch. But I don't. She is a mortal. Out of bounds.

I gently place her onto one foot while I unlock the door of her apartment, and then lift her up into my arms again and carry her inside.

'Does this mean we are married now, Mr. Harris? You just carried me over the threshold,' she says with a smile.

I grin back at her and wink. 'Oh, but that is old-fashioned, and times are changing, Emily,' I say.

'Maybe I like old-fashioned manners, Mr. Harris,' she responds in barely a whisper as I place her on the sofa.

I elevate her foot with two cushions and fetch ice from the freezer.

'Hello Liam, Emily.' The voice comes from the front door. Emily's mother has returned from her shift at the hospital.

'What have you done, my dear?' Emily's mother asks, inspecting the swollen, angry ankle. 'Well, it's not broken. But it will keep you out of mischief for a few days. I'll make us some tea.'

Emily looks at me. 'Then I'll be able to chase you.'

'You can, but you won't catch me.'

'There is more than one way to skin a cat,' she responds with a shy smile. 'Besides, you will be the one chasing me.'

I give her a crooked smile. I think I have already caught her.

Dudley sits in his reading chair knitting, when I enter our

apartment.

'Ciao, Dudley.'

'Hello yourself, Liam.'

'I told Emily that you were my uncle and you home-schooled me, if ever you should meet her,' I say, sitting opposite him.

'Mmmmm.'

'Mmmmm... is that all that you can say?' I say, unimpressed by his response. He looks at me and raises his eyebrows, unimpressed by my response.

'She damaged her ankle when we were indoor rock climbing. I wanted to heal it for her desperately so that she was not in pain anymore. But I didn't.'

Dudley bursts out laughing, scaring the cat away.

'Dudley! That's most inappropriate! Emily is in pain and it will be days before she can walk on it again!'

'It's not that, Liam. The vision of you engaging in a type of sport just blew my grey matter. Never, in my seventy-nine years have you even hinted at a desire to use your body physically, even though that's your body type!'

I smile at him, seeing the irony in his words. 'Actually, I did enjoy exerting my physical form. It kind of felt... liberating.'

'Then you should do it more often. Maybe this Emily girl is good for you?'

'And maybe she is making me feel confused. I seem to be thinking about her all the time. And... I don't like being away from her. But she is forbidden. Mother was sure to tell me what was allowed and what was not.'

'Friendship is allowed, Liam. Immortal and mortal physical intimacy is not. And by that, I mean in a sexual relationship. Anything that you do with her is okay, as long as you do not make love to her.'

I take a deep breath. It's bad enough that I'm stuck in this human physical form as an immortal. Now, I'm falling in love with a beautiful woman with whom I cannot express my love to her in the most intimate way possible, until I'm mortal. I now have a new incentive to find the anti-dote to immortality, fast.

As I retire for the night, I look at the whiteness of my bedroom ceiling in contemplation. Courage, temperance, wisdom, justice, patience. These I have. But now I have one more virtue to add to the words of my prayer.

I release a calming breath. 'Caro Dio, possa io avere coraggio, temperanza, saggezza, giustizia e pazienza – Dear Lord, may I continue to have courage, temperance, wisdom, justice and patience,' I whisper. 'And I pray, Lord, that you help me to find the answer to return to a mortal, and to help others as well. And my dream of Light is with me always, of being in Your unimaginable and indescribable presence one day, trusting in Your timing and wisdom. And love, Lord, thank you for love. If it is in your will, please let Emily and I be together, in Jesus' name I pray. Amen.' I say, feeling comfort from my spiritual connection before I slip into the unconsciousness of sleep.

Love.

But I can never tell her.

8

Storm clouds hang low when I start my work day with the remaining three Elevator Operators. I greet each one with a hand shake and a hug. We are interspersed amongst the thirteen elevators presented to the occupants of the building. I'm still the operator of Elevator Thirteen, the last one in the line of elevators.

The day proceeds slowly as the novelty of pushing your own button in the elevators attracts most of the occupants. Except the people with red glowing Life Watches. The *Society of Red*, I decide to call them. Those who fear death, and think it's the end of them. Finality. They don't know about the existence of God. Or choose to ignore Him, and all the evidence of the Creator that surrounds them. Or if they do believe in Him, they have no trust in Him, and have been swayed by those in power who try to control people, covering the truth with lies that are so well-embedded into education, companies and advertisements: you are god. You control everything about you.

The doors to the elevator open on the group floor, and a group of people crowd around, their arms covered by sleeves.

'Good morning.' I gesture for them to step in to my elevator, counting them as they enter. I hold my hand up. 'I am sorry, sir. I can only take ten people at a time. I will return for you,' I say. The man with thin grey hair, glasses and a walking stick takes a step back, his eyes wide with fear. I place my hand on his arm. 'I won't be long,' I say.

I step into the elevator and close the doors. 'It's a lovely day outside. Which floor would you like to proceed to?' I ask.

The words 'Mr. Moretti please,' and 'thirteen please' drift from their lips.

I nod. 'So you would like… more *time*?' I ask, raising an eyebrow.

They nod, some with a trickle of tears.

'You do understand that every mortal you know will die—friends, family—and you sign an agreement that forbids you from asking others if they are immortal. You cannot have intimate relations with others, mortal or not. You'll become lonely and depressed.'

'Better than death,' says a deep voice.

'Is it? And things get boring, you know. It's the same thing day in, day out. Tedious. Monotonous. With no end in sight. There will be nothing to look forward to. You'll have no purpose.'

'Still, better than death,' he says and rocks forward on his toes.

'Do you really think so? You will be witness to global decay, worse than it is now. Social divides. You'll have no value. No motivation to fulfill dreams. You'll feel worthless. Invisible.'

'But we'll still be alive!' he contends.

'And when the Earth eventually ends, and according to prophecy, it will. And what if you have missed your chance to step into the heavenly realm, freed from the fears and insecurities that plague us. Free from tears, death, ignorance, disappointment, war. No sorrow, no crying, no more pain. Living a life filled with happiness and love.'

There is silence in the elevator.

'And, you'll be forever on alert about being found out as an immortal, and the consequences of that.'

Someone clears their throat.

'You are trying to fill an emptiness inside you that can not be filled with immortality on the Earth. What you are searching for, you cannot find here.'

I turn and push button number thirteen, and the elevator pod rises. 'Are you sure about this? Have you spoken to God about this? You belong to Him, not to the Earth. There is only one true immortality.'

They nod. In unison. They don't realise they are making an eternal mistake. A very dark and emotional and spiritually painful mistake.

'Be sure to read the non-disclosure agreement,' I say once again and widen my eyes at them in warning.

The elevator doors open on the thirteenth floor. I follow them out then guide them to the office they seek. We enter.

'Mr. Moretti, I would like to introduce this group to you. They all, wish to speak to you about more *time*,' I say, inclining my head, my insides repelling at what they are about to do.

Mr. Moretti closes his eyes before his head bobs to me in the affirmative. He turns to the new client. 'Welcome. Our experience in extended time is second to none. I have appointments available now, as individuals or as a group if you wish.'

They look at each other, then one speaks. 'As a group, please.'

'Mr. Harris, can I offer you tea or coffee while you wait?' he asks. My cue to leave the office.

'Thank you for your offer, Mr. Moretti, but I must get back

to work. Perhaps another time I will be able to have coffee with you,' I reply formally, as per my given script. I stand, but do not shake his hand.

I turn to the men and women and incline my head. I cannot wish them all the best. They are making a grave mistake.

I step out of the office and return to my elevator. My hand tremor is worse. I shake my hand out to stop the tremoring, then push the button to return to the ground floor.

He is still there waiting for me. His face, an ashen grey.

'Welcome, sir,' I say and gesture for him to enter the elevator.

He walks slowly, like he has no energy, and leans against the brass railing. 'I'm ready,' he says, his words like a mere breath.

I push button number thirteen and the elevator car begins to rise. 'Do you believe in God?' I ask. I am forbidden to talk about religion in my work contract. Instant dismissal if they find out.

He nods his head. 'Yes.' He drops to the floor of the elevator, his arm outstretched; his Life Watch glowing red. Time left. 0.

I push the stop button and the pod stops moving. I bend down and feel the side of his neck for a pulse. There is none.

He is dead.

I take off my cap and my white glove and touch my hand to the top of his head. 'Heavenly Father, I ask for Your forgiveness for any sins this man may have committed during his life. Cleanse him with Your grace and grant him entry into Your kingdom. May he be forgiven and welcomed into Your eternal presence, where he will experience Your boundless love and mercy forever. In Jesus' name I pray. Amen.'

I stand with my head bowed. I try to imagine what he sees now, in comparison to the Earth. My heart smiles. He is free, back with his loved ones, surrounded by pure love and light, standing with his hands in his pockets, a wide grin, younger, radiating pure happiness.

I open the communication compartment of the elevator, and

request help for the deceased. I navigate the elevator to floor 7A, using the button inside the communication compartment. It's the floor used for emergencies such as this. On arrival, I step out from the elevator and prepare the report, which the gentleman is removed with dignity.

At 10AM, I drive the elevator back to the ground floor, after cleaning the pod with bergamot, fussing about my work space, ensuring it is clean.

When I open the doors, I am staggered to see a mobile Emily. She hobbles at a slow pace towards me, holding another painted canvas in her hand.

'Good morning, Miss Finnigan. I am surprised to see you two days after your ankle injury. I thought it would have been at least two and a half days until you could put weight on your foot again!' I say with humor, trying to look at her ankle. The bruising is concealed by the black stockings she wears.

'It's still sore, Li—Alex. But I have one of many paintings to deliver. Can you take me to the thirty-third floor, please,' she says, the pupils of her eyes wide, soaking me in.

'Absolutely, step into my office,' I say, offering my arm for her to take as support.

'Thank you,' she says as the doors close.

I press my lips together in a half-hearted smile, and nod at her as the elevator car starts to ascend to the thirty-third floor.

She hobbles closer to me. 'For going out with me on Saturday, I mean. I had an amazing time with you, and it didn't quite end the way I wanted it to... Liam,' she says quietly, and limps even closer to me, her lips part as she searches my eyes and then focuses on my lips.

My heart accelerates as I feel my attraction to her. That invisible pull that tries to take over the actions of my body. I point to my name tag.

'Alex. I am Alex, Miss Finnigan,' I say in a husky voice, trying to deter her from the kiss that's coming.

She steps away from me then, and blinks at me with a look of panicked confusion over her face.

'So Alex, you're not Liam, is that what you're saying?' Her voice is shaky.

I reach out my hand towards her. 'No, I am saying that I haven't pressed every button so that you can escape from me.' I try to explain my feelings for her without saying them explicitly.

She stares at me. Her face is unreadable and I don't like it.

The doors open and she hobbles out of the elevator and our conversation is left hanging. When the doors close, I take my hat and gloves off, and run my hand through my hair before I put them back on again. The elevator stops at floor thirteen. The doors open and close again, before I am transported back to the ground floor.

Odd.

My stomach churns after my conversation with Emily has ended in disaster. I exit my elevator, about turn and re-enter, close the doors and hold its position on the ground floor so nobody can join me.

I take out my personal communication device to talk to Emily; totally against company policy, for which I could lose my job over. She doesn't answer. So I leave a message, 'Emily, I need to talk to you. Meet me over in the park under the ancient oak tree. The one that has a park bench under it, at noon. I really need to talk to you.' I fold my paper thin device into four and push it into my pocket, then release the elevator doors again.

It is difficult to stand still outside my elevator. I have way too much nervous energy flowing inside me. I need to see Emily again and make sure everything is alright between us.

I look over to my right and see Elevator Nine. The doors open. My throat tightens as I watch Emily hobble out and limp along the polished wooden floor to exit the building. She doesn't even turn to see if I am here. Not a backward glance. Not a wave of acknowledgement. Nothing.

My heart drops. I'm hurting emotionally for the first time ever. And I hate it.

I look out of the expansive glass windows. Storm clouds are brewing. I just hope that they hold their rain until after I have met Emily.

At 11.50AM, I close down Elevator Thirteen and bolt to the staff locker room and change into my civil clothes.

I make it to the old oak tree by 11.58AM.

I lean against the tree with my eyes close, trying to calm my anxiety. I have a terrible feeling in the pit of my stomach that she isn't going to turn up.

And by 12.07PM, she hasn't.

I step away from the tree and walk a short distance with my hands behind my head as I feel the emotional pain shoot through my heart. Once I have resigned myself to my failure, I turn back to the tree, walking backwards, as I head back to work.

It's then that I see Emily leaning against the tree. Her hands are behind her back, her eyes glued to me. She is wearing a faint smile that catches me unaware.

I hang my head and walk towards her with my hand over my heart. It's beating hard. Is this where it ends for us?

I slow my steps and stop in front of her. 'Please forgive me?' I say, looking deeply into her eyes, hoping with all of my heart that she will.

She places her hand onto my shoulder. 'I'm the one who should be sorry, Liam. You were working. I put you in a difficult situation. Will you forgive me?' she asks.

A tear falls from my eye. I have never cried in my one hundred and twenty-one years of immortality. Not even at the deaths of people in my family, or past protectors. I don't know whether to wipe it away or to leave it there.

I leave it there. It's filled with my sadness. My relief. And my heart of love for her.

'How can I not forgive you? You make me feel… you make me feel…' I place my hands over my heart, lost for the words to describe how I'm feeling about her.

I turn around and run my hand through my hair in frustration at not being able to express my feelings. I have kept emotions bottled inside me to protect myself and others when I became an immortal human. It's hard to say what I feel when I know I should be protecting her from me. I'm torn. When I turn back to her, she reaches out and latches onto my shirt and pulls me closer to her.

I still in front of her and become lost in her inner beauty. Her eyes are so full of life and of love. I move my lips closer to hers, and barely let them touch, before I press my lips firmly to hers in a slow, lingering kiss.

And I start to lose myself in her. Nothing else exists but this moment.

I pull away from her, afraid of the loss of control of my awareness around me. It's beautiful and soul touching and dangerous. My head starts to spin from the high I'm feeling. I'm pulled to her again by our fatal attraction, and kiss her with a passion I never knew I possessed.

It's an emotional hunger. It's new, and it's addictive. I want more of her, physically, but can't. When I pull my lips away from hers, I wrap my arms around her and hold her close, never wanting to let her go, sending prayers asking for forgiveness.

An immortal and a mortal cannot be together.

'Liam,' she whispers into my ear, and then kisses my neck and holds me tighter.

'I have to go,' I whisper in a low voice, my eyes still closed as I relish in her closeness to me.

'I know,' she whispers back, 'but I don't want to let go of

you.'

I kiss her below the ear and she runs her fingers through my hair at the back of my head. I blow my strong emotions out, trying to ground myself. 'I really have to go,' I say, and step away from her.

She stands with her eyes closed, and then opens them slowly. 'Where did you just take me, Liam? I want to go back there again,' she says.

I lower my head and lips curve up on one side, wondering whether it is my healing energy that has caused her reaction. I reach for her hand. 'I'll walk you to a cab. Your ankle looks swollen, Em,' I say.

'No. I'd like to just stay here and enjoy the floating high that you gave me. And ah... it's not the halo effect, Mr. Harris,' she says, looking up at me through her long eyelashes.

I step towards her and kiss her lightly on the lips. 'I'm glad I could make you feel happy, Miss Finnigan.'

'Oh, Mr. Harris, you make me feel far more than happy, and I think I will just sit here on this bench on this beautiful day... just for a bit.'

I look up to the dark clouds. Thunder rumbles in the distance. 'Je dois aller mon amour,' I whisper into her ear.

'And you said?' she whispers.

'I have to go... my love.' My voice is low.

She takes a deep breath and closes her eyes. 'Liam,' she whispers again.

I kiss her one last time before I leave her sitting on the park bench in a dreamy state, then return to the humdrum of Elevator Thirteen.

The heavens open up at 3PM. Torrential rain pours relentlessly and lightning illuminates the sky, thunder vibrating throughout the building. People run here and there in a frantic state.

And then Dudley arrives.

And everything slows down.

His appearance is not a good sign.

He wastes no time greeting me. 'Hanno Emily,' Dudley says in a serious, quiet voice.

'Th-they have Emily? By they… do you mean, the immortal seekers?' My voice cracks as my throat tightens.

'Sì,' he replies gravely.

'Dove?' I ask, heat flushing through my body.

'At the vacant warehouse down the road.'

I bow my head, clench my fists, then close my eyes, suppressing the anger inside me. I have done this to her. I have done this to Emily. My immortality has put her in danger.

We can never be together. It can never work.

'I have to go to her and have her released,' I say between clenched teeth.

'Then you are playing into their hands, my boy,' states Dudley.

'Yes. But I will not have them hurting her!'

Dudley looks around as people turn to look at us. He places a finger over his lips to quiet me. 'If you are certain about this, then wait. My sources tell me that one of the three will be here soon with a message. Contact me if you need me. I must not be seen with you or they will become suspicious. Dio sia con voi … the Lord be with you,' Dudley says, and then places his hand on my shoulder and pierces my eyes with his, before he disappears.

I bounce on my toes. I want to run.

I want to run and find Emily and protect her from the immortal seekers. An unexpected surprise visit that catches them off guard could be effective. But Dudley has told me to wait for one of the three. He is my protector and my guide, and he wouldn't tell me this if he didn't know something that I did not.

At 4.15PM precisely, an immortal seeker walks toward me, his chin jutted out, his face decorated with a smirk. He's holding Emily's necklace in his hand and swinging it around, periodically. He steps into Elevator Thirteen and leans against the brass hand rail with a smugness spread across his face I want to remove with my fist.

But don't.

I close the elevator doors.

'Alex... we must talk,' he says, touching my name badge with his grungy finger.

I look at the necklace. 'Of course, how can I help you?' I say, pretending to know nothing about the capture of Emily.

'We need information from you. And we are prepared to exchange it for your girlfriend, Emily. Meet us in the warehouse down the road at 5.15PM. Really, she's as pretty as a picture. My boys have been salivating looking at her. I have given them napkins to wipe away their drool.' He brushes my shoulder as if he is removing some lint. 'See you soon.'

He tries to reef open the elevator doors after tucking Emily's necklace into his breast pocket, unsuccessfully. I clench my teeth in self-control, and calmly open the doors for him. He walks off with perfect posture and shoulders back, taking confident steps.

He is fortunate he left the elevator when he did, as my fury was becoming palpable, one that I find difficult to contain, and have only ever used once in self-defense.

I pace the polished wooden floor at the elevator hub in between the few patrons who still choose to use serviced elevators.

Clock-out time for the day cannot come fast enough. And when it does at 5PM, I move like a bull at a gate to the staff changing area, then charge out the revolving doors to the empty warehouse a block away.

I walk the perimeter of the rusty iron warehouse taking note of structural features, escape possibilities, and weaknesses before

I knock three times on the workman's entrance door.

Within seconds it opens with a loud corroded screech and the blurted aggressive command of "Enter!"

Directly in the centre of the warehouse is a table. Emily sits there. Silent. Her hands shake as she sits between immortal seekers. I walk at a steady pace towards them and stop.

'Release her. It's me you want, not her!' I demand.

'Alex, do you know how we found her? From your scent! She smells of you. Our sensors glowed and we followed the location, and there she was, sitting on the park bench. And then we realised what she is. Our boss from the university advised us to use Emily to lure you. So here we are, ready to exchange one for the other.'

'I'm here. Release her. Now!' My tone is sharp.

'Oh, we will, as soon as we have detained you.'

The sound of handcuffs are behind me. My arms are secured behind my back. I look to the far side of the warehouse as I strengthen my mind and body for what is going to come my way. I will not let them see my fear. And I will not give them my knowledge of *The Change*. My immortal origins.

The moment I am handcuffed, the dominant one stands before me.

'Alex, I'm Evan. I need to prepare you to meet our university criteria.'

He pushes me forward, away from the table and takes me to the right side of the warehouse floor, latching the handcuffs onto a metal structure behind me.

He paces around me like I'm a prize, looking me up and down. Then he rips my shirt open, exposing my torso.

'Emily, come,' he sings, looking at her with a creepy smile on his face.

She is guided to me by the immortal seeker who sat on her left. He touches her, running his finger along her collar bones and over her neck. My body tenses, and blood roars in my ears.

'Jax, stand her before Alex,' Evan stipulates. 'Pedro, you must come and watch Emily,' Evan says, looking at me and smiling.

'Tell me, Emily dear, what do you see before you?'

Emily blinks rapidly, 'A man,' she replies, her voice barely audible.

'Come on, you can do better than that. In fact, if your answer is not detailed enough, I will apply one punch to his body for each poorly described answer. How does that sound?'

Evan raises his fist and punches me in the gut. Hard.

'NO!' Emily yells, and struggles in the arms of Jax. Her eyes fill with tears.

'What do you see before you, Emily?' Evan asks again.

Emily swallows hard. 'I see a tall dark-haired man with chiseled facial features, honey brown eyes. He has a strong neck and broad muscled shoulders. His chest is well-defined and he shows abdominal muscles that indicate mid-body strength and fitness. He is wearing an open white long sleeved buttoned shirt, and acid wash jeans with a black leather belt. His shoes are much like hiking boots,' Emily says, shaking.

Evan takes a handful of her hair and smells it like it is a sort after delicacy. 'Well done. Your boyfriend must be proud of you, except you forgot one thing.'

Evan turns to me and punches me hard in the gut again.

I cough, and gasp for air as I try to bend over to stop the pain.

Emily screams before a filthy hand covers her mouth.

'You forgot to mention this scar he has here, on his chest,' Evan says, moving my shirt to the side to reveal the immortality scar that all immortal humans are brandished with, over and over again when the repairing nanobots have healed the scarring from the hot branding iron that sears our skin like we are cattle..

From my peripheral vision I see him squint and move his head to get a better view. Then he moves my shirt that partly covers my other pectoral muscle to look for the symbol.

I want to look down at my chest to check that my immortality scar is covered by a floral tattoo that I have to have renewed each month, as the repair nanobots keep erasing it.

He walks away from me with his fists clenched to either side of him, and then walks back and stops in front of Emily. He looks her in the eye before he lands another punch to my abdomen.

He grabs her face then, in his unclean hands, and speaks to her, his mouth almost upon hers.

Emily closes her eyes in disgust.

'Did he do the deed with you, Emily?' Evan asks in a gruff voice.

Her eyebrows draw together and she squirms.

'Answer me,' he spits into her face.

'NO!' Emily yells back at him before she empties the contents of her stomach, some of it landing on his face.

He uses the back of his hand to flick away the vomit, then turns to me and lands a punch in my face, almost causing me to pass out.

I feel blood dripping from my lip and my nose. My eye starts to close over as it swells. But I stand tall, staring at the opposite side of the warehouse. I refuse to make eye contact with anyone.

'I'm sorry, Alex. I'm so sorry...' Emily starts to whisper to me, until I hear the sound of a slap.

Then silence.

I remain still, burning with fury as I stand handcuffed with my hands behind me, unable to protect the woman I love.

Unprovoked, another punch is delivered to my stomach, followed by a kick to my thigh.

I clench the pain inside of me and refuse to buckle over as agony sears through my body. I will defy them and stand strong.

'Get her out of here. She is useless to us!' Evan yells.

From my peripheral vision, I see Pedro dragging Emily to

the workman's door. He opens it and steps outside with her. But doesn't return.

After a few moments, inside the door now stands a lone figure. Dudley. With a wooden walking stick.

'Benvenuto Dudley. Era ora che tu fossi un brutto bruto!' I mouth to him.

He nods, ever so slightly.

He walks at his own sweet pace toward the immortal seekers who stand before me.

'Gentlemen,' he says, addressing Evan and Jax, his voice deep and authoritative.

They turn at once at the sound of Dudley's voice. The element of surprise.

Dudley stretches his hand out towards them, his crooked bony fingers stiff and long. 'Do sit at the table so we can have a civil conversation. Release Alex from the post. He will do you no harm. This garbage of beatings and threats is old Hollywood rubbish made for the human psyche over a hundred years ago. It is old and dated. We are beyond that in this twenty-second century.'

Evan and Jax move as Dudley says, following his instructions like they are under his spell.

I rub my wrists where the metal handcuffs had cut into them, and then join them at the table, wondering what mind control Dudley has used on them.

'Right... questions...' Dudley says, straight to the point.

'Where is Pedro? Did you kill him?' Evan.

'Of course not! I gave him permission to start a new life,' Dudley answers, waving his hand around in the air like a butterfly as he often does.

Evan and Jax look at each other, bewildered.

'But you can't do that. You don't employ us.'

'Don't I?' Dudley raises an eyebrow at him and shows them

a university staff card. He pulls out his phone. 'Do you want me to call your supervisor?'

Evan and Jax shake their heads.

'I want to be released from my contract?' Jax says, his voice is as shaky as his hands.

'If that is what you desire—certainly.'

Jax looks at Evan, nodding his head. But Evan shakes his. 'No, Jax. We have a mission to accomplish to please our boss. Or he will kill us. Remember what he said?'

Dudley lets out a sharp laugh. 'I know him well. He is going to kill you anyway, boys, whether you are successful at your mission or not. I have the gift of seeing into the future. He persuades everyone to do his dirty work and promises them great things, and then he kills them. But I, on the other hand, can give you freedom, and a new life.'

'But he will find us!'

'Not if you change your hair, change your clothes, change your name, move away from the area, and I will give you this.' Dudley holds a small red crystal between his two fingers. A ruby. 'This, my boys, is the university sign that will protect you. All employees carry one with them. They will recognize it and leave you alone, if they find you. I can help you. All you have to do is to say the word.'

Evan and Jax focus on the crystal before they look at each other.

'I can read minds, too, boys. Would you like me to tell you what the other person is thinking? And Alex, what was that with your greeting? I heard your thought loud and clear—"Welcome Dudley—about time, you ugly brute!"'

The immortal seekers' eyes widen and they shake their heads vehemently at Dudley's suggestion of mind reading.

'Why do you seek my nephew, boys?' Dudley asks.

'The university is conducting tests on immortals. They torture them to reveal the secret of how they became immortal. And they're trialling their own anti-aging protocol. But you would already know that, since you work with them… right? '

'Correct. I was making sure they have been honest with you. And they have. How does torturing another human sit with you? Do you support it?'

'My job pays the bills and allows me and my family to live comfortably. I have no opinion on the morals of the testing.'

'Let me put it another way. If your son was mistakenly labelled as an immortal, and taken to the university for testing, how would you feel about it?'

Evan looked down. 'I would never allow that.'

'Then why would you allow it to happen to another human, regardless of their life status? When you stand before God to account for your life, where does that leave you? You do believe in God, don't you?'

Evan lifts his head and looks to the ceiling of the warehouse. He nods. 'Yes. I believe. And you're right. I have no excuse.' He looks at the table and shakes his head.

'And you, Jax?' Dudley asks. 'Do you approve of torturing another human? How would you feel if it was you? I can easily arrange for a little taste of how that feels for you.'

Jax drops his chin to his chest.

'I thought so.'

There's silence in the warehouse.

'Tell me. Are you happy doing this job?'

They look at each other.

'It pays good money.' It was Evan who spoke.

'But are you happy?'

He shakes his head.

'How about we come to an agreement. You leave your job. Stop the pursuit of immortal humans, and start a new life with a new identity in a new town. There will be no more wandering around being suspicious of people, nor the violent struggle to apprehend a suspect. And no more guilt that you were part of the process to torture others.'

Neither Evan nor Jax speak.

'I am giving you an option. What do you want to do?' Dudley asks. He taps his walking stick on the ground, creating an echo in the empty building.

'Why would you help us? We have done nothing but cause you grief,' Evan says.

'Why not? Did you choose to become immortal seekers, or were you forced? Your type, have to turn off love for other people to do what you do. And love is the key that will open up a whole new world, and release you from your heavy burdens. It's getting harder to switch over to being a loving and kind husband and father after a day at work, isn't it? You're wife and kids don't look at you the same way anymore. Sometimes they're scared of you.'

Jax sniffs, and a tear rolls down his cheek.

'Love is the key to the happiness that you are searching for,' Dudley adds.

Evan stands up, his fists clenched. 'STOP!' he yells, and then lets out a small cry.

Dudley stands and walks around behind them both. He places one hand on each of their shoulders and they calm. Evan sits down again. 'What will it be, boys?'

'Help me, please...' Jax says with his head bowed.

'And you, Evan?'

'Yes. Help me also.' His voice is subdued.

'Good choice,' Dudley says, his voice gentle.

Dudley sits at his chair again, and takes out two rubies. He gives one to each of them. 'This is for your safety. If you are approached and questioned. Show them your ruby, and they will leave you alone.'

Dudley pulls two wads of cash out of his pocket. 'This is to help you get started. Find the people who still accept cash as a currency. They will guide you as to where to go. They are safe.'

He places the money on the table before them. 'Now, leave your immortality scent detectors here, take the money and the ruby, and go. Don't look back. Go to your family and explain what is happening and why you are doing this, for them, and pack your belongings and go. I will contact your supervisors at the university and let them know that I have contracted you both to another job. They will be satisfied with that.'

Evan and Jax do not move at first. Then they look at each other and narrow their eyes.

'Pedro is already ahead of you.'

Jax stands, pockets the ruby and grabs the wad of cash. He takes a step, but stops. He looks at Dudley. 'Thank you.' Then he leaves.

Evan reaches over to the ruby and the money, and drags it toward him slowly. He inhales deeply, stands, and leaves.

'Don't look back,' Dudley reminds him and watches until he has left the warehouse.

'Bel ragazzo. E 'tempo di lasciare i nostri nuovi amici,' Dudley says to me as he puts his arm around my shoulders.

'Yes, it's time to leave. I don't know whether I can call them my friends, and I'm certainly no pretty boy with my face smashed up like it is now. Thank you, my Protector,' I say. 'And what is with that type of walking stick? I have never seen you with that one, old man!'

Dudley's belly bounces as he chuckles. 'I found it on the road on my way here. It makes a great prop.'

I start to laugh but then stop. It hurts too much. 'And the university card and ruby and money?'

Dudley points to his head. 'Psychological, my boy, psychological. The university card I took from Pedro. If they had looked closer, they would have seen his name and photo on it. The ruby is just the power of suggestion I planted into their minds. People from the university don't carry rubies around with them. And the money. That was the icing on the cake. At heart, all they want is a happy life with their families. And I suggested how they could do it. Their lives may be happier.' Dudley presses his lips together and raises his eyebrows.

'Perhaps,' I say.

Dudley stands and pushes the scent detectors onto the floor, then stabs them with his new walking stick, breaking them until they are irreparable.

I stand then, wincing in pain and we both walk to the warehouse half-size door and duck through it as we exit the old warehouse and out into the mist of the night. I groan in pain as the reality sets in of my beating. I start to button my shirt to pull my collar up around my neck, when Emily appears from behind an old barrel, limping.

'Liam, please forgive me. I'm so sorry,' she says between sobs.

I take a deep breath and look into her eyes, checking to see how she is faring after her traumatic experience. Her eyes are wide as she takes me in, and the blood on my body and my shirt. She takes a shaky breath, her face pale.

'No, Emily. I'm sorry. You would never have been forced to come here and witness what you did had it not been for me.' I take her fingers in mine. 'I'm the one who is sorry. And I'll understand if you don't want anything to do with me,' I say.

A tear slides down her face and she shakes her head slightly. 'I forgive you. They chose to do this. Let me take you home and tend to your cuts and bruises. It looks painful,' she says with a softness in her tone.

I look to the ground between us and close my eyes for the briefest time until pain shoots through my left eye.

'Uncle Dudley, how rude of me, this is Emily Finnigan. Emily, this is Uncle Dudley. I'm sorry I could not warn you of his ugliness before you met him for the first time,' I say, smiling at my Protector.

He lifts his walking stick up off the ground and stabs it onto my shoe.

'Ah,' I say, exaggerating the pain to make him feel bad.

'Emily, it's my pleasure to meet you. Your accurate observation of Liam's body was well spoken. You did save him from further unnecessary beatings. He should be thankful for that. And I think you should be the one to tend to his spilt blood, for I would find it difficult not to add extra antiseptic to seek revenge for his comment about my birth into this unfortunate beauty-challenged body of mine. I must return home before the rain returns. Good evening to you both,' Dudley says, inclining his head to Emily before pulling his collar up to cover his neck.

'Buona notte e ringraziamento, Uncle Dudley,' I call after him as he walks away.

'Good night, and you have already thanked me. Has anyone ever told you to speak English in front of your English speaking friends?'

I hang my head and smile, splitting my lip again. I squeeze my eyes shut at the pain before I dab at the blood with the sleeve of my shirt.

'That wasn't French, was it, Liam?' Emily says as she watches Uncle Dudley walk away.

I shake my head. 'No. It was Italian.'

Emily narrows her eyes at me. 'It is definitely not the halo effect, Mr. Harris. Let's get out of here and get you cleaned up.'

'Yes, let's,' I respond, hailing a cab and wincing at the pain that shoots through me.

I sit on the sofa in front of the fireplace. Emily kneels in front of me, looking up at me with a wrinkled brow before she dabs my swollen lip with honey to help with healing. She then holds ice cubes, wrapped in a clean cloth, against my lip.

'This will help with swelling. Before you go to bed, coat the cut with a turmeric paste and allow it to dry, then rinse with lukewarm water. It will help with swelling and pain.'

I cover her hand with mine as I take over holding the ice to my lip. I close my eyes, enjoying the cold sensation against my skin.

She unbuttons my shirt and opens it, and her eyes dart over my abdominal injuries. She runs her fingers over the bruising that has already appeared, before she applies ice packs, making me shiver.

'I'm so sorry, Liam,' she whispers.

'It's not your fault, remember,' I say, looking into her wide sad eyes before I move my eyes down to my chest, looking for the floral tattoo that covers the scar of immortality, compliments of "Here now. Here forever".

The immortal scar, like the number eight on its side, is there. But it's hard to see. I cover it with my hand. I don't want Emily to know I'm an immortal human.

I close my eyes when I feel Emily's warm, gentle fingers as she tends to my injuries. 'Thank you, Emily. I like your touch much more than my uncle's.'

She giggles quietly. 'I just had a vision of him adding vinegar to your wounds... and I... aahh… like looking after you…'

She sits next to me on the sofa and rests her head on my shoulder. I feel all the tension in my body release. And I feel, for the first time in my life, content. If only she and I could be a "we".

I enter my apartment feeling sore and sorry for myself, and slump onto the sofa chair opposite Dudley, placing my hand over my forehead.

He is knitting again.

'Yes, I have a headache. Yes, my injuries are hurting. But worst of all, I feel so useless and powerless compared to you. You make them retreat without any physical violence!' I say to Dudley.

He chuckles under his smile. 'Liam, we are given different gifts. Mine is… well… many that are different to yours. You, on the other hand, are a seeker and a healer,' he says.

'Yes… that I am limited to use as an immortal. That makes a lot of sense, right?' I mumble with my eyes closed. 'Thank you again for saving me today. I would have ended up at the university as a subject for experiments. I'm forever in your debt.'

'It's my absolute pleasure to be there for you. And I give abundantly with the generosity of my heart, without expecting anything in return. You owe me nothing, my boy. You know I love you, Liam, as if you were my own. And today, I answered your question you have asked yourself for the last one hundred and twenty-one years.'

'You did? Well, thank you. When I replay our day's events in my mind, I will discover the answer to the question I never directly asked you.'

Dudley smiles at me again. 'It's one of my gifts… and you're welcome.'

I hobble over to him and plant a kiss on his head. 'I'm taking my sorry, beaten and bruised body to bed to be healed by the nanobots. Buona notte.'

'Yes, good night, my friend,' he says. 'I am starting to feel my age tonight and will be retiring soon myself.'

I walk up the steps to my bedroom slowly.

'And Liam,' Dudley calls, 'I am coming to visit you in a

dream. And then you will not call me ugly anymore, Young One!'

I raise my hand in response to him. 'Yeah, yeah, Ancient One, in your dreams,' I call over my shoulder.

I release a calming breath as I lay my damaged body onto the bed. 'Caro Dio, possa io avere coraggio, temperanza, saggezza, giustizia e pazienza – Dear Lord, may I have courage, temperance, wisdom, justice and patience,' I whisper. 'And I pray, Lord, that you help me to find the answer to return to a mortal, and to help others as well. And my dream of Light, Lord, it is with me always, wanting to be in Your presence one day, trusting in Your timing and wisdom. And love, Lord, thank you for love. If it is in your will, please let Emily and I be together, in Jesus' name I pray. Amen.' I say, feeling comfort from my spiritual connection, then feel my injured body being repaired by nanobots. It feels like a soft touching of a feather under my skin, and a dulling of the pain until there is pain no more, but I am conflicted. My body heals and my mind heals of the trauma, but Emily's mental pain will stay with her. My heart aches for her, caught in this mess that was created by the immortal seekers.

Tiredness overcomes me. I think of my mother and father. I could really do with their comfort and words of wisdom right now. I look to my left and see the lesser red ball of caution. It still glows. The danger is not finished, even though Dudley has dealt with the immortal seekers.

Only one thing remained—Emily. Where is the danger?

Love could not be a danger, could it? I will talk to Dudley about Emily tomorrow.

Unable to focus my thoughts anymore, I set my mind for the continued healing of my injured body during my unconsciousness, as I slowly give in to the delta sleep zone.

'Guardate su di me con occhi di misericordia, possa la tua

guarigione mano resto su di me, possa la tua vita che dà poteri flusso in ogni cellula del mio corpo e nelle profondità della mia anima, la pulizia, purificazione, mi restituendo integrità e forza credo...' I whisper, and close my eyes. 'Look at me with eyes of mercy, may Your healing hand rest upon me, may Your life giving powers flow into every cell of my body and into the depths of my soul, cleansing, purifying, giving me strength and integrity.'

I open my eyes, at a revelation in the words I have spoken. Powers flow into every cell of my body. That's it. Here now, but *not* forever. I know what I need to do to become a mortal human. I can't wait to tell Dudley about my insight.

7

Tuesday.
7 days.

Rain is beating against the windows when I wake in the muted light of the morning. I take a deep breath, run my hand through my hair, accidentally brushing my hand against the side of my face. It's a little sore, but the swelling has gone down substantially.

I close my eyes and cautiously run my hand over my chest and abdomen, feeling for any discomfort from the blows I received yesterday. Remarkably, I have no pain.

I sit and swing my legs over the side of the bed and stand, apprehensive about my right leg after Even's ferocious kick to my thigh. Not even a twitch of pain. In the mirror, I inspect my injuries more closely. My reflection tells me that I look fine. Those body repairing nanobots are impressive. If only they didn't make you immortal. How am I going to explain the extreme healing to Emily?

As I descend the steps for breakfast, there is no cooking bacon aroma. For the last one hundred and twenty-one years of my immortality, one of my protectors has religiously prepared a cooked breakfast for me. I snigger. Dudley probably has some outrageous eating plan that will cheer me up from my feeling of helplessness. He is irrevocably dedicated like that. He always has my best interests at heart.

I stop at the bottom step when I see Dudley, ready to smile at him and wish him good morning in Italian.

He's still sitting in his reading chair.

His eyes are open and staring straight ahead without blinking, nor without moving towards me, acknowledging my presence.

A chill runs down my spine.

There's a knitting needle protruding from his chest.

I suck in an extensive amount of air as the feeling of suffocation descends upon me like a concrete weight, and then struggle to walk forward to him, my legs stiff.

I stop by his side and touch his hand before I drop to my knees with my head lowered.

He is dead.

Dudley is dead.

Nausea rises, and my throat tightens. I can't breathe and I feel faint. My heart beats fast and my mouth is dry. I try to swallow, but can't. From my chest rises a deep, knowing sob of heartbreak, and tears run profusely down my cheeks as I lean forward and put my head against the floorboards.

I slam my fist against the hardwood floor three times as I hurt to the core of my being, wailing. 'Mio caro Dio, mio Signore, my dear God, my Lord,' I weep with increasing weakness, before I curl up in the fetal position and rock myself in deep grief over the departure of my protector, my guide, and my friend.

'Noooooo!' My voice cracks. 'Noooo...' I weep.

Numb to the bone, I rise before him and place my hands over his eyes and close them. I put my hand over my heart where pain sears through it, and then kiss his forehead, letting my tears fall onto him. 'Che Dio vi benedica e ti protegga, e può ora camminare alla presenza del nostro Dio Onnipotente, per sei stato fedele fino alla fine. May God bless you and keep you, and may you now walk in the presence of our Almighty God, for you were faithful, to the end,' I speak over him.

I remove the knitting needle from his chest and open his shirt, exposing the wound.

I need to try to heal the skin so his death doesn't look suspicious, although I know that it is.

Dudley would never have taken his own life. Ever!

I place my right index finger over the wound and close my eyes. I breathe in through my nose and project the white light of healing, the perfect colour, into and around the entry site of the knitting needle. The area warms under my finger. And once coolness spreads to my finger, I breathe a slow breath between my pursed lips, then remove my finger. Has my first attempt at healing been successful?

I open my eyes and inspect the area with focused attention. It has not healed. Perhaps when I am mortal, my healing gift will be active.

A tear runs down my cheek. 'Who has done this to you, my friend?' I whisper.

I go to the kitchen and grab a knife, cut my finger and place the blood over his wound. In my chaotic thinking, I'm experimenting to see if my bio-nanobots will heal the surface of his skin.

They don't.

My mind wanders to the makeup artist bag in my room. I have it to create bruising or cut effects on my skin like I am mortal to hide my immortality. I go and retrieve it and return to Dudley. I clean the area of the wound, then glue the entry site of the knitting needle together with superglue, then proceed to use foundation to mask the injury.

I leave his body and find an identical clean shirt to the one he wore, change his shirts, and throw his bloodied shirt into the fire for incineration.

I inhale deeply before I call for a doctor. And within thirty minutes he has arrived.

I stand in the background as I watch him examine Dudley.

'Has he been unwell, Mr. Harris?' the doctor asks.

'Not that I know of. My uncle never complained about feeling sick. I don't recall him ever visiting a doctor. Last night though, he did mention that he was feeling his age. He has never said that before,' I say.

'Well, in my opinion, I do believe his old age caught up with him. That is the cause of his death. Natural causes. Please accept my condolences. I will call an ambulance to come for him. They will take him to a morgue to prepare him for burial.' The doctor takes photos, then places his hand on my shoulder and leaves. I hear him talking on his cell phone outside the door.

While I wait for the ambulance I fill the room with Dudley's favourite piece of music, *Adagio for Strings*. I sit with him, holding his hand in mine in the final moments before his Earthly vessel is taken away. Although, I know that he no longer dwells in the physical form of bones, tissues and blood.

Once his body is removed, I sit where he had been and let my emotions come to the fore. I am overtaken by an ache in my heart. And I cry. Grief. My debilitating, unbearable profound sense of sorrow. A void inside me, left by his loss. I feel empty inside. He has taken a part of me with him. I cover my face with my hands as my body heaves with the convulsions of sobbing from deep within me. It's a reflection of love. My love for him.

Deep grief comes from deep love.

I'm drowning in an ocean of tears, and I suddenly understand why people want immortality? It's about never having to say goodbye. It's about never feeling the agonizing pain of loss. Of loneliness. Of being left behind.

I stand, lost in the confusion of my thoughts, and somehow phone work to inform them of my circumstances, and my reason for my absence today. I wander around the apartment aimlessly. Lost. Staring at objects but not seeing. Staring out the window, but not present.

I sit on my bed. Empty. And alone. Close my eyes and lie down, hands crossed over my heart. It's beating fast. My heart, that if it is ever damaged, will be repaired by nanobots so I cannot die.

'Dudley,' I whisper, my voice cracking, 'I don't want to say goodbye… I want to say see you again when I step into eternity… but… will I ever—'

I cover my face with my hands as I let out a silent scream, rolling onto my side. This hurts so bad. I don't know if I can move forward. Not this time. It feels too hard.

'Lord, my Heavenly Father, hold Dudley in your arms and tell him that I love him. I miss him. And thank him for looking after me. And Lord, help me to find the anti-dote to immortality.' I take a deep shuddering breath. 'Lord, I thank you and praise you for the life of Dudley. I pray that he is clothed with eternal immortality, and is dancing with the angels in that place you have gloriously prepared for us. Thank you, Lord. You are our Protector and Deliverer, and ever faithful. In the name of Jesus I pray. Amen.'

I open my eyes, and panic invades me. Beside the glowing Earth energy mass, my constant companion day and night for the last one hundred and twenty-one years, is the red globe of caution. Except it is gray, like life has left it.

My heart beats wildly. It's hard to breathe and my head spins. I close my eyes, searching for words in conversations with my mother before she passed. Before I knew the explicit details of my human immortality. No, no. It's not conversations. It's letters.

I get out of bed and find the old leather box of letters from my parents in my cupboard. I lift the lid and her perfume floats around me, like she's here. With me. I finger through the twenty letters and find the envelope with the red circle on it. I pull it out and open the envelope, sliding the letter out. It's handwritten and my heart stutters.

Liam, my love,

I have instructed your protectors to place a glowing red globe on your bedside table when they are aware of danger, for you, or for someone in your circle. Your protector can't tell you who is in danger, but it is a sign that something untoward is coming, to prepare your heart. I wish I could be there with you, to comfort you, and to hold you.
Until we meet again, my son.

I love you,
Mama

I still, close my eyes and frown. Did I let Dudley down? Did he die because of me? I shake my head, feeling the heaviness of guilt. I want to reverse time and save him. If someone was going to be stabbed with a knitting needle, it should have been me. I would have survived it.

I let the words of my mother wash over me, then open my eyes. One day. One day I hope to meet you again…

I lie back on my bed. Empty. Exhausted. 'Il coraggio, la

temperanza, la saggezza, la giustizia, la pazienza - courage, temperance, wisdom, justice, patience,' I whisper, searching for some kind of comfort.

'And love,' I add.

Love is what Dudley was talking about when he said that he answered my one hundred and twenty-one year old question.

Love was the key to opening the gate for me to become mortal. It was caring for someone more than I cared for myself. I would have died to protect Dudley, and I was willing to be the sacrifice instead of Emily. Love was euphoria, but with it came pain. The pain of loss.

I had found the key to make me hungrier for my mortality. Now to find the door to open it. The door to my dream of light.

I roll on to my stomach and stare out the window at the dull, grey, lifeless day. It is exactly what I am feeling inside right now. I wondered when the sun will shine, literally, and metaphorically.

Time—it would take time—there is a time for sadness, and a time for happiness.

Now is the time for sadness, a parting of our souls, just for a short while, I pray… and then we will meet again.

Tiredness burdens me, and I let sleep sprinkle its magic dust over me.

Night has fallen when I wake. I wander to the bathroom to splash cold water over my face to spur me to lift myself out of my sadness. To keep going. For Dudley. He wouldn't want me to drop my bundle and sink into the sea of despair.

In the study, IDcom is flashing. I walk over to it. There are three alerts.

'IDcom,' I say. A ping sounds on the augmented reality, and a message is projected as a 3D hologram. 'Open messages.'

Request completed...

Incoming… Emily Finnigan – Message 1.
FROM: Emily Finnigan
DATE: 7 May 10:10
TO: Liam Harris
SUBJECT: Missing in Action

Hi Liam,

You aren't at work. I hope you're okay.

X Emily
#Liam'spersonalnurse

Emily Finnigan – Message 2.

FROM: Emily Finnigan
DATE: 7 May 13:13
TO: Liam Harris
SUBJECT: RE: Missing in Action

Liam,

Seriously. Let me know that you are okay. I'm worried about you.

XX Emily

Emily Finnigan – Message 3.

FROM: Emily Finnigan
DATE: 7 May 19:00

TO: Liam Harris
SUBJECT: RE: RE: Missing in Action

Liam, Alex, Mr. Harris,

I am beside myself with worry.
I am coming over to see you.

XXX Emily
#worrywart

'IDcom,' I say, 'Write a note to Emily telling her that I will see her tomor—' There's a knock at the door. 'Cancel that please,' I say.

Request completed...

I run my hand through my hair and sigh. I want to be alone. My eyes widen as I remember my complete healing from my beating. I run to the bathroom and find the make-up and apply it to look like bruising. Then I hesitate before I start towards the front door. I'm going to politely usher her away.

The knocking continues, even as I open the door to her. She looks up at me and cocks her head to the side, pulling her eyebrows together. 'Liam, are you okay?' she asks. 'You look terrible!'

Her eyes search my face, looking from my bruised eye to the split on my lip, and then look into the depths of my eyes. I cannot conceal the emotional pain. I want to burst open in grief, and tears. I want to see her, but I don't. I hang my head and close my eyes. I may as well tell her. I can't hide my heart that I wear on my sleeve. 'He is dead.'

'Who, Liam, who's dead?'

'Dudley.'

Emily steps towards me and closes the door behind us, then wraps her arms around me. 'No-no… I'm so sorry. When? How?' she asks in a whispered voice in my ear.

'I woke this morning to find him sitting where I spoke to him last night. He said he was feeling his age, Emily. He was old. I never thought once that he meant that he was going to die.' I sob into her shoulder, unable to control the deep sadness within me.

She doesn't say anything. She just holds me in her arms.

'I'm so sorry for your loss. I'm so sorry,' she finally whispers. 'I'll make some tea. Come to the kitchen with me,' she says in a quiet, calm voice, holding my fingertips and leading me to the kitchen.

I follow her like a lost puppy, comforted by her presence.

I sit opposite her at the table with my hands cupped in front of my lips.

'Thank you… thank you for coming over,' I manage to say.

She doesn't speak, but places her warm hand over mine and pulls it towards her in a comforting gesture.

I look down and shake my head. 'I have never been without him,' I mumble with sadness. I look up at her.

She has tears in her eyes. 'Death is a difficult time, Liam, no matter what you believe in,' she says in a quiet voice.

'What do you believe in, Emily?' I ask. I need her to believe in a spiritual life after the physical death of the human body. I want her to be on the same page as me.

'I believe that you will see him again. You will be united with him in your own death, with the freedom of your spirit that is encased in your human body.'

I look into her eyes then close mine in relief. I want to tell her that I love her, but not today. She may hear the words as those born out of pain, a wrestling, grabbing at something to hold on to as I swim in the darkness for a while.

'Can I do anything else for you? Help you with plans for the funeral? Let anyone else know of Dudley's passing?' she asks.

I shake my head. 'I'd just like you to hold my hand... please,' I say.

A tear rolls down her face as she stands and walks around to me. She holds out her hand for me to take. I place my hand in hers, and she leads me over to the sofa where we sit in silence, our hands connected.

I rest my head on her shoulder after a while, and she puts her arm around me and kisses my forehead. How can silence be so loud?

Her steady breathing and the warmth of her body lull me to sleep. When I wake later in the night, my head is resting on her chest, my arms wrapped around her and our legs entangled together.

I moved slightly, and feel her fingers move through my hair. She is so soft and warm. I have never been so close to a mortal human before. 'Oh... Emily. I'm so sorry,' I say when I sit up in alarm, running my hand over my face, embarrassed by falling asleep while she is here to see me.

'It's okay, Liam. There is no need to be sorry,' she says quietly, touching my arm. 'I can stay with you tonight if you like, considering...'

I look at her, tempted by her suggestion of company. But, I think I need alone time now, to sort out the direction of my life. 'Thank you, but—' I can't find the words to say to her.

Our eyes connect before she stands and walks to the door and opens it. I follow her, standing closely to her, almost falling into a heap on the floor at the thought of her leaving me.

'Thank you,' I manage to whisper.

She places her hands on the side of my face and kisses my lips, lightly.

'Ow!' I respond, lying, pretending that my lip is still sore. I pull my eyebrows together and put my fingers on my damaged lip.

Emily places her hands onto my shoulders and looks into my eyes. 'Call me, at any time. Okay?' she say, and waits for my nod before she leaves.

I close the door, turn around, squeeze my eyes shut and put my hands behind my head. The temptation to pull her into my arms and kiss her deeply was hard to resist. I want to wrap my body around hers and create our own bubble where nothing bad can ever happen.

I don't go to bed that night.

I can't.

I'm alone. Truly alone for the first time in one hundred and forty-nine years. And it feels like a punch in the gut, a twisting of a knife in the heart, a smothering over my face making it hard for me to breathe.

6

Wednesday.
6 days.

7 AM.
A knock on the door.
I open it to a young man. He looks the same age as my immortal age, twenty-eight. Wearing a trilby hat that matched Dudley's, holding a leather briefcase and a parcel wrapped in brown paper with string tied around it, a note attached to it.

He holds out his hand. 'Liam. I'm so sorry for your loss. I'm Aurelius. Your new protector. Call me Aurie.'

My breath hitches and I stumble backward. He's unexpected. It's too soon for him to be here. I'm not ready.

'Let's sit over here, Liam.'

He guides me to the sofa in front of the fireplace, then sits in Dudley's wing chair. I want to tell him he can't sit there. That's Dudley's chair. I close my eyes. I'm overwhelmed.

'I'm here to deliver two things to you, from Dudley, my

184

mentor, and friend.'

I open my eyes and look at him through my tears.

'This box is to remain on the dining table. Dudley said you will know when to open it. He said… you will need to heal first.' Aurie stands and takes the box to the table, then returns to the wing chair. Matisse meows loudly, like she is calling Dudley, and my chest tightens. He opens his leather briefcase and pulls out a letter, and hands it to me. 'Dudley wanted you to have this letter. He loved you like a son.'

I take the letter from him and nod. Words are jammed in my tight throat and I can't get them out. I swallow. Hard. Aurie takes out another letter and hands it to me. 'This letter is from me. I have some news you want to hear. Read it when you are ready, and contact me on the details I have left you on the letter.'

I walk him to the door. I release a deep breath and my throat relaxes. 'Aurie. I need to be mortal. I think it's something to do with TED. Can we work on it?'

Aurie raises an eyebrow and smiles crookedly at me. 'I'll see you soon.'

I close the door after him and head to the kitchen to make a cup of tea, leaving the two letters on the table. Apparently, a cup of tea solves everything. Does that include reading the contents of two letters?

I sit at the table with the letters before me. They have no pull on me. So I leave them there, unopened. I'm not ready to read them. Not yet. Not today. I need to fill the hole left by Dudley with precious memories of him. And stitch them up with threads of his love, threads of our friendship.

The hot cup of tea fills my stomach enough to get me to work. I don my elevator uniform and stand obediently outside Elevator

Thirteen as I have been groomed to do, greeting people politely and helping to remove burdens from their day.

But my burden remains. Hidden behind my mask. That ache in my chest, my constant reminder of my loss. The day means nothing to me as I mourn the loss of my friend. My protector. My guide.

At 9AM, a group of mid-life women stand before my elevator. I know what they want without even glancing at the arms for their red glowing Life Watches. It's that despair they have mixed with a look of hope that I can help them. They falsely believe that immortality on the Earth will bring them happiness. Tragically, all it will bring them is the feeling of being trapped. No escape. Loneliness. Intrusive thoughts and panic.

'Good morning,' I say and invite them into the elevator with a practiced smile. One I can put on no matter the circumstances. 'Which floor would you like to proceed to?' I ask, knowing very well what their answer will be.

'Floor thirteen please,' a woman says, then rocks onto her toes.

'Would you like… more *time*, I assume?' I ask, raising an eyebrow.

She nods her head. I look at the other women, and they too, nod.

I push button number thirteen, and the elevator pod rises. 'Are you sure about this?' I ask them.

They nod. In unison.

'Be sure to read the non-disclosure agreement,' I say and widen my eyes at them in warning. 'Ha! Imagine being two thousand years old! I mean… what will the Earth look like and how much more destruction can people governments do? And what is so important that you need two thousand years for… to achieve a dream perhaps?' I give them a crooked smile.

The elevator doors open on the thirteenth floor. 'Just a

question. Do you believe in God?' I clear my throat. 'Something to think about.' I gesture to them to exit the elevator, then follow them out then guide them to the office they seek. We enter.

'Mr. Moretti, I would like to introduce these lovely women to you. They all, wish to speak to you about more *time*,' I say, inclining my head, my insides knotting.

Mr. Moretti nods. He turns to the new clients. 'Welcome. Our experience in extended time, and our ability to resolve matters of time is second to none. I have appointments available now, as individuals or as a group if you wish.'

They look at each other, then one speaks. 'As a group, please.'

'Actually... I need more time to think about it,' the shortest woman says.

'Mr. Harris, can I offer you tea or coffee while you wait?' he asks. My cue to leave the office.

'Thank you for your offer, Mr. Moretti, but I must get back to work. Perhaps another time I will be able to have coffee with you,' I reply formally, as per my given script, before I stand.

I turn to the remaining women. 'I wish you all the entire best,' I say in a smooth, calm voice, as per my script.

I step out of the office and return to my elevator. Not one but three women follow me. We step into the elevator and I close the doors.

'As you consider your options about time, read widely, discuss eternal life deeply, and pray for the only answer that is correct,' I say as the elevator pod begins to descend.

'Thank you,' the shorter woman says, as the three step out onto the ground floor of the Great Hall.

At 10AM, the elevator doors close, and my lift ascends to the thirteenth floor. When the doors open, Mr. Moretti stands waiting for me with his hands behind his back. 'Lock the elevator at thirteen,' he demands, and then proceeds to his office.

I assume I am to follow him. But I stand, waiting at his door, for him to invite me in. He simply gestures, pointing to the seat for me to sit in.

'I offer my condolences at the passing of your… uncle,' Mr. Moretti says. Darkness settles over his face.

'Thank you, Mr. Moretti,' I say, lifting my chin and narrowing my eyes at him. He is as trustworthy as a politician.

He stands, then. 'I will see you in four more days, Mr. Harris, oh and, ah … did your uncle knit the scarf you wore around your neck this morning?' he asks.

I frown, cautious of his words.

'I saw you enter on the security camera this morning wearing a knitted scarf,' he adds.

'Oh, I see. No, my uncle did not knit the scarf for me,' I say while I stand. My heart begins to pound and an odd tingling sensation travels up my spine. I shake his hand and look into his eyes, wondering why he suddenly has an interest in my life.

I re-enter the elevator and return to the ground floor, troubled by Mr. Moretti's remark about Dudley knitting. Nobody could have possibly known that Dudley is a knitting nerd, his recently added hobby.

At 4PM, a group of ladies enters my elevator. All of them exit, except one.

It's Emily.

She stands opposite me and leans on the handrail. As the elevator descends, she pushed the stop button.

I sigh.

'How are you?' she asks, frowning.

I look down. 'As expected, I guess,' I say and look into her eyes.

'How's your lip? I'm sorry I hurt it kissing you last night,' she comments as her eyes wander over my lips.

I look down again and smile crookedly, remembering the soft touch of her lips on mine, and the feigning of the pain. I should be an actor. 'I think it needs more of your kisses to make it better,' I say in a quiet voice as she closes the space between us, and then runs her finger lightly over my bottom lip. She looks deeply into my eyes before she brushes her lips over mine, lightly, and I melt at her tenderness and pull away from her. 'I will have no choice but to tell Liam that you have kissed another man,' I whisper.

Emily smiles at me with a twinkle in her eye. 'Can you tell Liam that I'm taking him to the movies tonight, and that I'll meet him outside the building at 5.15PM. Okay?'

'Maybe I will. Maybe I won't,' I reply, and set the elevator to move again.

I smile at her as she steps out onto the polished wooden floor and walks away from me. My day is getting better. The sun is beginning to shine.

At the end of my shift, I walk out into the cool night air at 5.10PM. Covering my neck with the scarf Emily has knitted for me, I note a dark shadow to my left.

I turn to the right and masquerade between a large pole and a palm tree and watch a vaguely familiar silhouette pace nervously.

Two minutes later, a round figure descends the steps in his business suit. He stands, partly concealed behind the landscaping, but clearly slides his hand into his pocket where he retrieves a yellow envelope. He folds his arms and hides the envelope at his side.

The person clothed in the colours of the night meanders near him, then removes the envelope from the hand of the suited man before he walks off in my direction with his hands in his pockets.

I shrink further behind my cover, memorizing the face of the man who lurks, and then turn to see that is Mr. Moretti who has delivered the envelope.

I watch as he enters the building until he disappears from sight, then I step out to wait for Emily.

She appears before me right at 5.15PM.

'You okay?' she asks the moment she sees me.

'Ah… yes. Why?'

'You look as if you are paranoid or something.' She frowns. 'Uncomfortable.'

I shrug. 'One of those days,' I brush off.

'Did you talk to Alex by any chance?' she asks.

'Would I be standing here if I didn't?' I say, raising an eyebrow, playing along with her game. Her lips curl up and she tucks her arm through mine as we begin to walk.

'We, Mr. Harris, are going out to dinner to celebrate Dudley's life, and then I am taking you to a movie,' she says with a confident voice.

'As long as the movie has fast cars and exploding aliens in it—I'm in,' I say, teasing her.

'But of course,' she replies, punching me in the arm.

We walk in silence for some distance then stop. Emily turns to me, her hand caressing the back of my neck. 'How are you?' she asks.

'Still sore,' I say, putting my fingers over my lip where it had split.

'Sorry,' she whispers.

I pulled her against me and wrapped my arms around her. 'Pas besoin d'être désolé par l'amour!' I whispered into her hair. 'No need to be sorry, my love,' I translated for her.

She stepped back from me. 'And emotionally?' she asks.

I inhale deeply and lift my eyebrows. 'Struggling. But distraction helps. I'm putting off going home because I know it will hit me that Dudley is never coming home.'

Emily nods her head in compassion. In understanding. 'Let's keep walking to the restaurant,' she says with her hand over her heart.

'Indeed,' I agree, inclining my head to her.

After ten minutes, Emily stops outside an Italian restaurant and looks at me.

'Appropriate,' I say to her, thinking of Dudley's remarks and bantering between us in Italian. I follow her inside where we are escorted through the restaurant to our table.

We are seated opposite each other, close enough for an intimate conversation. It's perfect for the occasion. As the waiter fills our glasses with water, I ordered a red wine, Dudley's favourite.

'I hope you approve of the restaurant, and that I have not added salt to the wound,' Emily says, looking at me through her long black eyelashes.

'It's perfect, thank you.' I reach over and give her a hand hug.

She looks at the menu, but I do not. Instead, I watch her, thankful that our paths have crossed.

She looks up at me.

'Let's make a new tradition,' I say, 'whoever asks the other on a date does the ordering. I'll eat whatever you order for me,' I suggest.

She looks at me and giggles.

'What?' I ask, narrowing my eyes at her.

'I was wondering if I could order—' She blushes and doesn't finish her sentence. But then she adds, 'Sounds like a fun tradition to start. Until of course, when we don't go out anymore, and then it becomes a memory that makes one of us sad.'

'And what if we live happily ever after, and look back at our firsts with fondness?' I ask, and frown.

Emily nods. 'You're right. I shouldn't worry about the what ifs,' she says, then looks at the menu.

A waiter appears within a beat. 'Welcome to La Doce Vita. What would you like to order?' He pours red wine into our wine glasses.

'I'm doing a secret order for us,' Emily says, then points to each of the choices she has made for dinner. The waiter smiles, nods and leaves.

I grin at her. She is delightfully refreshing and she holds my heart in her hands. 'Dudley would have loved you,' I say and look at my wine on the table.

She reaches across and covers my hand with hers. I look up into her beautiful green eyes and panic starts to rise in my chest. I'm still immortal, and she and I can't be a "we". If I can't return to a mortal, she will get hurt. I don't want to hurt her. Maybe I should stop this now.

I pick up my wine glass and hold it up. 'To Dudley, may you enjoy your new life in the spiritual realm, blissfully happy in the company of your family for eternity… per Dudley, che tu possa godere la vostra nuova vita nel regno spirituale, beatamente felice in compagnia della vostra famiglia per l'eternità.'

Emily touches her wine glass against mine, and we drink deeply, lost in silence.

'You were everything to him. I saw it in his eyes when he looked at you the other night.'

I see tears forming in her yes, ready to fall from the catchment of her eyelashes. 'Yes. Yes, he did. And I cared for him in every way I possibly could, to ensure he lived a happy life. I loved him like a son loves his father,' I say, and then breathe in deeply to control my emotions.

The waiter steps into our view with our meals. A magnificent plate of pistachios and parmesan crumbed chicken thighs, deep fried, served with mash potatoes, asparagus, red pesto sauce is placed before me, while Emily has a traditional Italian lasagne.

'Ah, a woman with good taste, thank you,' I compliment her.

She smiles at me. 'You're welcome,' she says in a gentle voice.

'Why aren't you married?' I ask after we eat in silence for a while. 'And where is your Life Watch?'

'I … I have never felt the connection I have been looking

for,' she answers, looking at me, and then back to her food. 'And I don't wear the Life Watch because I am forb— I mean, I choose not to.'

I narrow my eyes at her answer. 'What connection have you been searching for?' I ask, interested by her definition of a "connection".

She looks up to the ceiling of the restaurant searching for words I guess, before she speaks, and then she looks back at me, her face glowing. 'Not just a chemical attraction of our physical bodies, but, a connection of the mind, and of the soul. A feeling like I belong with him, and that he will love me deeply until death do we part, and feel protective of me so I feel completely safe, and in awe of him. I guess, like it was destiny for me to meet him. That he was heaven sent,' she explains with a gentleness of spirit.

I look deeply into her eyes as she speaks and feel my heart start to beat as one with hers.

She is the one.

She is the one who has been chosen for me. I have absolutely no doubt. But we can't be together.

'You will find him, Emily, I'm sure of it. I believe that those of us who are destined to marry have had a soul chosen for us here on the Earth. I believe in love, even at first sight, the connecting of two souls so powerful that touches your heart and your spirit, the depth of your being, so that being parted from them can be unbearable.'

She takes a deep breath as she gazes into my eyes, her pupils dilate and her lips part slightly. I pick up my wine glass, keeping my eyes connected to hers.

'To happy endings,' I whisper.

'To happy endings,' she repeats, her voice barely audible.

'Why did you choose not to wear a Life Watch?' I ask.

'Why do you not wear a Life Watch?' she deflects.

'I hate that people constantly look at them. I hate that people consult with their time left to make decisions about their lives. I hate that others can see how much time you have left before death. One thing that I do like though, is that when the Life Watch turns red, you can pray for that person. Your turn.'

Emily stills and blinks before she speaks. 'I hate how it tracks you, measures your biodata, tells you what to eat or drink to give you extended time, that you are putting your trust in technology instead of the One who created you.'

I lift my wine glass to hers. She is indeed an amazing woman. And right at this moment, I love her more than I should.

'Are you a Pure One, may I ask, and if so, has your life partner already been chosen for you?' I need to know.

'You may not ask, and no to a life partner. I will choose who I spend my life with.'

When our meal finishes, I stand and hold out my hand for her. A powerful sensation enters my body as she places her hand in mine. I hope that she feels it, too. I no longer try to hold in my healing energy with her. She has already experienced it. I have nothing to hide.

Except my immortality.

When she stands, I raise her hand to my lips and kiss it. 'Grazie per la cena Emily, è stata magnifica,' I say into her ear so only she can hear it, then translate it, 'Thanks for dinner Emily, it was magnificent.'

She gazes into my eyes, places her hand onto my shoulder and blinks slowly.

She's very quiet as we walk to the cinema, hand in hand. 'Are you okay?' I ask after a while.

She lowers her head. 'Yes.' Her voice is quiet. 'You just... you just take my breath away sometimes,' she says.

I lower my head and smile. 'Shall I give you the kiss of life to return your breath to you? It would be my pleasure after all,' I whisper into her ear.

She smiles.

'So, what movie are we seeing, Miss Finnigan?' I ask, trying to change the topic of her focus.

'It's classified information,' she says, and looks up at me.

I hesitate and place my head against the door of my apartment before I go inside after my evening out with Emily.

In the pit of my stomach I feel the absence of Dudley with great intensity. And I want to cry. I inhale deeply then enter the quietness of my once warm and welcoming apartment.

Before I have even stepped fully into the room, Matisse is there to greet me. I pick her up. She gives me tiger kisses with her forehead against mine.

'Good evening, Matisse,' I say. 'Ready for dinner?' I place Matisse on the floor and she follows me to the kitchen. I feed her, then walk to the table. I run my hand over the two letters, then sit at the table.

I open the letter from Dudley, the smell of his aftershave permeating the room, a fresh masculine fragrance of precious woods, moss and patchouli.

My Dearest Liam,

You're reading this because I have left you. The glowing red globe of caution was for me. But I couldn't tell you. I need to tell you what a joy it was to be your protector. And that Aurelius is trained and ready to step into my shoes. He is a smart one, boy. He is also a Pure One. I have prepared something and boxed it for you and Aurelius has delivered it to you. You will know when the

right time to open it is.
Remember my love for you.
Until we meet again.

Dudley

My tear drips onto the letter, right next to the stain from his tear. Apt. I close the letter, bring it to my nose to inhale his scent, and put it back into the envelope.

I hesitate before I open the letter from Aurelius. I don't know him yet. But I decide to open it as Dudley is fond of him.

Liam,

I'm sorry for your loss. I too, am grieving. Dudley was my teacher, my competitor, my critic, always challenging, encouraging and supporting me to do better, for you. Dudley loved you more than words can describe.

I come to you with a knowledge that Dudley guided me to when he met me at the university. His university employee ID card is in the envelope. He asked me to give it to you.

We have an unfinished chess game, and I would love it if you could step in for Dudley. See you Saturday morning. 9AM.

At your service,
Aurelius

I flipped the university employee card over and over in my hand. Dudley was a man of secrets. This was one of them.

After my shower I lay on my bed. My mind is full. Dudley. The knitting needle. Emily. My human immortality. And now, Aurelius. A *Pure One*, like Emily. Is he the one she is waiting for? Am I simply the person to connect them?

The thoughts are too heavy on top of my grief.

I drift off to sleep with my arms crossed over my chest. Like I'm protecting my heart. I don't want to hold the glowing Earth energy mass. It's reminder of my immortality is too heavy, right now.

In the depths of nothingness in my unconsciousness in sleep, I see a vision of Dudley. He stands before me. Younger. Perhaps around thirty years old. He lays a hand on my shoulder and thanks me, tells me he loves me, and to keep dreaming of the Light. Then he smiles at me and fades from view. The nothingness of deep sleep blankets me then, and time passes by unnoticed.

5

Thursday.
5 days.

As the first rays of the new day speckle in through the blinds, I catch sight of a knitting needle on my bedside table. My heartbeat races and my adrenaline spikes. I sit up and glance around the room. Nothing. Then quickly change into jeans and a T-shirt and head to the kitchen, checking rooms along the way.

The apartment is empty, but an uncomfortable feeling of intrusion lingers.

I forego breakfast at home and grab some on the way, then change into my elevator operator uniform to start my short day.

At 8AM, an elderly gentlemen stands before me. He's well dressed in his charcoal grey suit. His hair is white and he sports an impressively manicured moustache. I approve.

I gesture for him to step into the elevator. 'Top of the morning, sir. The day is too beautiful to be inside this building.

Which floor would you like to travel to?'

He rubs his wrist where his Life Watch would be. But it is covered by the sleeve of his suit. He frowns at me. 'I'm wondering if this is the *time* lift? My friend who is the same age as me, time age, came here, but now he looks like he's thirty again. Can't wipe the smile from his face.' He grins at me.

I smile and looked down at my shoes. This is what makes Earth immortality so appealing at first. I look back at him. 'Yes sir, this is the famous *time* lift.' I push button number thirteen. 'Have you thought about the fact that he may now be trapped in time, where there is no perceived end of time, until Earth time finishes? And then what will happen to him?'

'Hmmm. No I haven't.'

'Have you considered true immortality, instead of the Earth immortality offered here?'

'All my life.'

'Do you believe in God?' Now my signature question for those seeking more time.

'I do.'

'Then compare how you will be living in the true heavenly immortal realm, compared to continued living on the deteriorating Earth. What do you gain? What do you lose?'

The doors open on the thirteenth floor. I follow the new client to the office of Mr. Moretti. 'Be careful to read the non-disclosure agreement. They will own you.'

The gentleman stops walking and faces me. 'So you're saying it's like I'm betraying myself?'

'Certainly is,' I say, and see Mr. Moretti waiting for his new client. 'Do you wish to proceed?'

'No. I want to live the rest of my days with peace of mind, not owned or controlled by someone else, or a corporation.' He turns and starts walking to elevator thirteen.

I shrug at Mr. Moretti, turn and follow the gentleman back

to my elevator, open the doors and deliver him to the ground floor. To freedom. 'May you be blessed beyond measure, sir,' I say before he steps out of my elevator car and walks with a spring in his step.

The day goes by in a blur until I leave at 2:30PM.

And at 3PM, dark clouds gather overhead as I stand at the graveside service for Dudley. I'm the sole attendant, as expected. It's how it is meant to be as a protector. He had arrived in my life the day after the burial of my previous protector. And tomorrow my new protector will enter my daily life. But now, here I am with him as his borrowed Earth body is committed to return to the Earth, but his soul, his spirit, back to the presence of our Creator and His Son.

Everything seems to be in shades of grey as I stand and wait, except for the priest's vestment of purple.

When he starts the commendation and farewell, I feel a warm hand slide into mine.

Emily's.

I have memorized every facet of it since we first touched. I bring her hand up to my lips and kiss it. From then on, I close my eyes while I listen to the priest in his prayers of commending and entrusting.

I open them again as the coffin is lowered into the grave.

'Earth to Earth, ashes to ashes, dust to dust, in the sure and certain hope of the Resurrection to eternal life…'

'He's not there anymore you know, Emily. His spirit is free. The physical body is the only thing that chains us to the Earth. Death is not the end of existence,' I say, watching until the casket is resting in the ground beneath.

I pick up a handful of soil and drop it on top of the casket. 'Fino a quando ci incontriamo di nuovo, Dudley,' I say before I return to Emily's side.

'I know. I wonder what the spirit looks like?' she asks.

'Beautiful, spectacular, I would imagine. With an endless energy and strong life force that reflects the love of our Creator,' I suggest.

'Did I paint your soul, your spirit, Liam? Is that what kept me awake that night?'

'No—I don't think so,' I reply.

I thank the priest and then turn to walk away with Emily.

'What did you say as you dropped the soil onto Dudley's coffin?'

'I said, until we meet again, Dudley.'

She breathes out audibly. 'It is not the halo effect.'

I smile. 'Let's go to Flowers for Fleur Café!'

'I'd like that,' she says.

'Thank you for coming to Dudley's funeral,' I say to Emily when we sit inside the café. Our teapot, cups and afternoon tea arrive quickly.

'I wanted to be there for you, and for Dudley. I liked him from the moment I met him, you know, after I moved beyond his ugliness. Life must have been tough for him.'

I look down and smile. 'How could I have been so lucky to have met you?' I say with affection, shaking my head filled with awe of her.

'I don't believe luck had anything to do with it, Liam. Is it meant to be,' she says.

I reach over and grab her hand, and kiss it. I want to tell her that I love her. But I can't. She is mortal. I am not.

Darkness has grown as we walk out of the café. Emily steps ahead of me and starts dragging me along like an anchor.

We cross the road and into the park where I catch sight of what has attracted her. It is our oak tree, lit up with fairy lights.

I let go of her hand and start running towards it. Emily squeals in delight chasing me, then grabbed hold of my coat and tugs me back, stalling my winning way.

She arrives at the trunk of the ancient tree before me, turns and leans back on the rough bark, panting. I pull up in front of her and place my hands on the tree trunk on either side of her.

'I win,' Emily exclaims with a smile that lights up her face.

'But I get the prize,' I say in a low voice as I moved my lips to hers, teasing her, brushing my lips across hers, but not kissing her. I have to stop this. Now. I don't want to break her heart. I want her to find her happily ever after. And it can't be with me.

She puts her hands on either side of my face and kisses me. I frown during the kiss, knowing that this is the last.

I pull away. 'Thanks for today. I have to go. I have a list of things I need to do for Dudley.'

Emily tilts her head on the side with a slight smile. 'Anything I can help with?'

I lower my head and shake it. 'It's something I need to do on my own.'

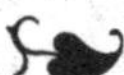

Saturday.

It's 9AM and I open the door to Aurelius. He holds a large leather suitcase in one hand and a chess board box in the other. I nod my head to him as he enters, and we both go to Dudley's room in silence. There, we sort through his possessions to donate to charity, put them in boxes and leave them by the front door. I leave Aurelius to arrange his new bedroom to his liking.

'I'll show you the apartment,' I say to him.

'No need. This is already like my second home.' He walks over to the table and opens the chess set and starts to set it up. He opens the digital photos on his personal communication device, finds a photo, and places the chess pieces in the place on the chess board where he and Dudley left the unfinished game.

'Tea or coffee, Aurelius?' I'm standing with my hands in my pockets, watching my new protector, wondering if his wisdom is on par with Dudley's. Somehow, he feels more like a brother, than an uncle or father figure, like Dudley was. A wave of grief rolls over me.

'Whiskey. And call me Aurie.'

My eyebrows shoot up. I go to the kitchen and grab two glasses and the bottle of whiskey. I sit at the table opposite Aurie, the chessboard between us, and pour a third of a glass of amber liquid for both of us. Dudley would be laughing right now.

Aurie holds up his glass. 'To Dudley,' he says, and I touch my glass to his before I take a swig at 11AM. 'It was my turn in the chess game. So we'll pick up from there.' He peers down at the pieces.

I sit back in my chair and take in his features. Brown, straight unruly hair falls over his brown eyes, framed by black glasses. His nose is straight and in balanced portion to his face. He's almost the perfect description of a model and a nerd. His black T-shirt is tight over his muscles. No wonder his is a *Pure One*. I straighten my back and run my hand through my hair, conscious of my new protector and his highly likeable physical features.

He makes his chess move. I look down and make mine. I wonder if he is aware that I have been playing chess for one hundred and twenty-one years with my protectors. He's only—

'Thirty-two. I have a degree in nanotechnology, physics and biology, with a PHD in nanobiotechnology. I'm single and on a world changing quest. You are my fifth subject… well, besides the chimps.'

Okay, so physically he is older than me. And Dudley has been quintessentially specific with who he has chosen. I make my chess move.

Then he makes his, almost immediately. 'I have tested your blood and immortality nanobots in the lab.'

I make my next chess move, remembering that time Dudley requested a vial of blood from me, then let more amber liquid coat my tongue before I swallow it, feeling the warmth spread throughout my chest.

'Successfully.' He moves his chess piece. 'Checkmate.'

I sit back in my chair and look at Aurie. 'Wh—'

'My mother and father decided to become human immortals when I was eight. By the time I had to choose a career path, I noticed their marriage fall apart, and violent fights they healed quickly from. Father thought he was invincible and could do anything he liked. And I mean, anything. Every night I would lie awake to my mother crying, praying for her mortal life back. So I decided to do something about it. And here I am.'

'And your mother now?'

'Mortal. Aging. Gracefully and happily. Thankfully. I didn't even want to imagine myself being the same age as my parents, or getting older than them.' He makes a move in the game.

I look at the chess board. My king has no legal moves to escape.

Game over.

'I'll return you to mortal status, then disappear. It's for my safety. If I'm found out, I can't continue the work I'm doing now. This is your gift from Dudley,' he says.

I put my hands over my face. This has turned my world upside down, tilted it and flipped it back again. Hope rises in my chest.

I let out a loud sigh of relief. 'Thank goodness. I was worried about Emily.'

'She's a delight. I can see why she's a Pure One, like me.'

'A Pure One? And?'

'And?' Aurie frowns at me. He's finally lost by a question.

'Should I be worried that she will be attracted to you, as a Pure One?'

Aurie laughs and leans forward. 'She is an incubator for the Pure Ones, the original humans, as we were created in the beginning. I will have babies when I find the Pure One I want to spend my mortality with. I haven't found her yet. But I will.'

I place my hand over my chest and close my eyes. Emily can't be mine. I'm not a Pure One. I'll be a damaged post-immortal human, now mortal. When she finds out—

'The process of detonating the self-repairing immortality nanobots will also purify your DNA of any impurities. You will become a Pure One.' He hands me a university employee card. 'When you leave employment at the Great Hall, this is your new job, where you'll be safe.'

I take the card from him. I can't believe what I'm hearing. It's incredulous. 'Is there any ri—'

'Risk from returning to mortality?'

I nod.

'Death.' His face is deadpan. A hearty laugh erupts from me. Death is a horror word in our society so filled with the fear of death, focused on immortality and no aging. 'At the age set by your telomeres,' he adds.

'Whe—'

'Today I'm here to make the change for you.' Aurie stands from the table and gestures for me to follow him. He enters Dudley's room and I follow him in. He hasn't moved in like I thought he would, instead, he has set it up ready for the change. There's a machine and wires and recording devices. 'TED—'

'The burst of electromagnetic energy, a transient electromagnetic disturbance. Banned by all governments in 2030 when it was used as a weapon in the world war.'

'Correct. You'll have questions, but I can't answer them, for your own safety. And, your brain and neural network will not be affected. Our process and procedure has been perfected, and is safe.' Aurie gestures to the bed.

I inhale deeply. This is it. It's what I have been wanting for over a hundred years. To be able to die so I can have eternal life. I'm terrified, and I'm excited.

I close my eyes and say a silent prayer. 'Let's do this, Aurie.'

Within ten minutes the procedure is finished. Painless.

'You kidneys, liver and immune system will break down the nanobots and clear them from your body, where they will be excreted in your urine,' Aurie says after checking my vitals. 'You're done. Welcome to the mortal world as a Pure One.' He pats me on the shoulder.

I feel no different as I rest on the bed. I get up and walk around the apartment while Aurie packs up his technology. He shakes my hand before he leaves, and I have no way to thank him for what he has done for me.

A memory charges at me then. A conversation with my mother, just before she passed away. I was at the age when I became immortal, twenty-eight, but in Earth years, forty-nine. I had not aged.

'Mamma, how will I know when I become mortal?'

'You will cut yourself, or bruise, and it won't heal quickly. You will catch viruses and they will make you feel sick. You will feel tired instead of full of energy all the time. And when you become mortal, if you find the way to reverse your immortality, the blue ball of light will no longer glow. But do not be afraid. It will be a day of rejoicing, for you when you become mortal, you can die and return to the spiritual realm.'

'Yes, Mamma, but, what happens if I get lost when I am mortal?'

'Dreams, my child. We will send dreams to guide you. And remember, books are knowledge, and knowledge is power.'

I go to the bathroom and take out a razor. I cut my arm to see if the nanobots repair it within five minutes. I continue to bleed after eight minutes, so I apply pressure to stop the blood but watch to see what happens with my skin. There is no fast healing like with the nanobots.

I look to the ceiling and close my eyes. A tear rolls down my cheek.

I. Am. Mortal.

Sunday.

'IDcom.' A ping sounds on the augmented reality, and a communication app is projected as a 3D hologram. I scan Emily's business card. 'Write a note to Emily asking her to meet me at the ancient tree today at 1PM. Thanks, Liam.'

Request completed...

I pace the study room from the window to the wall and back again, looking at my cut every couple of minutes to see if it has healed. Being mortal again is a novelty. And I'm not sure I can believe it after one hundred and twenty-one years of immortality. No fear of death. Now I feel like I have to keep checking that I am not in danger of a mortal injury.

After ten minutes I receive a reply from IDcom. It's a yes. I have an urgency to spend the rest of my mortal life with Emily. And I need to start now. I don't want to waste any moment of my precious time. Time that is now ticking away, moving closer to the end of my life.

I push my hand through my hair and push the thoughts of death from my mind. I have to be careful not to become obsessed with it.

The sun flickers through the dancing leaves of the ancient tree while I wait for Emily. I've been here for an hour already, ahead of time, rehearsing words in my mind. I'm anxious, worried that I will be too much today, my thoughts running superfast like I have to do everything pronto.

The trunk of the tree is rough when I lean back on it, resigned to whatever happens, happens. I have to trust in myself and the relationship I have built with her.

I smile when I see her in the distance. My heart flutters and adrenaline surges through me. As she comes closer, I put my hand over my heart. I hope that I am enough for her. I finger the small rock in my pocket, then take it out. The most perfect one I could find at the market stalls on my walk here.

'Bonjour, or should I say, ciao?' she says, stopping before me.

I grin. 'Hi,' I say. 'You look lovely, and smell divine.'

Emily lowers her head and smiles shyly, and my heart melts. 'That cut looks painful.'

I lift my arm and look at it. 'Yeah. It kind of is.' Emily runs her finger along my skin around the cut, and I shiver at her touch. I take her hand in mine and lift it to my lips and kiss her hand softly, looking into her green eyes.

I hold out the perfect, smooth cerulean coloured rock to her. She frowns. 'Penguins give a polished rock to the female they are courting, in hope that she accepts it—'

Emily's lips are on mine.

I pull away from her. 'Ti amo,' I whisper before I place my

lips on hers again and hug her close to me.

She presses herself into me like she is trying to become one with me. 'Je t'aime,' I whisper breathlessly, and step away from her, running my hands through my hair while walking a little distance away from her.

Overcome with my feelings for her, I turn around and face her. 'I love you,' I say.

Emily stills. Frozen like a statue with her hand over her heart. She doesn't say a word.

My stomach churns and my chest tightens. Does she not feel the same way about me?

Have I read her body language wrongly, or made an utter fool of myself?

I turn away from her and put my hands on top of my head. I lift my chin and look up to the sky to hold my tears.

She is there then, behind me, wrapping her arms around me. 'I love you, too,' she whispers.

I lowered my head and let my tears fall. I turn around and pull her against me, picking her up off the ground and burying my face against her neck. I carry her back under the ancient tree and place her feet onto the ground. I lean in, place my finger under her chin to lift her lips to mine. And kiss her.

I pull away and look into her eyes, and run my fingers down her arm to her hand and hold it, then lower myself onto one knee in front of her. 'Marry me, Emily... will you marry me?' I ask in a voice thick with emotion.

There's a deafening silence and my heart beats hard against my chest.

A tear rolls down her face. She looks from my eyes to her hand captured in mine, and back to my eyes. I try to control the butterflies that are fluttering about psychotically in my stomach, and wait for her answer with patience.

Please, don't let it be no. My chest is tight and it's hard to breathe. 'Although it is the male penguin,' I say to calm me down, 'who offers the smooth rock to the female, it is the female who chooses her ma—'

Emily's finger is against my lips. 'Yes,' she whispers, then places her lips on mine with tenderness.

I stand then, relieved. My anxiety has vanished into thin air. 'Thank you,' I whisper, and place the smooth rock into her hand. She's now mine, for keeps.

'Let's get married soon,' she whispers. 'Life is too short, unless you are one of those immortal humans.' She raises an eyebrow at me. 'And if you are, my answer is no.'

The rain starts to fall then. 'I am mortal,' I say, the words feeling rough and odd in my mouth. But it's the truth. I grab Emily's hand and pull her through the park to hail a cab. I'm out of breath as we slide into the back seat together. Is this part of the change from my immortal body to my mortal one?

We race from the cab and into the foyer of her apartment building where she presses the button before I can, and then stands back and smiles at me.

'Something amusing, Miss Finnigan?' I ask.

'Yes. But I can't share it with you because we're not married, yet. And I know you are old-fashioned,' she says, her cheeks reddening.

'Is that so?' I question before we step into the elevator, accompanied by another couple.

Once they step out onto the third floor and the doors close, I turn to Emily and pull her towards me, seeking her lips on mine.

She threads her fingers through my hair as we kiss, and moves her hands to wander over my body. Heat curls within me. I step back from her. 'Not married and old-fashioned, remember,' I say.

The elevator stops and a man joins us.

I narrow my eyes at Emily and shake my head before I look to the floor of the elevator with a wry smile. At the ping of the elevator doors opening, I grab her hand and walk her to her apartment door and knock on the door like I'm delivering an errant child.

'Hello you two, come in!' Emily's mother voice is elated. 'Why didn't you use your key, Emily?' she asks.

I look at Emily and raise an eyebrow, waiting for her answer.

'Liam is a knocker. He likes to knock—politely. Apparently, he is old-fashioned,' Emily says, looking at me and raising her left eyebrow.

We entered the apartment and move towards the living room, where I sit on the single sofa. I close my eyes for a moment, slowing time to bring me into the present.

When I open my eyes, Emily is frowning at me. 'Why are you sitting over there?' she says.

I place my hand over my heart.

She sits on the floor in front of me and puts her hands on my knees. 'I'm sorry. I will behave, for now,' she whispers out of earshot from her mother.

'Thank you,' I mouth to her.

A pot of tea turns up with three tea cups. Mrs. Finnigan joins us. 'Liam, I'm sorry about the loss of your uncle,' she offers in a solemn voice.

'Thank you, Mrs. Finnigan. I will miss him dearly. It has been difficult at home without him. Tonight will be no exception,' I say, looking into my cup of tea.

'You're welcome to stay the night if you think it will ease your burden a little,' she offers.

I look at Emily. Her eyes light up like a Christmas tree.

'Thank you for your kindness. I will consider your offer,' I reply.

'Liam, I must thank you. My daughter has never been happier since she met you. It has been a very welcome and pleasant change,' Mrs. Finnigan says.

I smile at Mrs. Finnigan. 'She has done the same for me—'

'Ma,' Emily interrupts, 'Liam asked me to marry him tonight. And I said yes.' Her voice is soft.

Mrs. Finnigan is silent. She stares at Emily with her mouth gaping open.

My heart starts to beat faster. I know we have only known each other for a blink of an eye, but she *is* the one for me. I have absolutely no doubt in my mind, after living for one hundred and forty-nine years.

Then, as time seems to stop, Emily's mother lets out a high-pitched shrill, barrels over and hugs her daughter. 'I knew it, I knew it! When Liam came to the door that morning, I knew he was the one for you. I'm so thrilled.' Mrs. Finnigan clasps her hands in front of her face and closes her eyes. A wide smile spreads over her face before she hugs me.

I look over at Emily. Her eyes connect to mine. I'm thankful to be able to stay here tonight. It's safer here than in my own apartment. I'm a marked man.

4

Friday.
4 days.

I organise a locksmith to replace all of the door and window locks at my apartment during my brisk walk to work. I arrive at work with a couple of minutes to spare and glance at the cut on my arm. It's still there. Healing slowly. I pull out a band aid and place it over it. A memory flashes into my mind of my mother putting a band aid over a cut on my knee when I was eight. I smile and a warm feeling radiates from my chest. Happiness.

The moment the building is open for business, a woman walks toward me with steely determination. 'Good Mo—'

'Floor thirteen,' she says. No pleasantries. No manners. And steps into the elevator.

I raise my finger to push number thirteen, but stop. I turn to her. 'What is your business on the thirteenth floor, madam?'

She pulls her sleeve up and reveals her red glowing Life

Watch. She holds it up to me and raises her eyebrows. Two days, four hours, 22 minutes, 10 seconds.

'I see you have *time*,' I say.

'I have no *time*. I am about to die!' she shrieks.

'But you have *time* to consider true immortality. Earth immortality is not what you want to have.'

'Listen here. Take me to the thirteenth floor.'

'No,' I say, and open the elevator doors for her to exit. She will hate me for it. And I am okay with that.

The morning is peppered with red glowing Life Watches who present themselves to me. And I take not a single soul to the thirteenth floor. My conscience will not allow it.

I am done.

As word gets around, the day drags on with no people with red Life Watches, and less people to deliver to building floors now that elevators can be independently operated. And many patrons prefer it that way. They can keep their own business to themselves without at least one person knowing where they go and at what time.

After rising to the viewing platform with a young couple, Elevator Thirteen settles on the ground floor with a sigh and the doors open.

She sits on the white leather sofa alone, presumably waiting for someone. She holds a painting in her hand. She looks my way, her red hair falling over her shoulder and then our eyes lock; green eyes to honey brown, lost together. She makes her way to me in haste and enters the elevator right away, leaning on the handrail opposite me.

'Hi, Alex,' she says, humour dancing in her voice.

'Hi yourself, Miss Finnigan. It is lovely to see you today. Where can I take you with your artwork?'

'To the thirty-fourth floor please, Mr. Harris.' She tilts her head to the side. 'Alex, do you think I should marry Liam?'

I narrow my eyes at her and take a deep breath. 'No, Miss Finnigan. I think you should marry me, instead.' My voice is serious. 'Liam is much too dangerous for you,' I add.

'Why do you say that?'

'Well, he is not as controlled as me, nor polite. He is more likely to sweep you off your feet and take you to some exotic place to marry you on the beach, whereas, I would marry you right here in the elevator, with elevator music,' I say, without any change in my expression.

Emily bursts out laughing, then calms her expression. 'Well, that is very tempting, Alex. But I would have to judge whether it is you or Liam to be my husband by a kiss. So I will reserve my decision, for after you have kissed me in the elevator,' she replies, breaking into a gentle smile before the doors open on the thirty-fourth floor, and leaves the elevator.

The elevator returns to the ground floor. The doors open and a familiar person steps in to accompany me. It's Pedro, the man who left the warehouse with Emily before Dudley made his appearance.

'Good morning,' he says to me, nodding his head, once.

'Which floor, sir?' I ask, keeping my eyes on him the entire time, reading his body language. He looks at the floor numbers on the elevator wall. 'The thirty-ninth floor.'

'Very good, sir. It is a superb day to look out over the city,' I say and push the button, keeping my eye on him, adrenalin spiking in my body. He is the one who took the envelope from Mr. Moretti. I wonder if I am on his hit list.

Pedro moves to stand opposite me in the lift. I straighten my body posture and tense my muscles. I'm mortal now. Death can come easily. Too easily. 'Dudley has passed away, Pedro,' I say in a voice that implies weakness, remembering the conversation with Dudley about his perceived fragility being a weapon.

'Yes. I know. It was quite quick. He didn't suffer a torturous death like my boss wanted him to,' he says.

'Yes, thank you for that. He was a good man,' I add. My heart is thumping.

The doors ding and they open at the viewing deck. Pedro exits my elevator car.

I breathe a sigh of relief and close the elevator doors and return to the ground floor, breathing deeply to calm myself.

I am in mortal danger.

Pedro is nervous about something. His body language is his downfall. He would never make a successful hit man.

The doors close and the elevator returns to the thirty-ninth floor. My stomach churns.

Pedro is waiting to enter my elevator. Sweat is beading on his face, though the day is cool.

'Are you feeling alright?' I ask, making eye contact, trying to read his intentions.

He doesn't answer me, but steps into the elevator opposite me. I wait thirty-five seconds with the elevator doors open.

'Close the doors, Alex,' he commands.

'As you wish, Pedro,' I say, noticing his right arm straightened beside his leg, his hand gripping something long and thin, and the end of a cream coloured knitting needle visible.

'You do know that I can stop the elevator and put a lock on its movements and doors, preventing them from ever being opened except by an explosive device . If you choose to kill me, you will be imprisoned in here with my body as it goes through the process of decomposition after death. At first, I will urinate and defecate because I have no muscles stopping me from doing that. My body will bloat as bacteria begins to multiply and feed off my internal organs. I will smell strongly of rotting meat, and fluid will leak from every possible orifice of my body. It will not be pleasant for you, the survivor, to see what will happen to your body when you die either of thirst, probably, hunger, or from inhaling deadly bacteria from me.'

Pedro winces.

'Or I can take you to a man who is a master of helping people out of seemingly impossibly situations.' I'm waiting for Pedro's reaction to Mr. Moretti's name.

Pedro stares at me. He narrows his eyes as I hold in the stop button. Sweat dribbles down the side of his face.

'Your choice, Pedro. What do you choose?'

He drops to his knees and points the knitting needle at his own heart, his hand uncontrollable with a strong tremor.

I sigh. 'Pedro, this will not solve the problem. What if you get the knitting needle stuck a little of the way in and it does not pierce the heart as you wish for it to? Or, what if you miss your heart entirely? What then? What sort of suffering do you want to inflict on yourself? Painless, apparently, like Dudley, really is the best way to go if that is what you desire—but are you immortal human?' I say, my voice calm, unlike the panic inside me.

He remains kneeling, whimpering. His eyes are screwed shut and his jaw clenched. I roll my eyes and bend down to remove the knitting needle from his hand and help him to his feet.

He clenches the knitting needle in his fist so I can't take it from him. But then his body goes limp as if he has given in, and I, too, relax in compassion.

He lunges at me then; with a ferocity I did not expect from such a coward of a man. I fall back against the wall of the elevator, causing it to rock in the elevator shaft. He makes a high pitched grating noise as he tries to stab the knitting needle through the thickness of my uniform.

His first attempt hits a brass button. In the second it took for him to register his attack had failed, I place my hands onto his shoulders and shove him backwards. Hard.

By the second attempt, I reach out my right arm towards him and clench him by the throat. He is short of statue and his arms are not long enough to touch me. I squeeze his throat with my fingers. 'I will kill you if you continue,' I say to him in a low, rough voice, piercing him with a death stare.

He smiles, drops the knitting needle to the floor and grabs my arm with both of his hands. With my left hand I swing a swift hook to his head, knocking him out cold. As I shake the pain from my clenched fist, I press floor number thirteen.

When the doors open on the thirteenth floor, I look to see if Mr. Moretti is within view. He's nowhere to be seen. I lock the elevator car in position and proceed to drag Pedro to Mr. Moretti's office and slump him against the wall.

Mr. Moretti enters from the back room, almost the instant our presence is made. His eyes widen at the sight of Pedro. 'Mr. Harris, nice to see you again. This is most unexpected.' He sighs and clamps his hands together in front of him.

'I did not know where else to take him. I will leave him with you,' I say, incline my head to him, then turn to leave his office and walk at a brisk pace back to the elevator.

I close the doors, send the elevator down two floors and push the stop button. I clean the elevator and use a bergamot fragrance to eradicate any stale odour from my confrontation, then re-engaged Elevator Thirteen to travel to the ground floor.

Relief surges through me. I have survived a mortal combat with Pedro. I'm sure he will come for me again.

Thirty minutes later the elevator doors close and I ascend to the thirty-fourth floor. The doors open. 'Miss Finnigan, nice to see you. Are you wishing to travel to the ground floor?' I ask in my formal elevator operator voice.

She enters and nods. The doors close and we start to descend, until she pushes the stop button.

'Mr. Harris, it seems you have information I seek,' she says to me, stepping into the centre of the car.

'I do?'

'Yes, you do. When does Liam plan on taking me to the exotic destination to marry me?' she says shifting closer to me.

'Oh, Miss Finnigan, I cannot answer that. It is privileged information,' I say.

'What if I exchange something with you?' she suggests.

'And what would that be?' I say, mesmerized by her.

'A kiss. You know I don't know whether to marry you in the elevator with elevator music, or Liam, whom you have declared to be a dangerous person,' she says, her head tilted to the side.

I look to the floor and then back into her darkening eyes.

'Alright. That sounds fair. Will you please sign this waiver before our lips meet?' I pull a piece of paper out of my pocket and hand it to her.

I love you, to the ends of the Earth,
To the depths of the oceans,
And beyond the blue sky
that holds the Earth in a bubble.

She smiles when she reads it, takes out a pen and signs it, and hands it back to me. I grin and place it back into my pocket and hold my hand out to her. I connect my eyes to hers and pull her towards me, slowly. I place my fingers under her chin, lift her lips to mine, and kiss her, gently, then pull away.

'Mmm. Is Alex old-fashioned like Liam?' Emily asks, opening her eyes.

'It depends. Are you going to marry me, or Liam?' I say, placing my hands on either side of her face, looking at her lips again.

'Well, Liam has blue eyes. I love blue eyes,' she answers. 'But you wear a uniform. I love men in uniform!'

I smile to myself. 'Maybe you could marry us both. He would never know,' I suggest.

'Liam, I mean, Alex,' she whispers, and steps back from me. She frowns. 'Tell me when Liam is planning on marrying me. Information exchange for another kiss.'

'Okay.' I sigh. 'The word on the street is two days. Be ready in two days. He will pick you up at 8AM, take you to an exotic location, of which I am not able to tell you, and marry you at sunset on the beach. That's all that I am allowed to tell you, Miss Finnigan,' I say, and watched a tear teeter on the edge of her eyelashes.

I step towards her and catch her tear with my thumb, then kiss her softly as the elevator descends to the ground floor.

'Have a nice day, Miss Finnigan,' I say in my elevator voice as she steps out of my car.

'I will, Mr. Harris. I'm going shopping,' she says in a happy voice before she hurries off.

I arrive at my apartment minutes before the locksmith. Although new locks could never deter a professional burglar, perhaps new locks would discourage Pedro, whom I assume had broken in and killed Dudley by his words in the elevator, and then entered uninvited again, leaving a knitting needle on my bedside table.

As the locksmiths leave, Emily arrives.

'Bella!' My heart flutters the moment I set my eyes on her.

She gives me a chaste kiss.

'Beautiful!' I whisper into her ear and breathe in the apple fragrance of her hair. 'I was about to call you,' I say as I brush my lips along her jaw line.

'Who were those men?'

'Locksmiths. I've changed every lock in the apartment, for safety and peace of mind. I'm thinking of selling this place. What do you think?' I say, waving my hand around the apartment as

Dudley would have.

'I don't mind where I live, as long as I'm with you,' she says.

I pull her against me and wrap my arms around her. 'I'm taking you out to dinner,' I say, changing the subject.

I take her hand in mine and double lock the front door before I lead her to a waiting taxi.

We sit in silence. I have a surprise for Emily and my stomach is in a knot. I kiss the back of her hand and take a deep, calming breath.

'Vous êtes belle… you look beautiful,' I whisper into her hair as we walk inside the French Restaurant. She looks up at me with a smile and sparkling eyes.

Emily sits opposite me at our quaint table, our legs tangled around each other, unseen to others.

The champagne I have pre-ordered arrives within a minute of our seating, along with one dozen red roses.

I lift my glass to her. 'Pour ma belle épouse d'être… to my beautiful wife to be,' I say, connecting my eyes to hers.

She touches her glass to mine. 'Thank you,' she says in a soft voice, then sips the champagne. 'Mmmm, that tastes divine, Mr. Harris,' she adds.

'I agree, Dom Perignon Brut Vintage. Did you know that champagne was enjoyed by French kings and rulers since before medieval times?'

Emily raises her eyebrows at me.

'As per our dinner rule, I've taken the liberty to order for you. All you have to do is to enjoy,' I say, looking into her breath-taking green eyes.

'Ah, Mr. Harris, you will make a beautiful husband. I'm so glad that you'll be mine,' she says.

I take her hand and kiss it, interrupted by the arrival of our entrée: twice baked blue cheese soufflé with light cheese sauce and poached red wine pears.

'Dance with me,' I say after we have finished our entrée. She smiles and places her hand in mine. I walk her to the dance floor and hold her close as we sway to the music.

We return to our table after one song, and our main meal arrives. I have ordered the pan fried free-range chicken breast stuffed with Camembert and cranberry, with green shallots mash, chilli dressing and red wine for Emily. And lamb cutlets with potato dumplings, heirloom glazed baby carrots and green piston sauce for myself.

Emily closes her eyes in pleasure as she savours the tastes embedded into the dish by the chef. It pleases me more than I thought it would.

'Em... I would like to give this to you,' I say. I hand her an invitation, an off white hand-made cotton rag paper. My writing is in gold ink.

She takes it from me and looks into my eyes. I watch then as she opens it, the small coloured hearts cascading from inside the invitation and onto the white linen tablecloth.

To My Dearest, Beautiful Emily,

I love you. I request the honour of your presence on May 13th, to become my wife in the sight of God. Our journey will start at 8AM, when I meet you in the beautiful gardens of your apartment building. At 5.30PM we will meet at sunset on the beach of Emerald Bay where our hearts and lives will be sealed together as husband and wife.

I promise to love you, cherish you, and adore you forever, til death do us part.

All my love, Liam xxx

She looks up at me with tears in her eyes. 'Liam Harris, I could never have dreamed of someone as beautiful as you,' she whispers.

My stomach flutters. She had spoken words of adoration. For me. A mortal. But she is wrong. She is the one who is beautiful.

We dance again before we share our dessert of crepes flamed in Grand Marnier, orange zest and vanilla ice cream. Then I whisk her off in a cab back to our ancient oak tree, adorned with a thousand fairy lights.

I stand under the treasured tree beside the love of my life, looking sky bound as the magic of the old oak tree enchants us. Then I kneel on one knee in front of her and take her hand in mine. 'I love you, Emily. Deeply. Truly. Madly... marry me?' I ask her again, this time holding open a box that houses an exquisite diamond ring.

She gasps. 'Yes, Liam, yes. The answer will always be yes.'

I push the engagement ring onto her finger and kiss it.

She moves her lips to mine then, and I fall deeper into my desire for her as we kiss. I move my lips away from hers, slowly, and step away from her. I place my hand over my heart.

Emily steps forward and puts her arms around me. 'I can't wait,' she whispers into my ear.

I gaze into her eyes, considering all the possibilities before me. 'Let's go,' I say. I lead her across the park grounds in haste and hail a cab. When it stops, I open the door and Emily climbs in. I bend over to follow her in, but hesitate. 'See you tomorrow. I love you,' I say.

Emily frowns at me.

'Not yet, my love.' I shake my head at her. I want our first intimate night to be as husband and wife, and to be romantic. I give her a chaste kiss, step back and close the door of the taxi, then watch as she is taken away from me.

I cannot sleep as deep yearnings for her run through me. Patience and control. We will be together soon.

'Caro Dio, possa io avere coraggio, temperanza, saggezza, giustizia e pazienza – Dear Lord, may I have courage, temperance, wisdom, justice, patience, and love,' I whisper. 'And I pray, Lord, that I will be a good husband for Emily. Supporting her. Encouraging her. Uplifting her. Honouring her always. Serving her. Please give me the wisdom and strength to be the kind of husband you need me to be as witness and an example of Your love on this Earth. And my dream of Light, Father, of being in Your unimaginable and indescribable presence one day, trusting in Your timing and wisdom, in Jesus' name I pray. Amen,' I say, feeling comfort and the peace of being blessed, before I slip into the unconsciousness of sleep.

3

Monday.
3 days.

The reality of day hits me hard. It's the third last day before I learn of my fate with Mr. Moretti.

I grab an espresso coffee on my brisk walk to work to shock me into alertness. There are some things that need to come to an end today, to allow for beginnings.

My immortal walk upon the Earth has come to an end, while the beginning of my mortal walk is just about to sky-rocket me to places I have never been to before, emotionally, and physically.

I don my Elevator Operator uniform for the last time as a single mortal man, insert the honey brown eye contact lenses that irritate the living daylights out of me and slip on my white gloves, then walk the wooden floor in long strides in my polish black work shoes to Elevator Thirteen. I enter it, check it over and prepare it with bergamot scents, polishing walls, buttons and railings, ready for the day.

Satisfied with its appearance, I stand tall outside my elevator and look about at the nothing more than an ordinary day. I have a few people with red Life Watches, insisting that I take them to the thirteenth floor, but I politely decline, ignoring their heart wrenching pleas.

At 10AM, the elevator whisks up to the viewing platform on the thirty-ninth floor. A group of tourists join me, and we coast down to the ground floor where they exit.

She sits on the white leather sofa alone, presumably waiting for someone.

She fidgets nervously, knotting her fingers together in her lap. She looks this way and that, her red hair falling over her shoulder. Then our eyes lock. Green eyes to honey brown, lost together.

She catches her breath and stands. Her floral dress swishes as she walks in her high heels toward me. She enters Elevator Thirteen and stands in the middle of the elevator car.

The doors close.

'Miss Finnigan, how can I be of service to you?' I ask her in my most efficient and polite elevator voice, with a coy smile reserved just for her.

'Mr. Harris, I would like to go to floor thirteen, please,' she answers.

I stiffen at her request. This cannot be true. Nobody asks to go to floor thirteen, unless…

I hold my breath. Adrenalin starts to surge through me.

'Floor thirty please, Mr. Harris,' she says a little louder, then leans over and pushes the button herself. She brushes her hand against mine and looks into my eyes.

I breathe out in relief.

Emily knots her fingers together, looks down at the elevator floor and then looks back up at me before she speaks in a quiet voice. 'Alex, I cannot marry you,' she starts, as tears in her eyes build. 'I cannot... marry you,' she says again.

Pain sears through my chest. I grab her hands in mine in panic and start to shake my head. My heart thumps, hard. 'Emily...' I whisper as I choke on her name, disbelief in the words I have just heard.

The doors open on the thirtieth floor and she steps out and disappears.

The doors close and I fall to my knees in the elevator. I feel as though I have been struck by lightning, shocked at the words that have just flowed from her beautiful mouth.

I shuffle to the corner of the elevator car and sit, close my eyes and let my tears fall. I've been such an idiot by asking her to marry me so quickly.

I brush the tears from my face, stand and take a deep breath. I have to get on with my job.

I release the door seal and the doors open. Emily is waiting on the thirtieth floor.

I don't speak to her as she enter. I cannot let my devastated emotions be released. I do not want her pity.

She is my only client.

I clear my throat. 'Ground floor?' I ask. I can't look at her. My heart is splintering.

She leans over and presses the button to the ground floor.

At the fifteenth floor, she leans forward and stops the motion of the elevator pod. 'Liam asked me to marry him again. And he gave me this,' she hands me the invitation I gave her last night. I look at it and then to her, confused. 'He also gave me this beautiful engagement ring. It took my breath away. My heart only belongs to him, and it always will. I cannot marry you in the elevator with the elevator music. I'm sorry, Alex,' she says in a quiet voice, her face etched with regret.

I lean against the elevator wall as I feel the blood draining from my face. I'm light headed.

She sucks in an awkward breath of air and stands before me with her hands on the sides of my face, looking into my eyes with sorrow. She kisses me then, tears falling from her face. 'I'm so sorry, Liam. I didn't mean to hurt you. I was trying to tell Alex how much in love with Liam I am,' she whispers to me.

I steady myself against the wall of the elevator while my emotions roller-coaster the highs and lows. I look at her, a pained expression on my face. 'But Emily, where you are concerned, I am he and he is me. And we will protect you from all of the evil this world has to dish out. We are one and the same. Alex loves you as desperately as I do,' I say, tears filling my eyes.

She brings her lips to mine, hesitating before she kisses me.

I pull away from her. 'I have to get this elevator moving again,' I say, re-engaging the descent of the elevator car. 'I love you,' I whisper to her before she steps out into the foyer.

'Et Je t'aime,' she whispers.

The elevator doors close and I am parted from her.

The hours pass slowly in the ordinariness on this particular day of extraordinariness.

That is what it would become at least.

My meeting is scheduled with Mr. Moretti for 13:13 on the thirteenth work day from our original meeting. Tomorrow is the day. But I have other plans.

At 1PM the elevator rises to the thirtieth floor and a hoard of women enter, bright and cheery, chatting like a bunch of forever friends. They all exit on the ground floor except for one.

Emily was hidden amongst them.

'Miss Finnigan, such a pleasure to see you again. Are you disembarking here on the ground floor as well?' I ask her, expecting her to be finishing up for the day.

'I will, but I have one more meeting, and then I can go and indulge in my preparations for tomorrow,' she answers with a shy smile.

I nod, smiling crookedly.

'Which floor then, Miss Finnigan?' I ask, officially holding my fingers up to press a button.

She gazes into my eyes before she answers. 'The thirteenth floor please, Alex,' she says under her breath.

I drop my hand to my side.

'Why are you going to the thirteenth floor?' Worry is taking hold of me.

'I have an appointment with a… ah… Mr. Moretti at 1.13 pm. His secretary contacted me and said that he wishes to meet me at that time. I thought it was a particularly peculiar time to request,' she answers.

'You can't go there,' I say under my breath, trying to keep my panic contained.

'I do need to go to the thirteenth floor, Alex. He said he had a special job for me to do for him,' Emily says, her voice assertive.

'No! I forbid you to go there!' I say with force in my voice this time.

'Alex. Let's get this straight. I am an independent woman. I make my own choices. You may advise me, but never forbid me. You do not own me!'

'Very well then, I advise you *not* to attend the meeting with Mr. Moretti,' I say, trying to quell my anxiety.

'Thank you for your advice, nevertheless, I choose to go to floor thirteen.' She stares into my eyes as if apologizing for her choice. But still, it's a challenge.

Anger rises inside me like a raging fire—anger at Mr. Moretti for involving the woman I love. He knows exactly what he is doing by involving Emily Finnigan in his silly little charade.

I have a great sense of foreboding. My world is about to come crashing down.

I press the thirteenth floor button of the elevator, sealing our fate.

We stand in silence as the elevator ascends, my heart aching.

I leave the elevator before Emily and go to Mr. Wilson's office at 1PM. Emily stands by my side.

'Enter,' he calls with an unusual brightness in his voice.

As we meet eye to eye, he starts to smirk at me. 'Well, well, Mr. Harris. I see you have brought your pretty girlfriend,' he comments, chuckling out loud. 'Pedro told me about her.'

Emily's fingers tighten around mine and her body stiffens.

'Mr. Wilson, I hand in my resignation as of now. I have completed all activities as assigned to me,' I say in a most formal voice and place the envelope of resignation into his hands.

He doesn't take the envelope so I drop it onto his desk. He pours himself a drink and gulps it down. 'Mr. Harris, Mr. Harris,. please sit in the black chair,' he says in a polite voice that repels every cell of my being.

'No, thank you, sir. Miss Finnigan and I will be leaving now. So I bid you farewell,' I say, turning with Emily to exit his office.

'Emily, are you aware that Mr. Harris is an immortal human?' he calls out a little louder than necessary.

She turns at once and faces him. Confusion spreads over her face and she looks at me, narrowing her eyes.

'Open your uniform, Mr. Harris, and show Emily Finnigan your scar of immortality.'

I close my eyes and sigh, look at Emily and shake my head at her.

Mr. Wilson charges at me and pulls on my blazer until the brass buttons pop off.

I stare at him with no emotion.

'Miss Finnigan, open his uniform. He bears an immortal symbol on his left pectoral muscle. You will see it as plain as day,' he commands her.

I continue to stare at Mr. Wilson while Emily reluctantly pushes my blazer to the side.

There is no immortal scar. Just my colourful floral tattoo.

Mr. Wilson's eyes widen as he looks at my scar free left pectoral muscle. Rage visibly fills his being. He picks up his whiskey and slams it down onto the desk, splintering the glass into fragments.

He looks down at the glass scattered about, picks up a large shard then lunges at me.

I fall backwards onto the floor under his heavy weight, gripping the wrist of his hand with the glass.

'YOU were the one who would solve all of our problems with the Here now, Here forever Scheme, Mr. Harris. Mr. Moretti has got the system set up now to receive you and extract your DNA. Your brain cells. Your stem cells. Your memories.' He sucks in a sharp breath. 'Your blood was what we needed to fuel ourselves to become immortal, like gods, and have supreme power, Mr. Harris. YOU... YOU were the one. Dudley knew about the plan and that is why I had Mr. Moretti organise to have him killed. I couldn't let him get in the way of our future.' Mr. Wilson is raving like a psychotic lunatic.

He holds the shard of glass above my chest on the left side. He is sweating profusely and his hand is shaking uncontrollably.

I place my free hand to the side of his neck and concentrate a burst of energy into his trapezius neck bundle of nerves, overloading his nervous system, rendering him unconscious at once.

He slumps over me like a sack of potatoes. I push him off and look over at Emily.

She stands as if in a state of suspended animation, her eyes open wide, breathing at a shallow rapid rate.

I stand and grip the lapels of Mr. Wilson's jacket, and proceed to drag him along the floor of his office.

'Is anyone outside, Emily?' I assert, hoping to snap her out of her shock with the sound of my voice.

She looks out the door.

'No. Is—' Emily gags. 'Is he dead?' she says, almost hysterical.

'No—he is unconscious,' I answer. 'Open the door,' I instruct.

Emily opens the door of the office and I drag Mr. Wilson's dead weight along the floor to Mr. Moretti's office.

It's 13:13PM

'Knock on the door!' I tell Emily.

She does so, surprising me with the urgency in her knock.

'Enter,' Mr. Moretti says with a voice full of hope.

Emily opens the door while I drag Mr. Wilson's body into the office.

'Close the door, Emily,' I say, looking into her eyes to determine how she is coping with the series of events that have just unfolded before her.

'Mr. Harris, this is most unexpected,' Mr. Moretti says, hesitating with his words. He steps away from us.

'Mr. Wilson is ready for you, Mr. Moretti. He went into a catatonic state as I informed him that the blood of the immortal, Pedro, was all that you required for success for your own immortality. Before he lost consciousness, he wished to proceed with the implantation of the slow release capsule you have been researching and preparing,' I say, trying to sound informed, although in reality, I have no idea what I am talking about.

'Very well, Mr. Harris,' Mr. Moretti says, after he considers my words.

He looks at my chest and narrows his eyes, but doesn't say anything. He looks back to Mr. Wilson. 'Can I get you tea or coffee, Mr. Harris?' he asks as if I have just delivered an ordinary individual to him on an ordinary day.

'Thank you, but no, Mr. Moretti, I must get back to work. But I will take up your offer of tea or coffee at another time,' I reply, as per the standard answer to his question. I incline my head to him as I have always done, then grab Emily's hand and leave the office with her in haste, dragging her back to Elevator

Thirteen and closing the doors before anyone else can enter the elevator with us.

On our descent to the ground floor I stop the elevator and pull out my personal communication device. My heart is beating fast. I call the police via the direct link number I had for emergencies as an elevator operator.

While I am talking, Emily falls against me and begins sobbing. I wrap my arm around her and hold her close. Then, as I finish speaking to the police, I slide down the wall of the elevator with her until we are sitting on the floor together.

I wrap both of my arms around her and hold her tenderly. 'I'm sorry you had to witness that bizarre event… I'm so sorry. We're here now, safe, together, and that's all that matters. I have handed the matter to the police. It is done. It is finished,' I whisper in her ear.

'I was so scared, Liam. I thought you were going to die. I thought that Mr. Wilson was going to slash you and you would bleed to death, and then he would turn on me,' Emily says between sobs.

'Ssssshh… it's all over. I would never let anything, or anyone hurt you. I will protect you with my life, always. I love you,' I say and kiss her forehead.

'What was that… thing… that you did to Mr. Wilson?' she asks, looking up into my eyes.

I frown, then grimace. 'It's something Dudley taught me to protect myself,' I try to explain, and kiss her forehead again, resting my lips against her skin as I breathe in her scent. 'Let's get out of here. I'm done. I want to push this whole fiasco out of my mind and move on. And… I do have something special happening tomorrow.'

Emily looks up at me and offers a weak smile. I lift my hand above me and engage the elevator to the ground floor, then stand and pull Emily up with me as we descend the shaft of Elevator

Thirteen for the very last time.

When the doors open, people are standing around watching as police storm the building. I wrap an arm around Emily to protect her from the sight of Mr. Moretti being escorted from the building premises, handcuffed, as is an unsteady and dazed Mr. Wilson.

They are followed by half a dozen police carrying boxes of evidence and strange canisters.

I turn Emily to see Mr. Moretti and Mr. Wilson bundled into police cars and driven away, so that psychologically, she will feel safer.

Then I take her hand in mine and lead her to the staff change rooms where I change out of my damaged Elevator Operator uniform and into my ordinary clothes.

In silence we walk along the polished wooden floors, out the revolving doors for the very last time, and into the brilliant sunlight.

I lift my face to the sun, thankful for my continuing chance at life as a mortal.

Emily rests her head on my shoulder and places her hands on my arm. I kiss her head and walk her to Flowers for Fleur Café and order a pot of tea.

'According to Dudley, there is no trouble so great or grave that cannot be much diminished by a nice cup of tea,' I say to Emily while she sits staring in silence.

There is no response.

'And, there is a Japanese proverb that says, as a bath refreshes the body, a cup of tea refreshes the mind,' I continued trying to get some sort of reaction from her.

But she remains silent.

I place my finger under her chin. 'A cup of tea solves everything,' I whisper to her. 'Speak to me, Emily,' I encourage.

She closes her eyes and takes a deep breath. 'What is this talk of immortality, and why do they keep looking at your chest for an immortal scar? Who are you, Liam?' she asks, looking directly into my eyes. Her face is sombre, and tears threaten to overflow.

I look at the table and take her hand in mine, thinking of the right words to tell her. I connect my eyes to hers. 'There are things I cannot tell you because it is not my story. I do not have the immortal symbol on my chest because I am mortal, but I do know the sign of an immortal. In this world, if there is someone you need to feel safe with, it's me, because of my knowledge of mortal and immortal humans. Please know that I will protect you always—your body, your mind, your spirit, your soul.' I'm nervous. She's worried about who I am. I take a calming breath. 'But you do have a choice. After the circumstances today, I'll understand if you choose to leave me. And I'll let you go if that is your wish.' I look deeply into her eyes. It's the only choice that I have. My heart is beating at a frantic pace and I feel nauseous. I know very well that Emily could choose to walk away from me.

She release her hand from mine, and look at her cup of tea. She picks it up and sips it, looking up at me through her long eyelashes. A tear runs down her face and she wipes it away with the back of her hand. She puts her teacup onto the saucer then walks around the table and stops in front of me. 'Hold me,' she whispers.

I stand, pull her close and wrap my arms around her. My heart races as I fear that we are about to part, and I will never see the love of my immortal, and mortal life again. 'I will love you for eternity, no matter what you choose,' I whisper into her ear.

She starts to cry into my shoulder and I hold her tighter, closing my eyes and burying my face against her warm soft neck.

She becomes quiet, and I feel my heart drop.

'Come shopping with me. I have some things to buy for tomorrow. I will feel safer if you are with me today,' she whispers, then softly kisses the side of my neck. 'I can feel you smiling against my skin, Mr. Harris. I hope that is a good thing?' she says running her fingers through my hair at the back of my head.

'Mmmmmmm,' I mutter in an incoherent state, realizing she had chosen to become my wife tomorrow.

I step back from her a little and look into her eyes. In a slow movement, I move my lips to hers and kiss her, lingering. She pulls away. 'Let's do some shopping therapy, Miss Finnigan. I'm eager for tomorrow's arrival,' I whisper.

'I am more than eager, Mr. Harris,' she says as I take her hand in mine to leave the café for a shopping date, my very first one.

That night as I prepare for sleep, I reflect on the three attempts to take my life in as many days.

Three has to be a significant number, didn't it?

I place my hands over my heart and recite the prayer I have said every night for the last one hundred and forty-nine years, perhaps for the last time.

'Il coraggio, la temperanza, la saggezza, la giustizia, la pazienza - courage, temperance, wisdom, justice, patience... and love, the greatest of these is love,' I whisper, finding comfort and solace.

I drift off into a much needed deep sleep, filled with visions of a conversation with my mother before she stepped into eternity -

'Mama, what shall I do when I find a woman who I fall in love with?'

'Liam, my dear child, you will feel a deep passion for her so strong that you will hardly be able to believe that a love like that exists. Treat her with kindness and tenderness. Tell her you love her every day that you are together. Marry her and treat her like she is your princess. You will

be her protector, her lover, her best friend. You will be her world. Never betray her trust, or destroy her dreams. Never raise your hand to her. Serve her with dedication, with the deep love that you will feel for her, as she will do for you. Respect her, and she will respect you. Love her passionately, and she will love you passionately. Adore her, and she will adore you. Pure, deep love never ends... it is a gift from God that must be treasured for eternity.'

'Yes, Mama.'

2

Tuesday.

I wake to a floral scent lingering in my room—frangipani, rose, lilac and lavender, I think. The sun touches my skin with warmth that radiates to my heart. I blink contentedly, and smile. Today is the day I marry the love of my life. My very long life.

I take an extended shower, enjoying the warmth of the water as it runs over my mortal body, and then dress in ripped denim jeans and a white shirt before packing my suitcase.

I look at the 18k gold wedding band with a full circle of round brilliant diamonds I have brought for my wife, kiss it and then close the case and push it into my pocket for safe keeping.

Then, before I close the door of the apartment I look around, thinking of its history, Dudley, and the future it is about to hold. My gaze lands on the box from Dudley that sits on the dining table, then I pull the door closed and descend the steps to the horse and cart I have organized to whisk Emily away to start our fairytale.

The air is crisp and the sky is a perfect cloudless blue as excitement drifts about me as I ride alone in the carriage, feeling the anticipation of greeting Emily this morning.

I see her before the horse and cart pulls to a stop. She waits on the garden seat in the sculptured gardens of her apartment building. She looks up at the sound of the whinny of the horse, and a slow, but magnificent smile spreads over her face when she sees me climb out of the carriage and walk towards her.

She runs at me. The happiness in her eyes and her smile lights up my world, then she kisses me as I wrap my arms around her. 'Ma belle Emily, ma femme d'être, êtes-vous prêt? My beautiful Emily, my wife to be, are you ready?' I whisper against her lips.

'More than ready, husband to be,' she whispers.

I kiss her again, but pull away as her mother comes toward us.

I step forward and hug Mrs. Finnigan. 'Thank you for Emily,' I say, giving her a quick kiss on her cheek.

I step back from her and watches as Emily hugs her mother.

I pick up Emily's suitcase and wrap my hand around hers and walk her to the carriage, helping her into the carriage like a gentleman should.

I sit beside her, kiss the back of her hand and watch the pure elation on her face as we ride in the horse and carriage, moving forward to the rest of our lives together.

We arrived at Sandals Emerald Bay in the Bahamas at 2PM. Emily is taken away from me the minute we arrive to be indulged by therapy staff to spoil her until our wedding ceremony, as I have organized.

I spend two hours in solitude on the beach, looking out over the blue ocean, praying and pulling calmness over me.

White organza material flows in the gentle breeze under the bamboo wedding canopy when the sun sits low in the horizon.

I watch Emily as she walks towards me along the beach, step by step, a beautiful smile conveys the pure happiness that dances around her.

She wears a halo of delicate white flowers atop of her red hair that is styled in an updo. Her off the shoulder long white wedding gown is very chic, glamorous, and in her hands, she carries a bouquet of white and lavender roses.

She comes to stop in front of me and our eyes meet, blue eyes to green, connecting in eye love.

I take her hands in mine. 'Beautiful,' I whisper to her, smelling the perfume of frangipani, roses, lilac and lavender, I think.

The minister commences our marriage ceremony while the sun sinks into the horizon, throwing hues of pinks and blues and purples over us. And while the gentle waves wash up onto the shore, we make our wedding vows with words that can never be unsaid, then exchange rings and seal our promises to each other with the tender kiss of husband and wife and the applause of family and friends.

Once darkness has settled over the island like a soft blanket, I hold my wife's hand and lead her to our dinner table to share our first meal as one.

I take my own seat opposite her and pick up my glass of champagne. 'To my beautiful wife, thank you for making me the happiest man in the world … I love you,' I say in a low voice, connected to her eyes in a depth I have trouble climbing out from.

'And to my beautiful husband, thank you for choosing me

to spend your life with … I love you,' Emily says in a voice that sings to my soul.

We share one entrée, and one main meal, exchanging words of adoration and true love.

'Mrs. Harris, will you dance with me?' I ask, after dinner is finished, holding onto her hand and rising from my chair. I walk around to her without breaking our eye contact.

'Yes,' she whispers, entranced by our love.

I walk her to the dance floor and turn and face her, then gaze at her from head to toe, breathing deeply before I pull her close. The music flows in and around us as we dance in each other's arms like we were the only two people who exist on the Earth.

'Mmmm … wife, we must leave very soon…' I whisper into Emily's ear.

'Why is that husband? I am enjoying dancing with you,' she whispers back.

'I need to be alone with you, Mrs. Harris,' I whisper, kissing her lips.

'Mmmm…' she sighs, as I take her from the dance floor and walk her the short distance to our private suite, pick her up and carry her through the door before placing her gently onto the wooden floor.

Never had I thought it to be possible to be intoxicated by love.

Never, had I thought it to be possible to love someone so deeply, so purely, so truly.

As Emily lays beside me, I watch her sleep. I adore her. I cherish her, and love her more than I thought was ever possible.

'Til death do us part.

Death. I had been an immortal human, unable to die, spending my time wishing to become a mortal, so I could die to return to the spiritual realm.

But now that I'm mortal, able to die, I don't want to die.

I want to spend my life loving my beautiful wife.

Ironic. Now I have to put my energy into not dying. Human life is far more fragile than we know.

1

I carry Emily over the threshold of the door to my apartment when we return home from our honeymoon. It's old-fashioned. Romantic. Gentlemanly.

I swing her around and place her on the floor before I move my lips to hers, caressing them with mine. I moan, and feather my lips across her cheek to whisper against her ear, 'Welcome home, Mrs. Harris.'

'Mmmm, I like the sound of that, Mr. Harris,' she responds.

'Which, home, or Mrs. Harris?' I ask, kissing her again, trailing my fingers over her shoulders and back.

'Mmmm, I like the sound of Mrs. Harris. It's like… we're married, Mr. Harris,' she says.

I smile against her neck as I litter it with light kisses. 'We are, Mrs. Harris,' I whisper.

Emily begins to unbutton my shirt.

'Soon,' I say, and kiss her tenderly before I move away from her and go to the box on the dining table prepared by Dudley before his death.

I open it without a clue as to what Dudley could have put in there. He did tend to be unpredictable, even eccentric at times.

I frown while I pick up a pair of pale blue baby booties, and a matching hat.

Emily is standing behind me then. She wraps her arms around me, her hands splayed over my chest. 'They're beautiful. How could Dudley have possibly known that I would conceive so soon?' Emily says, holding the booties in her hand and running her fingers over the softness of the wool.

Shocked, I turn and face her. 'What?' I ask.

She takes my hand and places it over her lower abdomen. 'We're having a baby,' she whispers, looking deeply into my eyes.

I stare at her for a moment, before I set my lips upon hers and kiss her with tenderness. I pull her into my arms then. 'You're having my baby?' I say as I hold her against me—my spirit is soaring.

'I love you,' she whispers.

I hear the sound of a loud click behind me.

The click of a loaded gun.

'Happy, happy families,' croaks Christopher Collins. 'Good for you—adding to the population of the world. Oh and ah... Liam, I loved watching you kiss your wife,' he adds with humour in his voice.

'What do you want, Christopher?' I ask in an impassive voice, masking the fury that's building inside of me.

'Your wife to be mine, and you, dead. Simple, really.'

I can see him in the reflection of a framed painting on the wall. His eyes are large and his nostrils flaring in time with his breathing.

As he walks closer, I angle my body to protect Emily. 'I

thought Mr. Moretti had helped you with your obsession, Collins,' I say to keep him talking.

He laughs out loud in an insane manner. 'He attached probes to my head, took blood from me and hypnotized me, except, he did not realize I was one of the fifteen per cent of the population who is unable to be hypnotized. I played along with his little game just to humour him. He still believes he cured me of my… *obsession*,' Christopher Collins blurts out, eyeing Emily with lust. He runs a hand through his hair. 'Aaaaah … watching you with her really turned me on. I want her more than ever, and I want her now,' he says walking closer to us until the barrel of the gun rests between my shoulder blades.

Emily is shaking. I tuck her head under my chin. I want to turn around and render Christopher Collins unconscious, but that would put Emily at too much risk.

I keep my arms wrapped around Emily as much as I can to protect her. If Collins shoots me this way, I will fall towards her and trap her under my body so that I become a dead weight, protecting her and our baby.

'Step away from her, Harris… DO IT!' he yells.

'Sorry, Collins. I don't like to share,' I say.

I can feel the gun shaking in his hand as it rests between my shoulder blades. I can also feel Emily dialling police on the personal communication device in her hands between us.

Christopher Collins walks away from us. In the reflection of the painting I can see his back towards us. I take a short side step with Emily to get us closer to the sofa chair so that we can use it to protect us from the monster in the house. But he turns, pointing the gun at me again.

He runs his hand through his hair. He's nervous and highly unpredictable. He turns his head slightly to the left as the sounds of police sirens come into hearing.

His agitation escalates. He panics and pulls the trigger.

I feel the bullet as it hits me in the back. Strangely it doesn't register as pain, just a blow, like someone hitting me. But then the searing pain spreads through me.

I look at Emily, staring at her as I become aware I am losing consciousness...

We lock our eyes together and fall, in what seems to be slow motion. I buffer my fall on top of her as best as I can with the little strength that remains in me. Once our bodies have settled into their final positions on the floor, I brush some hair away from her face.

My beautiful wife. My baby. My son. 'I love you both for always,' I say between choking sounds. I taste blood.

Emily gasps, nearly emptied of her breath. 'And. I. Love you. For always,' she whispers as my lips meet hers in our final kiss, as the blackness creeps down over me like the blanket of the night. Except, there are no moon or stars.

Out of nowhere there is a light in the darkness.

And silence.

But the silence disappears as I seem to leave my body, watching down upon my human form.

This scene is gruesome.

A man and a woman slumped on the floor together, bleeding.

No... not Emily and our baby... no... no... NO!

Christopher Collins squats beside our bodies, crying with his eyes squeezed shut, agony emblazoned over his face and the gun to his head.

Police are breaking down the door, splintering the wood everywhere. There is shouting, and guns held up, and then... a gunshot. Through the head. By his own doing.

Emergency services are everywhere: police, medics. They tend to us, checking for life signs, stemming the blood flowing from our bodies.

A mask is placed over my mouth, then Emily's, with a person pumping a bag of air to breathe for us…

… and then I'm carried away in spirit, angels by my side, to a place brilliantly illuminated, yet there is no sun or moon. There's eternal peace and joy, and love.

Pure, unconditional love.

Two others are with me. Emily, and my son. My son…

And I hear a voice, like rushing waters, 'Emily, my daughter, it is not your time yet. You are to return to the Earth with your son.'

'But I cannot go without Liam. I cannot,' Emily says.

I don't look at the Lord. I feel that I mustn't. I feel I must have permission to do that. I want Emily and our baby to stay here with me, where death is no more; nor grief, nor crying, nor pain.

But I feel Emily's spirit slip from me and fade away until I can't see her and our son any more. I let out a cry.

'Lord,' I say, 'I need to be with them.'

I feel His deep sympathy. He is love, so pure. 'I know. That's why I'm giving you a choice. You're welcome to stay here, or to return to Earth. Love is everything, and with love, all things are possible. What do you choose?'

'I choose to be Earth bound. I choose to be a protector, a healer. I choose to love Emily and my son until my final breath on the Earth at a much later date. I will return to You because of my knowledge and faith, and my love for You.'

After I say the words, I feel like I'm in suspended animation. Silence surrounds me as I start to retreat, in slow motion at first, until I'm back in my mortal body.

Unconscious.

I feel her presence before she places her hand on mine. Emily. Her hand, so soft and warm, tracing circles, spirals and scrolls on my skin with the lightness of a feather.

'Hi,' I say as I wake. But I hear no voice. No sound from me. I frown and turn my eyes to Emily.

'Hi.' Her mouth moves, but there is no sound.

My eyes widen, my heart races. I have no hearing. None.

I reach out to Emily. She takes my hand in hers, her skin warm and comforting, singing to my soul.

'I can't hear,' I think I say, like mouthing the words and feeling the vibration in my throat.

Emily draws her eyebrows together and shakes her head. 'I know,' her lips say.

My stomach begins to churn. Perhaps this is a dream—no—a nightmare. Being deaf, unable to hear the voice of my wife or my child, and the sounds of nature and music would be a nightmare. Devastating.

Emily reaches for a pen and paper. 'We are alive,' she writes, her words soothing my erratic heart. 'And for that I am eternally thankful!' she adds. 'I think I saw a glimpse of heaven?'

Tears flow from my eyes. I *know* she saw a glimpse of heaven. Like me. 'I'm scared, Emily,' I think I say, engulfed by the realization that my hearing was damaged when I was shot.

Emily holds my hands with tenderness as she lifts them and places them on either side of her face.

Breathing in a haphazard manner, I explore her face with my fingers: her lips, her hair, her neck and shoulders. A tear rolls down my face. 'Kiss me, Emily. I want to feel your lips on mine,'

I think I say, as I struggle in the darkness of no hearing, trying to hold on to something I am familiar with. Touch.

And then her lips were there, brushing against mine, kissing with a depth of emotion, and love.

She pulls away and my heart settles.

She takes my hand in hers and places it against her stomach. Our son has grown. How long have I been in a coma? I let out a shuddering breath and look at the beautiful shape of her round stomach. A tear rolls down my face. Our baby is safe.

Emily writes on the piece of paper and hands it to me. 'Our son is strong. I feel so blessed that you will get to meet him. That you are still here to be his daddy.'

I look up and smile at Emily. She is right. We have everything to be thankful for. She wriggles in beside me on the bed and places her head on my chest. I feel the kick of the baby against me and my heart skips a beat.

I feel her tears drop onto my skin. She traces her finger over my left pectoral muscle in a continuous pattern. She sits up and writes on the paper again. 'You have a scar now where the bullet went through. If it makes you feel any better, I have a matching one. I'll show you.'

I frown and shake my head from side to side. I never wanted her to get hurt.

She takes hold of my fingers and moves them to touch the top of one of her right breast. I can feel the raised scaring of her skin. It's the shape of a figure of eight, except on its side.

I raise my eyebrows in disbelief. It is so like the symbol of immortality.

'At least we have matching scars,' I think I say, trying to find my sense of humour.

And then I quieten, as a deep sadness rolls over me.

Emily strokes the side of my face. 'Talk to me,' she mouths, and wipes away the tear that has escaped.

I don't know if I can pronounce my words properly. I take a breath and concentrate hard on using my word muscle memory to talk. 'I… I will understand, if… you choose to leave me. I am damaged. I am no good. I don't want to be a burden to you and our son. Don't feel obliged to stay with me because you are my wife. I never want you to feel trapped. It would kill me if you became miserable. I want you to be happy, and, if that means leaving me, then I will accept it. I love you more than my own life, Emily.' I try to say the words without releasing tears, but fail miserably.

Emily grabs the piece of paper and madly scribbles on it. She holds it up for me. 'For better, for worse, for richer, for poorer, in sickness and in health, until death do us part,' she mouths it to me as she points to the words, before kissing me. She writes on the paper again, and mouths it to me while she points. 'I love you more, Liam. So that means you're stuck with me, if that's okay.'

I let out a sharp breath and nod my head, then move my lips to the top of her head and kiss her there. She snuggles next to me, and I feel her even breaths as she drifts off to sleep in my arms. Her warmness and her beating heart comfort me for now. I know that anger and self-pity will come as I grieve my hearing loss.

I close my eyes to try and sleep with her by my side. The sound of silence terrifies me. Except it's not silence. It's tinnitus. Three sounds, not one. High-pitched. Buzzing. Shoosh. I breathe out that breath God has given me.

I focus to calm myself. I'm in hospital. I'm in a safe environment. Yet still, my heart hammers in my chest. Anxiety to the extreme. And then I think… the nanobots that repair and restore. I *can* have my hearing back! My body shudders at the thought of nanobots inside me again.

I slowly close my eyes. Faith. I pray the familiar words I spoke every night for one hundred and twenty-one years:

'Il coraggio, la temperanza, la saggezza, la giustizia, la pazienza - courage, temperance, wisdom, justice, patience... and love, the greatest of these is love,' I repeat into the depths of my consciousness, finding comfort and solace.

And I find something else I didn't expect to find: a luminous white light.

I reach for it in my darkness and pull it towards me, feeling it energize and lift me. And then it becomes brilliant with the colours of gold, blue, purple, and scarlet, surrounding me with His Love.

And I hear a voice like rushing waters, reminding me.

> *'For I know the plans I have for you, plans to prosper you and not to harm you, plans to give you hope and a future.*
>
> *Then the eyes of the blind shall be opened, and the ears of the deaf unstopped.*
>
> *He made the storm be still, and the waves of the sea were hushed.*
>
> *Blessed is the man who remains steadfast under trial, for when he has stood the test he will receive the crown of life, which God has promised to those who love him.*

I breathe in the words spoken from a Voice of Love, and float in the heavenly presence of peace, drifting on the whisper of hope that sings to my soul. Without my hearing, I will be able to hear the unheard through my other senses, and become a healer as I have prayed for. Yes, I will weather the storm with patience, and courage. 'Lord,' I called. 'I want to protect my family? But

I will fail without my hearing. Please tell me what to do,' I feel myself saying.

And then I know the answer, placed in my mind. Protection is not only a physical act. It's a spiritual act. Prayer. The most powerful weapon. And love, love protects.

I bow my head. I know that everything I need will come at the perfect time. I have to trust in God's timing. Life is a gift, no matter what. I just have to unwrap my gift.'

'Thank you, Lord,' I whisper.

The colours of gold, blue, purple, and scarlet recede from me then, leaving me to the dark world of my mortal body.

The storm had started, and I had entered it.

Tears streak down my face as I think of my three lives in one; the immortal human, the mortal human, and the non-hearing mortal human, prophesied to see life more clearly than ever before.

Am I blessed or cursed?

I choose blessed.

For in everything there is a purpose. The best things in life are unseen as they work for our greater good.

I recite the words of my prayer:

'Il coraggio, la temperanza, la saggezza, la giustizia, la pazienza - courage, temperance, wisdom, justice, patience, and love. The greatest of these is love. And my dream of Light, Lord, being in Your unimaginable, indescribable presence one day, where no eye has seen, no ear has heard, and no mind has imagined what You have prepared for those who love You. And trusting in Your timing and wisdom, in Jesus' name, I pray,' I say, feeling comfort from my spiritual connection before I slip into the unconsciousness of sleep...

For it is but a short time that we are mortals on the Earth. Our lives are like a breath; their days like a fleeting shadow. True immortality is eternity with our Creator, where there is no end,

and no suffering.
And unconditional love.
That breath you just took. It is a gift.

Choose kindness. Forgiveness.
And *love,* without judgement.

ACKNOWLEDGEMENTS

Writing ideas come to me from several places – a single word or a melody of three words, a stunning photograph or art, or a single event in time. A Dream of Light came to me in a single event in time, when I was staying at the Peppers Salt Resort at Kingscliff on the Tweed Coast, New South Wales.

My family were staying there as my eldest son, an elite triathlete, was competing in the Kingscliff Triathlon. One day at the resort, we were waiting to catch the elevator. It arrived and the doors opened, and it was full of people and there was no way all five of us could fit in. So we stepped back and waited for its return. When it did, the doors opened and the elevator was empty. I gasped. And from that moment, a new novel was conceived.

All my love and gratitude to my wonderful and patient husband, Bradley, as he journeys through my novels with me, listening to me rave about parts of it and wondering what on Earth I'm talking about. And to my children, adults now, Declan, Claire and Riley and their partners. It takes time to write a novel. Time, that is indeed precious in human relationships. Time you can never get back. And I always stop writing to converse with you, to help you, to make sure that you are all okay. Thank you for when you approach me while I am typing words of my story, that you stand and wait next to me to finish my sentence before you talk to me so that I don't lose that train of thought, those words in that precise moment that I may not get back. Thank you for your patience. You are all very kind and understanding.

Thank you to my lovely mum and dad, for your forever support of my writing, always delighted when you have another of my books in your hands.

Thank you so very much to you, my readers, for giving your precious time. It makes my heart overflow with joy, even if one person loves my story. That's all I need.

To my writing and author friends. Thank you for inspiring me with your books and never giving up on our craft of storytelling, especially in this time of invasion by AI. People want and need stories written with human intelligence, a human heart and human love, to feel the emotion and empathy in words for our spiritual connection and understanding. Our light.

And to my *Heavenly Father*. Thank you for being in my life story. Thank you for being the Author of my life story. I couldn't make it through without You. Thank you for Your rescue packages You give me when I am struggling, in the way of people, animals, and nature. You spoil us, even when we don't deserve it.

Soli Deo gloria.

Books written by *Julieann Wallace*,
under her own name and her pen name, *Amelia Grace*.

Amelia Grace

THE GIRL WITH THE FLAXEN HAIR (2024)
(Adult Fiction)
Print book and eBook

Jane Piccadilly bought a mistake-house. In a hurry. While her white shoe sunk into something soft and offensive. There was always a mistake-number-one with something new, wasn't there?

And there was always only one mistake, wasn't there?

The mistake house was plain, like Jane. *Dear Alice's little girl*, Jane.
The middle of seven sisters. Daughter number four.
The one who was the least seen, but saw the most.
The one who would speak, but nobody heard.
The one who could slip out of a family gathering, and no one would see.
The one who saw the bodies, but nobody saw her.
The one who could pretend to be dead, and nobody noticed.
The middle, invisible child.

Neglected. Ignored. Overlooked.

Jane Piccadilly made the mistake-house an un-mistake.
Then the seven sisters moved in—Poppy the librarian, Violet the hairdresser,
Daisy the carpenter, Rose the photographer, Zinnia the botanist,

Flora the farmhand, and… plain Sunday Jane.

Then came the knocks on the front door, mysterious letters, the snake and the pig, the strange man with a carpet bag who sat on the bus seat, and the bones the dog fetched from the back yard.

It all pointed to one thing. *The unravelling.*

The unravelling of the mistake house with its secrets.

And the unravelling of plain Jane, the threads that held her past and her trauma and her guilt and her shame deep inside her, straining and breaking.

The truth always has a way of exposing itself.

Plain Jane wasn't so plain. Was she?

Julieann Wallace

YOU BEFORE ME (2023)
(Young Adult Fiction)
print book and eBook

Eighteen year old ARI FLORA COHEN is stuck living in a pre-technology time, until she ventures to the forbidden Beyond where she is captured. Finally released, she staggers home through elaborate underground tunnels, reeling from the lie about the non-existence of the world outside her home. What other lies has her mama told?

ELIAS WOLFE GREEN is Ari's protector. He finds her wild and unconventional and disagreeable. Nevertheless, he has a job to do, no matter how many times she tells him she hates him.

Elias follows the rules. Ari breaks them.

Ari has questions. Elias has answers, including the truth about her father who was taken before her birth, but he cannot speak of his knowledge. So Ari must find the answers herself.

She discovers she is living in a time called *The Unfolding*, where the truth of the world is being unwrapped, layer by layer, after the time of *The Boxing*, when the Earth was made singular by the covering of the stars and the universe with light pollution and surveillance satellites, when the truth of everything was hidden. She discovers there are four versions of everyone, and Ari discovers, her mama of love and light, is not who she thinks she is.

Distraught, wanting answers, Ari must dress as a boy and return to *The Beyond*. But disaster strikes.

Now you, dear reader, must choose the ending...

Amelia Grace

THE BOOK KEEPER
print book and eBook

COHEN DARCY leaned over and blew the dust off the top of a book that had mysteriously appeared beside his bed. The dust flowed into the air like a wave turning over on itself, leaving the worn, brown leather cover naked to the eye.

It was there he saw an embossing. The words were unknown to him—*Mutato Nomine De Te Fabula Narratur.*

Cohen stepped out into the new day. A new rainy day. A new day of unwelcome events. It had started with the arrival of the mysterious book, then came the seduction, the unlawful act of the CAI stealing his work, and the promise that his existence would never be the same.

That night, when he opened the book and found the owner, it belonged to GEORGIA HARRISON. Now his day was about to get even worse. He needed to meet her to get rid of the book!

He doesn't do books—or relationships. As simple as that.

Could he do a system restore of his life to an earlier time, and bypass the events of today?

INDESCRIBABLE. A love letter.
A picture book for teens and adults
print book, kindle eBook

A stunning, raw and heartfelt Christian love letter to God, for adults - emotive and moving - filled with wonder and awe and praise for God.

Dear Lord,

Here I am with pen and paper, in our sacred garden where we talk. Just You and me, surrounded by Your flowers, breathtaking and fragrant. Accepting me. Just as I am. And I'm so thankful. I'm overcome. I'm bursting with overwhelming emotion and my tears fall. I have no words as I inhale that sacred breath You gift me. It's just... It's just too much...

I exhale. I have no eloquent, silver-tongued words like a scholar to offer You, to write and to read to You with a whisper of deep love on the breeze. It's just me, Lord. With a God-shaped heart and a profound adoration for You. It's the work of Your hands, Lord, that gets me. Your fingerprints. Over all of creation. Over the heavens and the Earth. Over me.

And I'm undone. Please accept my heartfelt words, with love and praise. I exalt Thee.

www.ingramcontent.com/pod-product-compliance
Lightning Source LLC
Chambersburg PA
CBHW010306100726
47904CB00011B/2767